W9-CJM-066

THE TIP OF
THE ICEBERG:
A NOVEL

F. H. EINHORN

THE TIP OF
THE ICEBERG:
A NOVEL

F. H. EINHORN

A Targum Press Book

First published 2012
Copyright © 2012 by F. H. Einhorn
ISBN 978-1-56871-516-2

All rights reserved

No part of this publication may be translated, reproduced, stored in
a retrieval system, or transmitted in any form or by any means,
electronic, mechanical, photocopying, recording, or otherwise,
without prior permission in writing from both the copyright holder
and the publisher.

Published and distributed by:
TARGUM PRESS, INC.

Distributed by:
Menucha Publishers
250 44th Street
Brooklyn NY 11232

Printed in Israel by Chish

R07100 26924

Introduction

*L*ife is a chain of choices. The choices we make shape the people we become. They are a reflection of our goals; an expression of that which we consider important.

Although we tend to think that *bechirah* (i.e. free will) is the choice between good and evil, the Torah tells us otherwise. "*Choose life*" (*Devorim* 30:19), we are commanded. The options lie before us with one choice signifying life, whilst the other is death.

A choice might seem miniscule at the moment that it is made, but its ramifications go far beyond our comprehension. When a spear is thrown toward a target, the slightest deviation at the outset will translate into a great distance when it reaches its destination. Every choice leads us towards or away from our goals.

This story is replete with choices. Small choices, big choices...choices that seemed insignificant until their implications became painfully obvious.

A *chassid* once approached R' Yisroel of Tchortkov to receive his blessing before traveling overseas.

"I reserved a berth on the Titanic," the man said. "Here in Poland, I have no means of earning a living. I hope that in America my prospects will improve."

R' Yisroel fixed a penetrating glance on the young *chassid* and extended his hand in farewell. "Send my regards to the American deity," R' Yisroel requested.

The man was caught unawares. "W-What does that mean, *Rebbe*?"

"Do you think that Hashem cannot help you here, too?" R' Yisroel replied gently. "Do you have to travel to America to merit His sustenance?"

The young *chassid* canceled his reservation on the Titanic. He made a choice...and received his life in return.

Big choices. Little choices.

Imagine a penniless vagrant who was granted the gift of one million dollars. An anonymous benefactor hides this astronomical sum in the vagrant's voluminous sack without notifying him about his sudden windfall. Week and months elapse with the beggar trudging from one street corner to the next, begging for alms. He is unaware of the fortune he possesses.

Bechirah is a fortune. If utilized correctly, it can propel us to unimaginable heights...so long as we acknowledge its power.

*   *   *

A note to history aficionados

The story is set in the early 1900's. Historical accuracy has been maintained as much as possible to lend the events an authentic flavor.

In Plawo, Poland

The San River was a central focus of village life. The Zionist youth group, Bnai Yehudah, functioned primarily in a nearby town, but it attracted members from the wider neighborhood. Eliezer ben Yehudah, featured fictitiously as a guest speaker, bears the dubious credit for the creation of *Ivrit*.

In Manhattan, New York

Park Avenue was home to the New York elite during the early 1900's.

The Speyer School, Yankee Stadium and J.P. Morgan Chase Bank are all portrayed in accurate detail. During the Great Depression, J.P. Morgan Bank was hard-hit and its clientele stormed the doors in fury. The scene is portrayed as it was recorded in 1929.

Aboard the Titanic

The names and roles of all the crew members and passengers are authentic, aside from the fictitious main characters - the Hoferts and Bonairs.

Events that transpired aboard the Titanic - its glamorous appearance, amenities, and events leading up to and including the horrific tragedy - are all historically accurate.

Part I:
Manhattan, New York
1920-1930

Chapter One

*C*ongratulations, Estelle!"
The voice impinged on the stillness of my room, chasing away the demons of yesteryear. They would be back, those relentless memories, but for now they had been banished by my enthusiastic visitor.

"This is just wonderful, dear!" Melinda Bonair exclaimed. "As soon as I heard the news, I dropped everything and ran."

Melinda paused, obviously awaiting my response.

"Uh...Yes," I weakly stammered. "I've been waiting for someone to come and share in my excitement."

I instinctively closed my eyes in an attempt to conceal the damp evidence of my emotions, but Melinda was quicker than me. Her sharp, ocean-blue eyes registered surprise, displeasure, and finally sympathy.

"Oh, you poor dear," she murmured. "I should have known that this would be a difficult time."

I averted my gaze, unable to look pity in the eye. Over the years, I had learned to circumvent her overt expressions of sympathy, but today was different. Today I needed it more than I cared to admit.

"Melinda, I can't believe that I've actually graduated to this stage. A little bundle of pink considers me her mother."

I fell silent, contemplating the wonder of it all. I had entered the realms of motherhood on a beautiful, sunny morning at the tail-end of April. Suddenly, there was someone who thought that I was the center of the universe. There was a pair of brown, almond-shaped eyes that bore an uncanny resemblance to my own. For the first time, I felt the joy of being needed.

I have become a mother, Melinda. I have earned a title of distinction, but at what price?

"So, I told Barry that you could definitely come to me for a week or two," Melinda rambled. "After that, we'll hire a nanny until you can manage on your own."

Apparently, I had missed the first half of the monologue. Who had decided that I would convalesce at Melinda's palatial Park Avenue residence? Why wasn't I consulted before the decision was signed, sealed and set in stone?

Melinda's heels clicked against the hardwood floor as she busily arranged the many gifts she had brought. Darling little outfits were piled on the windowsill, while a vase of fresh flowers winked at me from the table. An abundance of tempting pastries appeared in front of me, dangling ceremoniously from Melinda's hands.

"Eat, Estelle. You must be ravenous!"

On that point, at least, we were both in agreement. While I munched on a crusty cinnamon bun, Melinda organized my belongings to suit her taste. She shoved my beloved, well-worn slippers under the bed with a snort of disgust and efficiently sorted my clothing onto several shelves.

Her ministrations aroused a wave of emotion deep within me; a surge of feeling that I couldn't define. Was it resentment at her intrusion, or maybe annoyance with her overbearing ways? Did I feel threatened by her unwanted involvement in my life?

When Melinda regally walked out of the room to check

on my newborn princess, I surrendered to the unbearable yearning for that which was no more. I closed my eyes to the fluorescent sterility of Mount Sinai Hospital and allowed visions of simplicity and warmth to dance on my closed eyelids.

I longed for my mother's warm and unpretentious ways. Now, more than ever before, I felt the ache of a void which I constantly sought to ignore. *Mamme* was far, far away, buried in a watery grave. The years that had elapsed since her untimely death had assuaged my pain, but they had not succeeded in assuaging my guilt.

"Estelle! She's just gorgeous!" Melinda breathlessly exclaimed. Once again, her entrance disturbed my ruminations.

"That little princess inherited your looks, my dear. Have you thought of a name, or is it still too early for that?" She paused momentarily, as though struck by a passing thought. "Oh, that was silly, wasn't it? You're certainly naming her after your mother."

I looked at this woman who sought to fill my mother's shoes, and I knew that she would never understand. The need to explain overpowered my hesitation, and I instinctively poured forth my turbulent thoughts.

"Actually, I don't think I'll do that," I said. "My little girl cannot bear my mother's name. She just can't."

Melinda stared at me with her mouth agape. If my mood wouldn't have been so low, I might have found it amusing. After all, how often did I get to see the high-powered Madame Bonair nonplussed?

"If I am to love this innocent soul, I have to give her a different name," I firmly concluded.

There was no point in further explanations. Melinda would never comprehend my feelings and she wouldn't lend credence to any expressions of guilt. How could I possibly clarify the events that led up to that fateful night? How could I justify my youthful folly which bore such tragic results?

Melinda rifled through the contents of her voluminous handbag. She extracted a monogrammed handkerchief and carefully folded it into a perfect square. Under my watchful gaze, she organized her assortment of peppermints and replaced them in their little sachet.

"Uh, I think I'll be going now," she finally stated. "I'll send Barry regards from his precious princess, and I'll start preparing our guest room. Be well, Estelle!"

I breathed a sigh of relief as the tall, slender figure disappeared from my line of vision. Never had I been so glad to bask in the quietude of my own company.

A slight tropical scent lingered in the air as a delicate reminder of the person who had graced my humble room with her presence. Melinda was everything to me. At times, I viewed her as my savior; my lifeline in a country I could not yet call 'home'. Recently, however, I had begun setting her in the cast of a smooth-talking con artist and this comparison made me immensely uncomfortable.

Barry laughed at my quirks, as he called them.

"That's Auntie Melinda you're obsessed with," he would say. "She's not worth a second of your thoughts! All fluff and glamour and nothing underneath."

My horrified response elicited a smile from my husband but I was left with the uncomfortable sensation of disillusionment.

How could I explain to him that our match had been orchestrated by his ubiquitous aunt? How could I possibly confess that I had been forced into this marriage with sugary coercion and honey-glazed threats?

"He's a good person, Estelle," Melinda had insisted. "Do you know how difficult it is to find a truly good person, with innate decency and sensitivity?"

My attempts to probe into Barry's religious standing did not meet success.

"Of course, he observes the Sabbath. Why would you think otherwise?" Melinda persisted. "I mean, he's not into all those nitty-gritty details, but he's definitely Sabbath-observant. Yes, definitely."

I was a young girl of nineteen and I didn't have the strength to refute her flimsy declarations. This was America, after all. I wasn't in Plawo, and I couldn't rely on my parents to sift through a host of marriage prospects.

Grab whatever you can, Esther, I told myself sternly. *Barry is Jewish. And...and that's about all I know of him. But...at least he's Jewish. Do you want to remain a spinster like old Muhme Gittel?*

That last thought really threw me for a loop. Muhme Gittel's petulant gaze seemed to bore into my conscience, urging me to avoid the mistakes she had made. Her graying hair and overt discontent hovered over me like a thundercloud, and I rushed to find protection under the umbrella of marriage. It wasn't a marriage I would have considered suitable for our maids, but now - in the emptiness of America - it became an option. Not an enticing option, but an option nonetheless.

It was too late to turn back now. My little girl had tied together our disparate backgrounds and goals to form a family.

"Isn't that so, little one?" I crooned, peering into her eyes. The nurse who had brought her in looked on with pleasure as I scrutinized the features of her littlest charge. I sought a spark of familiarity; a reminder of the family I had left behind. All I found was a miniature replica of Barry.

"You're Daddy's girl," I murmured. "But you're also mine. Mine and *Tatte's* and *Mamme's.*"

The nurse puttered busily around the bassinet, rear-

ranging the flimsy blankets and organizing the baby par-
aphernalia. She solicitously took the baby from my arms,
and unwound the many layers that encased Baby Bonair.

"Ain't she sweet?" the nurse commented, caressing
the baby's cheek. "I've seen many babies in my time, but
none as absolutely charming as this little Bonair."

I smiled proudly, acutely aware that the nurse probably delivered the same compliments to every new mother.

"Since the hospital moved here to Fifth Avenue, we've
been getting many patients of your caliber," she commented.

"Of my...caliber."

"You know, the rich Americans who demand preferential treatment and all," the nurse babbled. "We con-
struct a new building, ten spanking-new pavilions, and
– voila! Our ratings go up nearly overnight!"

*That must be why Barry insisted we use Mount Sinai.
It has obviously become somewhat of a status symbol.*

Status symbol or not, I was ready to bid the beautiful new building farewell. The sterile atmosphere, hushed
footsteps and muted voices seemed to envelop me in their
confining grasp.

When I arrived at Melinda's home, however, the
longed-for homecoming lacked the serenity I had envisioned.

"We have to think of a name," I told Barry as soon as
we were alone in our luxurious guest suite. "A name for
our...daughter."

Barry grunted in agreement, heaving our oversized
suitcases onto his bed. I flinched. Those bedspreads were
designer imports. Melinda would be furious.

"I was thinking of something...regal. Something aris-
tocratic. Like – like – Malka."

I held my breath. Would Barry also wonder why I
wasn't perpetuating my mother's memory, or would he

understand my hesitation?

"Malka," I repeated. "Sounds good, doesn't it?"

"Lisa," Barry countered almost instantaneously. "Lisa Bonair."

Lisa?! What sort of name is Lisa? I could just see myself introducing her to the family back home. 'Hello, Tatte. Please meet your darling granddaughter, Lisa.'

"Barry, that's not a Jewish name. It's good for school and for...for a passport, but I can't give her that name at her *kiddush*!"

Tears prickled dangerously at the corners of my eyes, and I felt their watery force dissolving my future. Was this what they meant when they described a new mother's unpredictable emotions?

"One thing at a time, Estelle," Barry calmly intoned. "The name bothers you? No problem. We can give her a name like...like...Leah! She'll be named Leah but for all intents and purposes, she'll be Lisa Bonair. We'll put Lisa on her birth certificate, on her savings bonds, on her school application, on her university diploma, and on her marriage license."

A bubble of mirth escaped my throat as I watched Barry weaving the newborn's future.

"But what's this about *kiddush*?" Barry continued, genuinely confused.

"A *kiddush* is what we make - "

"I know, I know," he interrupted. "I'm not such an ignoramus, Estelle. It's what people say on Saturday when they drink wine."

"Er...that's right. But there's another sort of *kiddush* we make when a baby girl is born. It's the occasion of...of naming the baby."

"So how does this ceremony work?" Barry asked impatiently. "Do I have to drink a bottle of wine and yell out her name between sips?"

I tried explaining the significance of a *kiddush*, but Barry was highly unimpressed.

"Let's make sure I got this straight," he said. "I have to get hold of a Bible and Saturday morning we say her name while standing near the Bible. Correct?"

I nodded, not trusting myself to speak. Barry had outlined the bare bones of the ceremony, but he had mercilessly chopped out its heart.

"I was planning a bash over the weekend, in either case," Barry continued. "While you worry about the Bible and the *kiddush*, I'll give our guests a good time. They won't soon forget Lisa's grand arrival!"

Ensconced on Melinda's plush sofa two days later, I acknowledged that Barry's promise was being fulfilled beyond his wildest expectations. Boisterous laughter washed over me in tidal waves, while winds of meaningless conversation buffeted me incessantly.

"Estelle, darling!" Melinda exclaimed. "Why are you sitting here, in the dark?"

I turned my face towards the wall, but Melinda caught me in the act.

"Don't worry, sweetheart," she said, stroking my arm. "It's alright to feel crotchety and anti-social. It will pass, Estelle. Believe me."

I grasped Lisa's little hand desperately, seeking normalcy in a world that had spiraled out of control. This was *my* baby! *My* firstborn! Why were all these unfamiliar guests crowding into my life and grabbing hold of the joy that was rightfully mine?!

The ruckus rose incrementally with every passing moment, and Melinda rushed into the dining room to ensure that no one was trampling on her imported rugs. Joy was one thing, but mindless ruin was quite another!

Lisa looked at me intently, and I found myself smiling

into her chocolate-brown eyes. *It's just you and me now*, I whispered gently. *Just you and me.*

She opened her mouth in the most adorable yawn, and I hugged her fiercely. Despite my incompetence, she accepted me as her mother. I had never swaddled a baby this small, but Lisa would teach me. She would be patient while I mastered the skills I had neglected to learn when my brothers had urged me to try.

A rustle at the door caught my attention, and I reluctantly turned to accept another party-goer's warm wishes.

Oh. Barry.

His hair was tousled and his eyes bore that unmistakable gleam of hard-core liquor swigged one time too many.

"Estelle, isn't it high time to do this *kiddush* thing? Look, the day's running away from us and you said we have to do it on Saturday."

I nodded, not trusting my voice to articulate a coherent response.

Barry scratched his ear and leaned over to re-tie his gleaming lace-ups. With an exaggerated groan, he straightened his back and ambled toward the decorative fireplace.

"Here you go!"

I looked at the book he was clutching in his hand, seeking its title. The cover was bare.

"It's yours for the taking, Estelle. A Bible. Imported from the Jewish bookstore on the Lower East Side."

Gingerly, I took the book he had tossed in my direction. *Please, Hashem! Don't let it be a New Testament. Don't let Barry embarrass You to such an extent!* When I turned the book over, I noticed its gold-embossed Hebrew lettering, and exhaled my tension in a cloud of relief.

Chumash Devarim.

"Here, let me put that down for you," Barry offered.

He put the *chumash* on the arm of the sofa, and gently lifted Lisa from her cradle. With a smile of fatherly pride, he cooed to the infant and she obligingly opened her eyes to gaze at her Papa who adored her.

"Uh...Where should I put her?"

I was just as non-plussed as my husband. How does one make a *kiddush* in a home where inebriated revelers are supposedly celebrating the occasion? How does a baby receive her name with only a guilt-ridden mother and ignorant father in attendance?

"I suppose she should be lying on the Bible," Barry finally offered. "I mean, to make sure that the ceremony works."

"No!"

The cry escaped my throat and Barry flinched.

"Have it your way, Estelle," he muttered. "You can't expect me to know the details if you don't bother providing any information!"

Lisa was dutifully replaced in her bassinet, and Barry sauntered out of the room. I put my hand on the little *chumash* and choked out the few words I remembered from my niece's *kiddush.*

"...and her name shall be called in *Yisroel...*Leah *bas...*"

I paused, confused. *Am I supposed to mention my name, or Barry's? I don't remember!*

"...Leah *bas* Esther. Leah *bas* Boruch."

My baby has a name. I didn't know whether this ceremony bore any significance, but it was the best I could do under the circumstances.

Leah Bonair. Lisa Bonair.

Will she also mutter her daughters' names over a closed chumash? Will she even acknowledge that a baby girl's arrival shouldn't be celebrated with liquor and gluttony?

Chapter Two

*I*f there's anything I dislike more than chopping onions, it's chopping onions in the heat of summer. Barry doesn't understand why I insist on doing the cooking on my own, but this is one foothold that I refuse to relinquish.

How do I know that Gallita won't mix milk into some of her meat dishes? With her relegated to the cleaning tasks of this sprawling mansion, I can ensure that my family eats kosher.

Kosher. Really. Whom am I fooling?

Tatte would swoon at the thought of the foods being served in his daughter's home. What would *Mamme* say about daily forays to Tony's Bakery and weekly excursions to Roger's Butcher Shop?

They would think it's kosher, wouldn't they?

Nonsense. *Tatte* wouldn't step over the threshold of my home for fear of being contaminated by the American free-flying culture. His darling Esther, feeding her children platefuls of poison. *Tatte*'s grandchildren, nourishing their bodies on pickled meats and roasted tongue that never saw the glimmer of a *shochet's* knife.

Whom am I fooling?

THE SURIE MILLER
LENDING LIBRARY
3110 W. TOUHY AVENUE
CHICAGO, IL 60645

"Mom!"

Davey's home and dinner's not even thinking of making its way to the table.

"Hey, Mom! I'm home!"

"Hello, Davey. I'm in the kitchen."

Davey sauntered into the kitchen, slinging his backpack onto the black and white tiles. With a swagger only nine-year-old boys could carry off, he approached the refrigerator and scanned its bountiful contents.

"How was your day?" I asked, while increasing the tempo of my vegetable-chopping.

"Good," my son replied through a mouthful of roasted chestnuts. "I gave Mr. Houston my assignment and he said that I could return to class on try-base."

"On what?"

Davey shrugged his shoulders.

"That's what he said. Try-base."

The vegetables were done. All they needed was a bit of seasoning and they would be ready for consumption.

"Davey, he didn't say try- oh! You mean, trial basis!"

"Mmm...that's what I said."

I smiled into the bubbling barley soup. Dave could charm his way out of the tightest spots. He must have offered a penitent smile and a wide-eyed look of innocence along with that assignment to receive his teacher's forgiveness.

Barry had bribed him with a trip to the River Avenue Yankee Stadium at the end of the month, if he would manage to stay out of trouble. With utmost sincerity, Davey had pledged to behave as "good as Lisa" for the duration of the month. I wondered whether the promised adventure would curb Davey's rambunctious conduct.

As if reading my thoughts, Davey launched into an account of his planned trip, talking as though he'd been there already.

"Mom, when I go to the game, you won't have to make me dinner. Daddy won't eat anything either. So you'll make only for you and Lisa."

"Really, young man! Who told you that?"

"Yeah, 'cause there's this big concession stand by the stadium and they sell popcorn and soda...See? You don't need to make me dinner. We'll sit on the bleachers and scream when they play and we'll eat and then we'll scream again. We'll go all the way to...to..."

His forehead was creased in concentration as he tried to recall the precise address.

"To East 161st Street!" he crowed triumphantly. "Daddy told me. That's where the stadium is. And we'll eat there and clap and scream and...and...then we'll go home."

Davey's eyes blazed with intensity as he envisioned his outing. I tousled his hair fondly, hoping against hope that the trip would not join the heap of promising incentives that never came to fruition. If only Dave could channel his energy in a positive direction... His intelligence outstripped those of his classmates by far, and the greatest factor in his mischief was boredom.

"So that's what you do at a baseball game, Dave?" I asked.

"Yeah! You scream when someone hits a home run, you know? And then, if someone doesn't hit it, you scream again. Everyone cheers and claps."

Hashem, he must go to this game! Help him stay out of trouble!

I caught myself just as the prayer tripped its way out of my heart, on its way to infinity. How could I offer such an inane request? How could I pray that my innocent David should join the jostling, cheering crowds at a baseball game? Did I really want him to go?

Barry had offered Dave the trip on the spur of the moment, after hearing about his latest madcap escapade. It was a natural incentive for a young American boy, and I didn't think twice about it. Davey was as American as... as the President! Well, almost. He was raised on a diet of patriotism and equality, and there was no reason why baseball games shouldn't find their rightful place on the list.

But why did it have to hurt so much? Why did I have to juxtapose Zalmen's smiling face on Davey's slight frame?

"Davey, sweetheart."

Davey continued slurping his soup. With Barry stuck at the bank once again, he was free to ignore those cumbersome table manners.

"How about I tell you a story while you eat?"

My son looked up, surprised. At the ripe old age of nine, he hadn't been treated to suppertime stories for quite some time.

"I'll tell you a story about a great person," I continued, waiting to see a spark of interest in his eyes. While Davey settled down for a long narrative, I tried to remember an inspiring story from my youth; something that would inject some spirituality in my little one's life.

"A story about a truly great person," I repeated. "A person who devotes his life to fulfilling a goal."

"Yes!" Davey exclaimed. "Tell me about Babe Ruth!"

I tried to grasp the wispy memories of *Chassidic* stories, but Davey didn't give me the opportunity.

"Mom! Tell me a story about him!"

Who is Babe Ruth?

"He's a great man, Mom! Do you know how he performed in the last game?! He made his team win! He's the best outfielder they ever had! And he's more than six feet tall!"

Oh. A baseball hero. I should have known. This is America, Estelle. Kids today want to be baseball players, not Torah scholars. Did you really think you could raise a frum child in a vacuum?!

I knew all that. Over the past fifteen years, I had slowly exchanged my youthful ambitions for goals that fit into high-flying American society. My children, however, were my lifeline to the future and I felt obligated to preserve something of my past in their psyches. All I could muster was Davey's slight physical resemblance to *Tatte* and Lisa's inexplicable affinity for embroidery. The track record was dismal, and it was only getting dimmer as time marched forward.

"When I grow up, Mom, I want to be just like him! No, even better than him!"

Davey's enthusiasm barely penetrated my foggy ruminations.

"Like whom, son?"

I whirled around in surprise. Barry stood leaning on the granite countertop, a bemused smile creasing his tired face.

"Like Babe Ruth, Daddy! You know that he saved the Yankees during the last game? I could do that, too! My coach told me I have a good hand!"

Barry laughed; a deep, throaty laugh that seemed to release a day's worth of bank-related tension.

"You're educating your mother, Davey, aren't you? I've tried doing that for the past decade without much success."

Turning to me, he continued, "Davey will make a good Yankee of you, Estelle!"

I shuddered. Here I was trying to squeeze an iota of spirituality into my son's life, but he was just as intently leeching it out of mine. My sweet, innocent boy. I brought him into a world of baseball and parties, yet I expected him to intuitively reject it all. I wanted him to be a well-adjusted student and friend, yet to simultaneously strive for goals that existed in a different world; a different life-time.

Dave sauntered over to the window and leaned over with abandon. I bit my lips to refrain from shouting the "Careful, Davey!" that punctuated our every interaction.

"Hey! Huey! Ready for a game?"

The reply was indistinct, to my ears at least, but it apparently satisfied my young son.

"Bye, Mom! G'night, Dad! I'll be back later! Huey found this old mitt in Anderson's garage and we're gonna hit some good ones out there!"

He bounded out the door before either of us had a chance to respond. Barry laughed good-naturedly, no doubt attributing his behavior to normal boyhood development.

"Who's Huey?" I asked, as I carefully ladled some soup into a bowl.

"Nice kid," Barry grunted. "Lives in one of those tenements two blocks down."

"Not Jewish, is he?" I asked, subconsciously imitating his terse tones.

Barry shrugged, and I was afraid to probe the issue. The soup sloshed dangerously close to the bowl's rim, but miraculously stayed within its boundaries. I couldn't say the same for Barry's business concerns. In the past few weeks, he had been experiencing difficulties at the bank, although he never told me so outright. I sensed the anxiety and tension bubbling close to the surface, oftentimes dribbling out during dinner time.

"What's Lisa complaining about a trip that you refuse to let her attend?" he asked, slurping his soup much the same way as Davey had. His day must have been harder than I imagined.

"Trip?"

"Lisa insists that you don't let her go on this outing

with her class. A ferry ride, if I remember correctly."

I grimaced into the salad platter.

"Lisa can't go. Didn't you notice that she's been coughing something terrible these past few days? She can't go on a ferry ride. The water and the winds will surely aggravate her condition. I think I'll summon the physician tomorrow."

Barry frowned and I knew that my ruse had not succeeded. He could see beneath my rambling stream of words, and easily detected the kernel of fear that refused to be subjugated to reason.

"It's a ferry ride, Estelle. For goodness' sake, don't impose your illogical fears on the child! Do you really think there are icebergs floating around in that little stream?"

Clink. Clink.

The silverware spoke for me, expressing my displeasure in no uncertain tones.

"Estelle, it's been eighteen years! It's high time you put the tragedy behind you."

I brought the salad platter to the table. Glancing neither right nor left, I marched back to the counter and slid several chicken cutlets onto a plate. When the dishes were arranged on the table, I could evade Barry's gaze no longer.

"I killed my mother, Barry. That's not something you can just 'put behind you'. Not now and not ever."

Chapter Three

*T*he lawn needs mowing. Paul has been remiss again. It's awful. If you don't stand above them with reminders and warnings, they slack off.

I looked around at the expanse of green and inhaled deeply. This was my paradise; my getaway. Every detail of the garden had been planned to perfection, and the results evoked feelings of peace and serenity. A cascading waterfall in the center, surrounded by quaint stone ledges, tickled my senses and I strolled towards it with pleasure.

If only life were so simple. I thought a visit to the garden would distract me, but even the magic of greenery was powerless against fear. It was a fear so strong that it refused to be compressed into any crevice of my feverish mind.

Where is she? It's way past 4:00, and she still hasn't returned home. I knew that I should never have allowed that ridiculous ferry ride. Water is not safe as a sport. It's best viewed at a distance - a considerable distance.

When Lisa shouldered her backpack that morning, I said not a word. I figured that Barry had given her the go-ahead for her long-awaited outing. Contesting his authority was an absolute forbidden in my home. After all,

Park Avenue was my entire world! I had nothing and nobody aside from my husband and children, and I would
do anything to avoid confrontation.

Lisa went to school. The hours passed in mindless occupation. A stint of embroidery, a short inspection of Gallita's dusting capabilities, and preliminary dinner preparations carried me through the endless hours. As the
clock ticked past Speyer Junior High School's dismissal
time, my nerves stretched tighter and tighter against a
backdrop of paranoia.

*Where is Lisa?! Why isn't anyone calling me from
school?! Hashem, please save my precious daughter. My
Leah. I know that our life is a mere parody of a Jewish
existence, but...but You are my Father! Am I not still your
beloved daughter, Esther? Beloved, though estranged.*

"Hallo, Madame Bonair!"

Mrs. Portnoy's gray bun bobbed in the distance, and I
groaned. Of all people to meet right now, old Mrs. Portnoy
was definitely the least desirable. How did she uncannily
choose the most inopportune moments to put in an appearance?

"Hallo! I'm here! See me?"

Her affected Southern drawl was the last thing I
wanted to hear at the moment, but I knew better than to
insult our crotchety neighbor. If Hilda Portnoy decided
that 4:15 p.m. on a Monday afternoon was the right time
for a visit, no one would dare contest her absolute wisdom and perception.

"Good afternoon to you, Mrs. Portnoy," I replied.

"What do ya' say to that? Talkin' so polite and pretty
to me, huh?"

I smiled warily. There was no way of knowing what
would set her off, and I didn't want to serve as the next
portion of gossip fodder in Mrs. Portnoy's neighborly
rounds. Patting the spot near me on the stone ledge, I

waited for the feisty old woman to make herself comfortable.

"Nice garden you got here," she muttered. "Not that I expect anything less from some hoity-toity bank manager!"

Where is Lisa?! She should have been home at least twenty minutes ago! If she doesn't come home within the next ten minutes, I'll send Paul to the school building.

"Ho, if it isn't little Madamesoille Bonair, of the pretty shoes and blond hair!"

Lisa! She stood before me in the waning sunshine, flashing her dimples with charm. The French braid that Gallita had so painstakingly created was slowly coming undone, and flyaway wisps of blond hair glinted like spun gold. My beautiful princess had come home. Hashem had not exacted retribution upon me, despite my grievous history.

Thank You! I don't deserve such kindness! Mamme, you must have interceded on my behalf...

"Cat got your tongue, little girlie?"

Lisa smiled bashfully, and I desperately wanted to enfold her in my arms for eternity. But it wouldn't do. Not when Mrs. Portnoy was eyeballing her in stern expectancy.

"How do we greet a guest, Lisa dear?" I prompted.

Lisa obediently curtsied, flushing slightly under Mrs. Portnoy's disapproving gaze.

"You spoil that child, Estelle. Her life is all ribbons and bows and mollycoddled love."

Don't respond, Estelle. You know that it will only prolong the harangue.

"When will she learn to deal with adversity, huh? Ya think she'll be able to get on in life when she doesn't have to do more than raise her little pinky to call for a maid?!"

I nodded perfunctorily, glancing worriedly at my little

girl. She seemed unaffected by the diatribe.

"Well, ah guess that all she'll ever need to know is how to dress up for parties and mingle with the high-brow crowd. Just like her mama."

"It's not as though I attend parties all that often, Mrs. Portnoy," I foolishly interjected, in a vain attempt to protect my dignity.

"Nah. It's only every second night or so. Ah hear there's another one comin' up. Tonight, if I'm not mistaken."

I looked at Mrs. Portnoy in horror. Did she know something I was not privy to, or was she just throwing her weight around?

"Ya know, that big ball hosted by the Darwig's. Ah hear that only the bigwig moneybags are bein' invited tonight. No politics for the Darwig family. No sirree!"

Louisa Darwig's party! It had completely slipped my mind. Her chauffeur had delivered a thick, cream-colored envelope the previous week, and I had hastily perused its contents before stowing it away for future reference. It must still be lurking in elegant splendor on the hearth, patiently awaiting my attentions.

"I completely forgot about it, Mrs. Portnoy," I admitted. "Thank you for reminding me."

"Forgot, huh? So many parties to attend, ya' jest can't keep track of 'em all!"

I nodded woodenly, feeding right into the woman's agenda.

"Your money is a ticket to everything!" she ranted. "Ah don't think it's fair. Jest because Mr. Bonair landed a position in J.P. Morgan Bank, does that make you somethin' special? No, it ain't fair. Ah should be at these parties, too. Not that ah would know what to do there, with all those little cups and tiny little plates. How they get satisfied from these kid-sized portions is jest beyond me."

My mind had traveled to my closet, where a host of ball-gowns hung in silent splendor.

What shall I wear tonight? The Darwig's party is sure to be a grandiose affair, with all the powers-that-be in attendance. Barry would want me to appear my best. The taffeta confection might do it. I'd better check that the crinkles have been pressed.

I stood up and Mrs. Portnoy looked up at me from her perch.

"Ya goin', aren't ya?"

"I have to see to my wardrobe, Mrs. Portnoy. Your reminder came in the nick of time."

She smiled happily, bobbing her head in gracious acceptance.

"Go ahead, dear. I'll stay here a bit and rest my tired feet. Don't you worry 'bout me."

I turned to go, protectively clutching Lisa's hand in my own. Mrs. Portnoy would have to see herself out whenever her ailing legs agreed to carry her further. I had important matters to see to.

"Mom, could I come along tonight?"

"Mmm..."

Maybe the burgundy silk would be more appropriate. I have to strike a balance between simplicity and elegance, and I believe that the taffeta ball-gown is a bit too overdone.

Lisa threw her arms around me, and I smiled down at her in surprise. She was not usually disposed to spontaneous displays of affection, unlike her brother who projected his emotions at every opportunity.

"Mommy, what will I wear to the party?! I can't wait to see all the -"

"What party, darling?" I asked in bewilderment. "Is someone in your class having a birthday party?"

"No, not from my class. Your friend, Mrs. Darwig, is

making a birthday party."

"Lisa, sweetheart," I slowly responded. "The Darwig party is for adults. That is, for Mommies and Daddies. Not for little girls and boys."

"But...but you said I could come!"

She must have wrangled permission from me without my noticing.

"Lisa, Mommy didn't really mean that you could come. I meant...I meant that you could almost be by the party."

She sniffed, highly unimpressed with my efforts at appeasement.

"Mommy is going to choose a gown and put it on to see that it's in perfect condition. You could help me check the gown, alright?"

Lisa's rosebud lips turned down at the corners, but she offered not a word in protest. Spoiled, indeed! Why did Mrs. Portnoy think that we were spoiling our little girl? At her age, I had never displayed such unquestioning obedience!

While Lisa went to join Gallita in the kitchen for her after-school snack, I ascended the spiral staircase to the master bedroom. It was imperative that I choose an appropriate outfit for the evening immediately, so that Gallita could still press it to perfection.

The rose-colored tea-gown was already worn one time too many, while the burgundy silk was too extravagant for the Darwigs' stately affair. Was the mint-green lace a fitting choice?

Glancing at the large cuckoo clock hanging between the two bay windows, I stopped agonizing over the endless options. I pulled the mint-green gown off its hanger with decidedly graceless movements, and impatiently changed into it. The row of buttons marching down my back did not lend themselves to speed or alacrity, and I struggled to close them without losing my composure.

Glancing at my reflection, I noticed that the sleeves were creased beyond what could be considered decent, while the hemline had apparently lengthened when no one was looking. Gallita would have a lot to do before I could don this gown for tonight's extravaganza.

Oh, bother. I'll have to show Gallita precisely what to do and then hold my breath until the alterations are complete. I suppose I could always fall back on the burgundy silk if worst comes to worst.

I slowly made my way down the steps, marveling at the power of dress. Now that I was clothed in an elegant confection, I modeled my steps and gait to meet its standards. I felt a singular grace accompanying me down the winding staircase, swishing along with the gown's pretentious movements.

"Gallita," I called out.

Her smiling face and frilly apron passed me by in a blur of motion.

"Gallita!"

"Yes, Madame Bonair. I'm coming."

The young girl stood looking up at me, appearing for all the world like a servant of old. The comparison unnerved me, and I quickly traipsed down the last few steps to speak with her at eye level. If there was one thing I didn't want to be associated with, it was a domineering monarch.

"Look here, Gallita," I said, pointing to the drooping hemline. "This has to be shortened."

The clang of the door-knocker interrupted my detailed instructions, and I groaned in exasperation. If time would just stand still for several hours, maybe I would find myself looking forward to the Darwigs' affair. These stressful preparations leeched out every bit of enjoyment from a promising evening.

Gallita looked at me questioningly, and I gestured towards the door. Geniality must take precedence to my pressing concerns. After all, social standing places heavy demands upon its willing victims.

"Hello, girl."

Melinda, of all people! Couldn't it have been the post-man, or even someone as innocuous as a newspaper delivery boy?

"Where's Estelle?"

Gallita's soft footsteps mingled with Melinda's click-ity-clacking and I clenched my jaw in an effort to maintain control. I would be polite and welcoming, although it would probably force me into that burgundy silk that I had so wanted to avoid. Melinda was my savior, after all. The least I could do was greet her with warmth during her infrequent visits.

"Oh! Estelle!"

Her gasp of surprise brought me back to my senses. What was I thinking?! I was dressed in full regalia, mint-green ball gown and all, in the hubbub of an ordinary weekday.

"You look...ravishing! Just like you used to look during your opera appearances!"

I flinched, but Melinda forged on relentlessly.

"I just can't believe the coincidence! Here I am, prepared to offer you the opera world on a golden platter, and you seem ready to step onto stage this instant!"

From behind the pantry door, I heard Lisa's gasp of awe and I knew that she relished the opportunity to hear details of my past performances. Once Melinda started on this topic, there was no stopping her.

"Look, Estelle. Just look at this once-in-a-lifetime opportunity."

She rummaged in her voluminous purse and extracted a carefully-folded newspaper clipping.

"It's from the *New York Times*, see? The Opera House

put in an advertisement calling all performers to audition for the leading role in their upcoming performance. They need someone who....'sings like a nightingale'. I tell you, Estelle, as soon as I read these words I knew that only my beloved niece could possibly satisfy them."

"Melinda, I - "

"Don't thank me, Estelle," she interrupted, holding up her hand imperiously. "This is the least I could do for you. You know how much I enjoyed your performances in the past. If you secure the star role, that will be thanks enough."

"Aunt Melinda, I really don't think this is for me," I countered, in a desperate attempt to quell her enthusiasm.

"No, no, no. Don't underestimate yourself, sweetheart. I know that you'll be a shoo-in for the role. As soon as they hear you sing they'll cancel all other auditions!"

"I will not do this, Melinda."

My deliberate pronouncement stopped her short. The blazing fury in her eyes didn't surprise me. I would be treated to another one of her lengthy oracles concerning my blatant ingratitude and foolishness, and then she would haughtily depart without a backward glance. Within a week or two, she would be back in our family circle, warming herself in the glow that childlessness had denied her.

"After all I've done for you, Estelle, the least you can do is use your talents! Do you know how much money I invested in your education? How many strings I pulled to get you into the highest echelons of theater society? How can you forget all that? Is that the sort of gratitude your 'holy' parents taught you back in Poland?!"

I bit my lips fiercely. My honor was one thing, but my parents' honor?! I couldn't allow her to trifle with that!

"Had I known whom I was rescuing, Estelle, I'm not

so sure I would have bothered."

Her chilling words found their mark. I felt a warm blush of shame creeping up my neck and flaming across my cheeks. Melinda slung her purse over her shoulder and stomped out of the room. When Gallita started following her out, Melinda cast a withering gaze upon the poor girl and she immediately shrank back in mortification.

"I...I just wanted to show her out," Gallita stammered miserably. "I didn't mean anything bad."

"Don't worry about it, Gallita," I replied, shoving aside my personal hurt to deal with hers. "Melinda knows her way around the house, and she prefers to do things her way. I know you meant well."

While Gallita slunk off, ostensibly to nurse her wounds in private, I turned to face Lisa. Lisa of the inquisitive mind and penetrating gaze, who absorbed more than she let on.

"Lisa, darling, how was your ferry ride?"

She just stared at me, expressing more in her silence than she could have said with a thousand words.

"Did you enjoy the trip?" I tried again.

No response. Lisa looked at me intently, and I suddenly felt self-conscious in my party get-up.

"Mom, why was Auntie Melinda so upset?"

My innocent little girl. Your world is still divided so evenly between good and bad; between happy and sad. I wish I could grasp some of your innocence to slice through the stifling grays that obscure my vision.

"It was something about the opera," Lisa stated.

"Auntie wanted me to do something, but I can't do it," I said evenly.

Lisa fingered the lace on the sleeves of my gown. Her delicate hands seemed so young and fragile; too small to be grappling with my complex issues.

"Auntie told me that when I grow up I'll be an opera singer, just like you!"

I stared at her in horror, although I couldn't pretend to be astounded by her pronouncement. Lisa's voice was reminiscent of my own, with the same sweet pitch and unbelievable range. Melinda had uncovered my talent way back when I barely acknowledged it myself. It was self-understood that she would pinpoint talent growing up in her beloved nephew's home.

"That's...nice," I quietly answered. "But I think we have time before we make such weighty decisions, don't we?"

Lisa smiled benignly, neither agreeing nor disagreeing with my statement. As she walked towards her abandoned snack on the table, she hummed an unfamiliar tune to herself. I was gripped with sudden, inexplicable foreboding. Would her beautiful voice trap her in its compelling allure, or would she have the strength to avoid my grievous mistakes?

Melinda's newspaper clipping winked at me from the table, and I perused its contents once again. The auditions were to be held on Saturday, at the Manhattan Theater.

Tatte, I gave it up for you. Every time I stood on stage, I saw your face in the audience. It was your gaze that held me captive while I sang to mixed crowds, and it was your voice that rang in my ears when I listened to the echoes of my performance.

I folded the paper in half, and then in quarters. Resisting the urge to vent my fury and confusion upon the meaningless sheet, I walked over to the garbage can and dropped it in.

For you, Tatte. Only for you. So that you'll be proud of your only daughter; the daughter you don't care to know.

Chapter Four

C r-r-rash!

"You done it, Dave!"

The sounds of running footsteps pounding the cobblestone garden path followed the frightening clatter of shattered glass.

"I told you not to swing the bat so strong! You don't know what you're doing!"

"I do, too," I heard Davey protesting. "It was the best pitch, only in the wrong direction!"

His defense was met by raucous laughter. I didn't recognize the voice of his playmate, but of one thing I was certain. It didn't belong to any of the gentle and well-bred friends whom Barry had so carefully chosen for his only son.

"Go cry to your mama! I'm outta here!"

I hurried to assess the damage before Davey would barge into the house. Entering the living room, I was shocked by the profusion of glass shards scattered over the armchairs and braided rugs. The large French doors leading out to the veranda looked skeletal in the absence of their opaque glass innards.

Oh, Davey! Did it have to be the custom-made glass that you shot out? Couldn't you have chosen a simple window to destroy?!

The front door was tentatively pushed open, and I heard the swish of sneakered feet attempting to make a silent getaway. The child had been warned time and again that our garden was not a playground, but he continuously flouted our authority. Although Davey certainly deserved every bit of fright this incident was giving him, I couldn't help feeling a surge of pity coursing through my veins.

"Davey?"

The cat-like footfalls ceased their furtive movements and a worried little face peered into the living room.

"Davey, come in here please."

"Mom, it was a mistake! Honest. I meant to pitch that ball way over on the other side to Huey, but it flew in the wrong direction. I don't know why!"

Don't smile, Estelle. The child needs disciplinary measures right now, not motherly warmth and understanding.

"How many times have I told you not to play in the garden, David? And about this Huey - I really don't think he's an appropriate playmate for you."

"Huey's my bestest friend, Mom! He could pitch the ball further than anyone in my whole class!"

What should I tell him? I can't explain that his social standing is way below ours. I don't want Davey turning snobby on me. It's enough that his classmates are teaching him their haughty ways.

"Look at the damage, David. What do you think is going to happen now?"

Davey looked around at the glass-bedecked room and grinned easily.

"Daddy will call down someone to fix it," he said with finality. "And Gallita will clean up everything else."

His response bothered me, but I couldn't fault him for it. Mr. Barry Bonair's son did not have to concern himself with anything other than getting the most out of life. We had raised him as a prince and his attitude had been formed in consonance with his upbringing.

"Mom..."

I looked at him questioningly. The macho front had dissolved instantaneously, leaving a defenseless little boy in its place.

"Mom, could I be Davey again?"

The smile I had been trying to conceal finally burst out of its confines. Davey always knew how to mellow my anger and melt my frustration. I hadn't even realized that I called him 'David' whenever his conduct fell below par.

"Of course, my Davey-boy," I said. "If only you would try a little harder to remember Mommy's instructions."

"But I do try, Mom! I really do," he countered. "Just sometimes I remember too late."

I carefully led him out of the living room and watched bemusedly as he ran towards the door. He was going to look up Huey, no doubt, to continue their interrupted game.

I've failed him. How could I let him get away with such negligence and disobedience? As a parent, it's my responsibility to teach him; to guide him. I should have made him clean up the damage, or pay a pittance from his generous allowance.

Barry would laugh at my concerns. He insists that our children are entitled to live the good life. If we have the money, why withhold it from them?

I thought about Barry's reaction to the mishap. He would probably wave it off with his oft-repeated mantra. "Boys will be boys," he would say, and place a call to the glazier to demand express service.

But Barry did not follow the lines of the script I had created. When he came home later that evening, his face was like a thundercloud on the verge of bursting.

"What is going on here?!" he roared from his perch on the sofa. "The doors!"

I hurried into the living room, immensely thankful

that Davey was already sleeping soundly upstairs.

"Barry, it was a mistake - "

"Mistake?!" he interrupted. "How could an entire pane of glass disappear by mistake?!"

"Davey was playing in the garden and he pitched a ball in the wrong direction. He didn't do it on purpose and he was very sorry about the -"

"He was sorry, was he?! Sorry!" Barry snorted disdainfully. "The little prince was sorry for causing such damage. But don't worry. His rich Daddy will pull some greenbacks out of his pocket and all will be fine and dandy. Sorry, my foot!"

I cringed at this uncharacteristic tirade. Barry was usually calm to a fault. Nothing fazed him. I was the one prone to emotional outbursts and I knew I could rely on him to keep me anchored.

"It's just a door, Barry. The glazier will repair the damage and it will be as good as new."

Barry muttered darkly, ignoring my reassurances.

"Had a hard day at the bank?" I cautiously inquired.

"No, it was all peaches and cream," Barry replied. The sarcasm screamed out of his every word, and I shrank back in trepidation. Something serious must have occurred, but I was never one to probe into work-related matters.

"They think money sprouts like mushrooms after a rain," he complained. "Shattered a glass? No problem. Daddy will pull some cash from his never-ending cache and it will be alright. Having a school function? No problem. Daddy will finance a new wardrobe for the occasion. Overwhelmed by work? No problem. Daddy will hire another maid."

The diatribe would have continued indefinitely, if Gallita wouldn't have entered the room at this most inconvenient juncture.

"Uh, sir -"

"Don't 'sir' me!"

"Oh," she whispered. "Mr. Bonair, someone is here to see you."

"Lead him in!" Barry ordered. "Let the hordes descend upon New York's financial giant! If only they would know…"

I had no time to dwell on his baffling words, for the unknown visitor was already stepping over the barbs of our spiky conversation.

Oh no. This is a perfect illustration of Murphy's Law. Barry is not equipped to deal with the most genial of visitors right now, let alone an…Orthodox Jew!

"Good evening, sir," the man said in heavily-accented English. "I hope this is a good time for you."

"Perfect," Barry muttered. "Couldn't be better."

"Good, good," the man said with a trusting smile. "Maybe I could interest you in a short description of our *yeshiva* - "

"Speak in English, man," Barry ordered. "Don't throw in all those Hebrew terms."

"Uh…I'll give you a short description of our…our school. We have more than two hundred students learning there and most of them cannot afford to pay tuition."

From my position at the kitchen counter, I couldn't help marveling at the man's command of the English language. My brothers never mastered a single word of English, yet this *Yeshiva* man was holding his own in a conversation.

"I don't understand you," Barry interjected. His voice was cold and calculating, and I knew that this poor *meshulach* would not be seeing any profit from his ill-planned visit.

"Why are *you* coming to *me* for your students' tuition? You expect me to work myself to the bone so that those boys could sit like kings in your school?!"

"They don't sit like kings, sir," the man responded in even tones. "Our school exists with the barest of necessities and most of our students go to bed hungry more days than not."

"All the more reason for them to find themselves employment," Barry trumpeted. "I have no intention of being your slave, get it?"

I walked into the room, trembling with a mixture of shame and pity. The poor man must have been informed that Mr. Bonair was a generous donor. He certainly did not expect such an aggressive reception.

Carefully, I placed a laden serving tray on the glass-topped coffee table. I knew that the collector wouldn't touch my offering, but I had to maintain appearances. Visitors had to be served in style; even if they were Orthodox Jews.

"I didn't come to debate you, sir," the *meshulach* said. "I only came to ask whether you would be interested in offering assistance."

"This is all I can afford," Barry said, withdrawing a crumpled bill from his shirt pocket. "I hope it helps your starving students survive another day in their ridiculous occupation."

I stared in horror as the solitary dollar bill exchanged hands. The *meshulach* maintained his dignity, uttering not a word in recrimination or protest. He extended his hand in farewell, but Barry merely stared at the skeleton of our French door in obstinate silence.

I couldn't allow the man to leave in disappointment. After such an aggravating exchange, he deserved the satisfaction of a sizable donation.

"Excuse me," I said quietly, catching up to the *meshulach* when he was already at the door. "Will you please wait a moment?"

He nodded mutely, and I rushed up the stairs to retrieve some of the spare cash Barry always left in the bureau drawer. Barry wouldn't know the difference. For all he was concerned, I could be spending the money on clothing or accessories to supplement my bulging collections.

"I'm sorry about the...unpleasantness," I said, unsure whether the European would recognize that word. "My husband had a very hard day."

"I understand," the *meshulach* replied. "Thank you and may you and your family always be happy and secure."

"*Amein.*"

The man seemed surprised and I realized that I had unwittingly reverted to my childhood dialect. His appearance must have transported me back to the world of my youth, retrieving the speech inflections I had thought forever lost.

"Where is your *yeshiva* located?"

"In Poland," he said.

"Where in Poland?" I persisted.

"In a small town near Krakow."

"Did you ever hear about the Hofert family? My...The head of the family is a renowned *Rosh Hakahel* in Plawo."

The man creased his forehead in thought, and I could easily picture him swaying over a *gemara* as my brothers had done late into the night.

"The name does sound familiar..."

"He is a widower," I added, feeling the familiar sting of guilt pulling apart my innards.

"No, no," the man immediately rejoined. "No, his *rebetzin* is alive and well, *geloibt tzu Gut.* It must be another Hofert family we're discussing."

I bowed my head in acceptance of the inevitable. Did I really think that every Polish *yid* would know my family personally? Did I really wish to send regards to those who so adamantly refused to forgive my sins?

"May you know peace and happiness," the *meshulach* intoned, and I felt as though a Heavenly hand was blessing me from Above.

Peace and happiness...Hashem, I don't deserve true peace after I rent my family asunder. Happiness is not mine for the taking, for I have dumped Tatte's happiness to the depths of the Atlantic Ocean. But...but You know how much I rely upon You, Tatte in Himmel!

As the man stepped out into the balmy June evening, I was overcome by bittersweet nostalgia. He took along with him the whiff of the European *shtetl*, and the innocence and purity of its residents. If only he would leave some of that for me and for my American family...

"Estelle! Did that man leave already?"

"Yes," I said. "Yes, he's gone."

"Good riddance."

Barry was still sprawled out on the sofa, his tie askew and his suit unbuttoned. All at once, the enormous divide between our cultures yawned before me and I felt an inexplicable urge to bridge the gap.

"Barry, you really don't know what a *yeshiva* is?"

It was the wrong thing to say, and it was the worst timing for such an ill-fated mistake. Barry sat up, removing his tie in the process. His eyes flashed fire and I knew that this time I had overstepped my self-imposed boundaries.

"Do I know what *yesh*-whatever is?! No, I don't! And I have absolutely no interest in getting acquainted with an institution geared to self-righteous loafers."

Don't answer, Estelle. Anything you say will just add fuel to the flames.

"Don't look so smug, Estelle! Just because you grew up in those backwater towns doesn't make you a better

Jew! You don't have to rub my ignorance in my face!"

He's right. Is it his fault that he was raised in America while I spent my childhood in an enclave of Yiddishkeit? Does he have to pay the price for my mistakes?

"No, I don't know what that man's school is. And no, I don't know about *Shabbos* and *tzaddik* and all those other things you insist I should be aware of," Barry sputtered. "Do you know about Dow Jones? What about the stock market average? And the Smoot-Hawley Tariff Act? And a bull market?! Do I ever poke fun at *your* ignorance?"

I shook my head mutely, acceding to a point well-taken.

"No, I don't. And you know why? Because you were never exposed to the financial jargon. You have no connection to the banking system," Barry continued, slightly calmer now that he had made his point. "I respect your right to ignorance, as you should respect mine."

There is no reason for me to dispel my banking ignorance, I countered in my thoughts. *But your ignorance of all things Jewish is a travesty! Judaism is your birthright, just as it is mine. What will our children know, if their father knows next to nothing?!*

I didn't say it aloud, for I knew that the argument was a moot point between us. Barry felt that he was a good Jew just by identifying with his religion and being proud of his roots. He didn't see the necessity in adhering to age-old laws that appeared like old-world restrictions in the American free-for-all.

"Barry, what's going on?"

"I thought you'd never ask," Barry said with a smile. "I'm probably just over-reacting, Estelle. The bank is going through a hard time and I'm afraid that this hurdle will not be so easily overcome."

"Oh, I see," I said, though I didn't see at all.

"It's not just our bank that's experiencing difficulties.

This seems like a nationwide affliction. The stock market is severely unstable these past few days. Those in the know blame it on President Hoover's pending Tariff Act, but it's mere speculation and it does nothing to set things right."

I nodded, secure in the knowledge that the Bonair fortunes could withstand the toughest of storms. Barry, however, did not share my equanimity.

"You're lucky I'm a bank manager, Estelle. Forewarned is forearmed. I've begun withdrawing our savings from various investments just as a precaution. Not everything, of course, but enough to tide us over in the event that the stock market freezes temporarily."

Barry could have been talking about complex calculus equations, for all I understood. In my eyes, the American banking system was sacrosanct. Deposits and withdrawals came as naturally to me as eating and drinking. If there was one thing I wasn't concerned about, it was the Bonair fortunes.

"Err...Barry," I ventured, afraid to trigger another explosive outburst after calm had finally been restored.

"Hmm?"

"The glass."

"Right, the glass. No big deal," Barry commented, true to form. "I'll contact George at General Glaziers and have him do an express job for us tomorrow. Boys will be boys, huh?"

I laughed, releasing the tension of the past hour. Barry was finally following my script, and my teetering universe righted itself without causing any damage.

Chapter Five

*P*ray for me," Barry had said that blustery Tuesday morning, as he rushed out to work. "I don't know what you murmur under your breath, but whatever it is, I could sure use it today."

I stopped ladling Quakers' Best into Davey's bowl to examine Barry's complexion. Perhaps he was feeling under the weather, like Lisa. The comment was so uncharacteristic of him, that only a feverish mind could have formulated it.

"Mom, I'm going to be late!" Davey exclaimed, kicking the table leg for emphasis.

His no-nonsense remark brought my ruminations to an abrupt halt. Speedily, I filled up his plate with the steaming oatmeal and placed it on the table, along with the requisite cocoa and sugar.

Barry stooped down to grab hold of his briefcase, and as he straightened up I noticed that he was swaying slightly.

"Barry, maybe you should mark this as one of your sick days," I suggested.

"Oh, I wish I could," he replied. "But that would be a most cowardly cop-out."

I didn't understand, or maybe I chose not to understand. There had been ample indication that something catastrophic would grip the stock market system by its neck and throttle it to death. Barry had told me on more than one occasion that he feared for our financial security. He had taken several steps based on his premonitions, and there were stacks of cash stockpiled in various locations around the house.

But I didn't want to believe that the inevitable had actually come to pass. Would the great American empire truly be brought to its knees, with no prior warning?

Strolling through the streets that afternoon with Lisa and Davey in tow, I was forced to admit that Barry's anxiety had been well-placed. Hours had elapsed since I had seen him last, and I was concerned for his well-being. How was he holding up under a barrage of bitter consumers and disillusioned pensioners? Was anyone protecting the bank staff from the rioting mobs?

"Huey! Hey, Huey! Look here!"

Davey's voice caroused down the street and I followed its path in fascination. It led me towards a huddled mass of humanity sitting atop a pile of mattresses in the bitter cold.

Huey.

"Huey, what are you doing out here?" Davey asked curiously, surveying the bizarre scene.

"My papa said we have to leave the house," Huey explained matter-of-factly.

"But it's so cold! And why did you take out all your beds?"

Huey shrugged.

"Don't know. Mama said we should take everythin' out because the landlord said that the bad bank is gonna come soon."

Davey stared at his friend blankly.

"The bank?! Like, my Dad?"

"Your Dad works in the bank?" Huey asked with a spark of interest.

Davey nodded enthusiastically.

"Good. So he could tell the bad people there that it's our house and we have nowhere to go."

"Yeah, I'll tell him," Davey assured his shivering friend. "You just wait and see. My dad will get you back your house."

I averted my gaze from the awful scene. Mrs. Mcneil's desperate eyes followed me down the block, while her husband's smoldering stare shot daggers in my back. Worst of all was little Huey's innocent dependence upon Davey's empty promise. He appeared chipper and optimistic after their short exchange.

Blustery winds buffeted us from all directions, and I instinctively pulled my children closer to me. They shouldn't be seeing these distressing sights. Their innocent view of the world was undergoing a rude awakening on this black day, and there was nothing I could do to protect them.

As we continued walking along the Avenue, we passed people in various stages of agitation. Some were waving their fists and spluttering epithets that made me want to put my hands over my ears, while others were staring ahead vacantly.

"Mommy, why is everyone so sad today?" Lisa inquired.

Why, indeed. Could I possibly explain the complexities of their graceless fall from financial security? How could I introduce my children to the dark face of life; the face that looked upon poverty and hunger with eyes that had seen the underside of human nature?

Davey had been unnaturally quiet ever since we met Huey's family huddling in the frigid outdoors. He finally expressed that which had kept his active mind occupied.

"Mom, did Daddy really take away their money?"

"Of course not, Davey!" I exclaimed with horror. "Daddy would never take away someone's money!"

"B...but everyone is screaming about the bank," Davey persisted. "And our Daddy *is* the bank!"

"I'll explain everything when we get home," I said. "Lisa shouldn't be traipsing around in the cold today."

"Lisa, Lisa," Davey muttered.

That gives you another ten minutes, Estelle. What will you tell the children? How will you enlighten them to the fact that there are people out there who simply have no place to call their own? Children raised in a world of plenty cannot fathom the concept of grueling hunger and biting cold.

Just like you, Estelle, never fully understood what your childhood friends were grappling with. Even Anna remained a paradox to you.

Anna. Where is she now? I wonder -

"Every last penny! Do you hear?!"

Mrs. Portnoy's gravelly voice reached me from around the corner, and I braced myself for a most uncomfortable encounter.

"I saved and sweated every day of my life - for what?! So that my retirement fund should be wiped out by the powers that be?! So that all those high-flying stockbrokers should laugh at my naiveté?!"

There she was, her gray bun bobbing ceaselessly as she held forth before a crowd of neighbors and acquaintances.

"Whom do we have here?!"

Her eyes bored into mine, pinning me to my spot. I put my arms around my children's shoulders, waiting with a sort of horrified fascination for the axe to fall.

"Madame Bonair! Your husband must be laughing uproariously at my downfall, huh? I deposited my savings every month with him, you hear that? Every month without fail I brought him my business!"

I stared at her without uttering a word. Anything I would say would just add fuel to the uncontrollable fires.

"Look at me, Madame Bonair," Mrs. Portnoy demanded. "Look at me, a hard-working citizen who's been duped by the system. Justice will yet be served, you high-flying party-goer! Don't think that you can prance around with your luxurious minks while we huddle in rags! Justice will yet be served!"

I realized that the harangue would continue endlessly until I removed myself from the scene. People in trouble naturally seek to place blame, and I was a perfect victim. Standing stoically in the center of the wide street, I was asking for others to begin spewing their venom at me.

"Come, children," I whispered urgently. "Let's go."

They followed me obediently, sensing my shame and desperation. Davey couldn't resist looking back at the milling crowd, but Lisa kept her eyes fastened to the ground. I knew that her sensitive soul had been battered badly by the morning's excursion, but I hoped that the experience would help her grow and mature. It wouldn't hurt her to know that there were others less fortunate than her.

Our large mahogany door had never looked so inviting. I hurried up the path to the veranda, pulling Lisa and Davey after me. With fingers gone suddenly unreliable, I tried to fit the key into the lock but it mocked me gleefully.

"Here, let me do it," Davey offered.

I gave him the key and he effortlessly let us in. Without pausing to thank him, I closed the door firmly behind us and secured the two bolts. Gallita was at my side in an instant, taking off my mink overcoat and offering me a hot drink to banish the frigidity.

"Thank you, Gallita. I don't think that will be necessary."

"Oh, Madame! This has been a difficult day; very difficult."

Did Gallita know about the stock market's collapse already? How had the news penetrated our protected estate?

"What - what was so difficult, Gallita?" I inquired worriedly.

"The gardener came an hour late and I thought he wouldn't show up. And then the butcher promised he would be here by noon, but he still hasn't come!"

I breathed a sigh of relief. Gallita's concerns were miniscule when placed in context. What wouldn't Huey's parents do to be bothered by such details?

"Don't worry, Gallita," I reassured her. "It will all work out."

"And Mr. Bonair - he came home very early today. He said he doesn't feel good and then he went upstairs," she continued. "I asked him if he wants a cup of tea, but he said no. He doesn't want anything. Just that I should leave him alone."

The poor girl seemed close to tears. She was so devoted and concerned. It truly bothered her when one of the family members looked askance at her ministrations.

"I'll go up and see to Mr. Bonair," I said. "Why don't you help the children get settled in their rooms? Dinner should be ready soon."

Gallita bobbed her head enthusiastically, turning towards the children who were still huddled near the door. With an impish smile, Davey ducked behind his sister and escaped towards the living room. He would keep Gallita in a tizzy for the next few minutes, until one of them would concede defeat.

I climbed the stairs wearily, dragging the world's anguish on my shoulders. From the middle of the stairwell, I could already hear Barry's frenzied pacing, beating a staccato tattoo on our carpeted floor. His day must have been one long series of recrimination and retribution.

"Barry?"

The pacing stopped mid-step, and our bedroom door creaked open. He stepped into the well-lit corridor, shielding his eyes from the sudden glare. In his tortured facial expression, I saw Huey's hopeful stance, his parents' despair, and Mrs. Portnoy's fury. I saw mounds of shattered dreams and heaps of disappointment outlined in the furrows on his forehead.

"Are you going to ask me how my day was?" Barry inquired, half in jest.

"Uh...I imagine you'll tell me."

"Awful. Beyond anything you can imagine," he tersely stated. "Anger. Complaints. Demands. I felt like a caged animal terrorized by hordes of vicious onlookers."

I waited silently, unsure of how to respond. I couldn't in good faith reassure him that everything would blow over in a matter of days. Nor could I commiserate with an entity too large for my mind to encompass. Barry didn't wait for my response. He launched into a description of his day at J.P. Morgan; a day that would live in infamy forever more.

"As soon as I approached my desk, I knew that my premonitions had been well-founded," Barry said. "There was a flurry of messages heaped on one side, and several employees were cowering before me."

'What happened?' I asked them.

"None of them had the courage to answer. They stared at each other, at the floor, at the ceiling - anywhere but at me, their manager. Finally, Clemens mumbled something about rumors and reports that had them all concerned. He said that the stock market had opened with a whopping Dow Jones downslide. I assured them that I would look into the matter, and sent them back to their posts.

"I looked into the matter, Estelle. Actually, the matter looked at me - it stared me in the face with all the grace and discretion of a five-ton elephant! Within moments of my arrival, a commotion ensued in the bank's lobby. Hordes of people descended upon the tellers, demanding their money. They wanted to withdraw their savings and to redeem their bonds, Estelle, but...but there was nothing to withdraw!"

I gasped in horror. How could millions of dollars simply disappear like wisps of curling smoke?! How could people lose their safety nets in an instant of chaos and confusion?!

"They screamed, Estelle, and I couldn't blame them. Normal, sane people lost their composure before my eyes. They spoke in a manner that would put the lowliest riffraff to shame, oftentimes resorting to violence in an effort to express their indignation.

"But I was helpless! I couldn't create money from a pit of nothingness! I couldn't retrieve their fortunes that had been sucked into a maelstrom of disaster!

"So I tried to calm them down. I told them that the United States Government wouldn't let them down."

Barry shook his head at the memory of those traumatic moments.

"They didn't believe me, Estelle," he whispered. "It's no wonder. I didn't even believe myself. But they blamed *me*! Barry Bonair, bank manager, became the address for their vicious tirades."

He covered his face with his hands, allowing me a glimpse of the vulnerable child concealed beneath layers of prestige and success. I was furious that people had attacked this upstanding person for naught, yet I understood their frustration. The carpet had been pulled out from under their feet and it was imperative that they find someone to blame; someone to point fingers at.

"Foreclosures. Estelle, you have no idea how many families will be turned out into the bitter cold because the bank will have to repossess their homes."

"Huey," I quietly remarked. "Davey's friend has already been crowned homeless. I saw his family sitting on their mattresses, shivering in the cold."

Barry merely nodded. He had heard more than his share of similar stories. But this was Huey! A person with a name and a face and a family. A person with wants and dreams, who was now reduced to groveling on the ground for sustenance.

"Can't you do something, Barry? They need a home! There's no way they'll survive the winter without a roof over their heads."

Barry shook his head miserably.

"I wish I could help them, Estelle. Do you know how many others find themselves in similar situations? There's nothing I can do. Nothing! My hands are tied..."

I fell silent. I didn't want to join the multitudes who accused my husband of sitting idly by whilst their fortunes turned to dust. If Barry insisted that he was helpless, it must be so. Why didn't everyone else see it the same way?

"What about us, Barry?" I finally ventured. "Did our savings also run into the ground?"

Barry smiled; a tired smile that couldn't chase away the demons of morn.

"We lost a lot, Estelle. I won't pretend that my position spared me, but it did allow me to foresee a crisis. Over the past few months, I've been withdrawing large sums of money and concealing them in various safes and vaults. We won't starve, Estelle. Our children won't wander the streets in search of food."

Visions of Lisa standing on a street corner begging for alms flitted by on ravens' wings and I exhaled in relief. Davey wouldn't be forced to shine others' shoes and I wouldn't have to exchange my elegant wardrobe for heaps of rags. I felt it almost sacrilegious to feel so relieved when countless others were struggling with my imagined disasters.

"You're a lucky woman, Estelle," Barry said with a smile. "I don't know why I burdened you with today's traumatic happenings. Life will continue running smoothly for the Bonair family."

I'm a lucky woman. I can continue wearing my exquisite gowns and lacy hats, as I've always done. I can occupy myself with parties and tea-time gatherings...because I'm lucky. Esther Hofert of Plawo, born with the spoon of luck firmly entrenched in her mouth.

Don't you think so, Tatte? Don't you consider me lucky beyond description?!

Part II:
Plawo, Poland
1912

Chapter Six

*M*aria, the laundry basket is waiting in the courtyard," *Mamme* kindly intoned, as she did every Wednesday morning. "Do you have enough
soap to last the day?"

"Yes, yes," Maria hurriedly reassured her. "I will go
right now. Is Esther ready?"

I could imagine *Mamme* raising her hands in a gesture of resignation. *Where was Esther,* she was probably
wondering. Her darling, sixteen-year-old princess had
not yet put in an appearance since last night, and Mama
must be frustrated at the silent display of protest.

"Esther!" *Mamme* called out. "Esther'ke!"

I furtively peered into the kitchen, only to disappear
from view within mere seconds.

"Esther, it's time to leave."

Mama's voice brooked no objections. The door swung
open and I smilingly stepped into the room. My hair was
done up in a neat braid, similar to the hairstyles of my
contemporaries. It had that elegant twist, however, that I
insisted on forming every morning to the utter annoyance
of my practical mother. She couldn't understand my need
for individuality; the desperate urge to set myself apart
from my peers.

"Yes, *Mamme*," I cheerfully called out, forcefully biting the inside of my cheek when I discerned *Mamme's* annoyance. "I was sitting in my room, awaiting your summons."

Maria smothered a chuckle of disbelief before heaving the laundry basket onto her shoulders and heading in the direction of the river. Resignedly shrugging my shoulders, I gracefully turned on my heel and followed in her wake. Certain tasks could not be shirked, despite my coveted status as Shimon Hofert's only daughter. Supervising the maid on laundry days obviously fell into this category.

The winding path leading towards the San River was a study in contrasts. A neatly-paved cobblestone walkway meandered through the shrubs and trees, cutting into the wilderness with nary an apology. Each time anew, I felt a surge of righteous anger at the injustice of it all. How could a human hand dare to impinge upon this scene of untamed beauty?

"Maria, doesn't this path seem misplaced?" I inquired dreamily.

"No, it is good," replied the washer-woman, shifting the laundry basket with a groan of pain. "I like this path."

I barely listened to her response. My gaze was focused on the distant horizon, seeking the precise distinction between water and sky. Lost in thought, I didn't notice that we had reached our destination.

"Esther, stop!" Maria cried, clutching my elbow in consternation. "Oh, what would your Mama say? You nearly walked into the water!"

"Nearly but not quite," I replied with a smile.

I sat down under the shade of my favorite elm and leaned upon its sturdy trunk. A pleasant breeze blew through the trees, playfully teasing the stately crowns of foliage. I languidly smoothed down my ruffled skirts and tucked runaway wisps of chestnut hair behind my ears.

Thwack, thwack! Drip. Thwack, thwack!

Maria was assiduously completing her assigned task under my lackadaisical supervision. Washing laundry was a full-day affair and Wednesdays had been assigned solely for this time-consuming chore. Although Maria had been stationed at our home for nearly a decade, Mama did not yet trust her implicitly. Perfection in household tasks ranked high on Mama's list of priorities and she demanded nothing less from her household help.

Laundry days were such a bore. I was forced to sit on the riverbank for hours in a stretch, watching Maria cleaning our linens. If only Maria would be more of a conversationalist, the chore would be bearable. She generally spoke in monosyllables, conserving her energy for what she considered truly important. Like washing laundry, for instance.

Closing my eyes, I gave myself over to the one passion that remained mine alone. I felt the sun dancing lazily across my eyelids, and I heard the water swishing smoothly a short distance away.

I sang. Here, at the riverbank, I didn't have to worry that my voice would carry too far. It was my sole source of pleasure in an utterly tasteless task.

Maria grunted in pleasure, as she did every week. She enjoyed the musical accompaniment to her repetitive motions, and she was certain that I sang solely in her honor.

A short while later, I spotted another laundress standing at the far end of the river, diligently scrubbing a white shirt. Maybe she would be receptive to my friendly overtures. Ambling over to where she stood under the glaring sun, I was surprised that she did not seem familiar in the least. I couldn't place her face with any of the Plawo families...and there weren't many faces that remained unknown to me. In a little town like ours, the lines between family and friends were often blurred beyond distinction.

"Hello!" I called out.

The girl looked at me with blatant curiosity, but she offered not a word in response.

"Whose laundress are you?" I inquired politely, attempting to begin a conversation that seemed doomed from the start.

"Laundress?!" the girl finally said. "I am nobody's laundress!"

I blinked in surprise. Well, really. Did she think I was oblivious to the task she was completing at the riverbank?

"Do you want me to believe that you're dunking clothes in the water as a sport?"

I tried to keep the sarcasm out of my voice, but from the girl's flushed cheeks I realized that she'd detected it.

"For your information, girls tend to help out their mothers. At least, that's how it works in *my* part of town."

I was floored. The girl had just knocked the wind out of my sails, and I didn't even know her name.

"Which part of town is that?"

Pointing towards the far side of the river, she replied, "Right over there. I live in that small cottage with the thatched roof."

Oh. The school teacher's daughter. So that's why I didn't recognize her at first glance.

"Nice to meet you," I said politely.

It was time to make a quick getaway. I had nothing in common with this girl, nor did I seek a friendship with someone so far removed from my sheltered world.

"Same here," she replied quickly. "My name is Anna Podolsky. What's yours?"

"Esther Hofert."

"Oh, now I understand! You must be the daughter of Shimon Hofert, the richest man in Plawo."

I nodded, not quite understanding what my identity had clarified.

"That's why you thought I was a laundress! In your

perception, people who do honest and upright work must be servants, correct?"

Anna laughed; a tinkling sound that made me want to share her mirth.

"I also do honest and upright work," I said in my defense. It wouldn't do to have myself portrayed as a lazy good-for-nothing living off her family's largesse.

"Give me one good example," Anna demanded.

"Well...I...I come here every Wednesday to supervise Maria," I triumphantly declared.

"Isn't that splendid?! You come to relax at the riverbank and then you have the audacity to term that 'work'! Isn't there anything else you do?"

"Not really. I mean, I sometimes deliver *Mamme*'s baked goods to my brother's house. And...and once in a while I accompany my sister-in-law on a walk through the streets."

The words sounded lame in my own ears, and from Anna's expression I figured that they echoed much worse in hers. What *did* I do all day? There was never a need for my assistance, considering that I was the youngest child and the only unmarried sibling. *Mamme* had ample assistance on a daily basis and my efforts were simply superfluous. It wasn't that I was lazy. I was just not needed.

"On Tuesdays, I accompany *Mamme* to the market place," I desperately added. "We go from stall to stall and choose the finest produce for - "

Anna had turned her attention to the laundry and I stared at her energetic movements with a twinge of envy.

"I even help *Mamme* decide what fabrics to purchase for our wardrobe. And it's not as though I stand near the Town Hall in the center of the marketplace, waiting for *Mamme* to finish her shopping," I said. "I go from one stall to the other, and - "

"Spare me the details," Anna interrupted. "The description of your hard work is truly overwhelming me."

I bit my lips in consternation. Apparently, first impressions were not my forte. Not when it came to a strong-willed, self-assured stranger who had no compunctions in grinding my coveted status to dust.

"You must feel so fulfilled when the laundry is sparkling clean," I ventured.

"Mmm...I wouldn't exchange my hard work for your endless hours of leisure. Not even if I was blessed with your beautiful voice."

"But...but I'm lucky!" I countered. "I don't *have* to do anything. It's not like I'm shirking my responsibilities!"

"What could be worse than that?" Anna replied. "Not to be needed by anyone or anything? Sounds pretty awful to me."

She's right. My friends envy my easy life, but they don't perceive the stark emptiness that accompanies me at every step. They begrudge the hours spent tending to their younger siblings or helping in the kitchen, but they would never be satisfied with endless hours of nothingness.

Splash!

"Oh, bother!" Anna muttered. "When I do this without company, I'm more adept."

"I'm sorry."

"Sorry won't remove the mud."

"You don't have to be so rude," I blurted. "Don't they teach you any manners in your part of town?"

Anna looked up at me, and a mischievous twinkle dominated her large green eyes.

"I was wondering whether anything could pull you out of your self-induced complacency."

Huh?

"I figured that a spoiled only daughter requires some toughening up," she continued. *"Spoiled Princess."*

"Wh-what did you just say?"

"Nothing you would understand," Anna smugly replied.

"Try me!"

"*Spoiled Princess.*"

"That's not Polish," I slowly contended. "What language are you speaking?"

"English, for your information."

I gazed with newfound respect at the girl standing before me. My preconceived notions of an uneducated country bumpkin skittered into the water.

"You know the English language?" I asked incredulously.

"Apparently."

Anna was intently focused on her laundry, and I was miffed. Never before had someone displayed such blatant disinterest in my presence. My friends knew that when Esther arrived, scintillating conversations would follow. What did this self-assured upstart think - that she was too good for someone like me?!

"Will you teach me what you learned?" I queried.

Anna shrugged noncommittally, but I was not one to give up so easily.

"Will you?"

She finally turned around to face me head-on.

"You sure are determined, aren't you?" she asked with a smile. "I would never believe you had it in you."

"That's not supposed to be a compliment by any chance, is it?"

Anna laughed, that sweet, tinkling sound that made the world seem so much brighter than it had moments before.

"Listen, Esther," she said. "I would gladly teach you some English, but I can't tutor you free of charge."

I was taken aback. Anna had very successfully backed me into a corner. There was no way that I could ask my parents for funds in order to learn the English language. They would be scandalized by the mere suggestion of such outlandish aspirations!

"I can't do that," I admitted. "My parents wouldn't agree to such an arrangement. They didn't even allow my brothers to attend the school of Baron Hirsh, although all their friends were enrolled there. No, my parents wouldn't allow it."

"Your parents? What do they have to do with this?"

"Just because I'm Shimon Hofert's daughter, doesn't mean that I walk around with a stuffed purse!" I blurted, annoyed by her overbearing attitude. "I'm not such a *spoil prin-cess* as you think!"

"You're a great student!" Anna merrily remarked. "Repeating a phrase during your first lesson...That's an accomplishment."

"You mean, my last lesson," I muttered darkly, visions of English fluency withering in the summer heat. "Without my parents' permission, I can't fund these tutoring sessions."

"Who's talking about funds?" Anna asked in surprise.

"You just told me that you won't tutor me free of charge."

"Of course not! I expect something in return. Don't you know anything that I don't?"

Now I understood. Anna was hungry for knowledge, and on this point we were on equal ground. I had always pestered my big brothers to share their learning with me, but they had shrugged off my requests with a laugh. At one point, Zalmen had finally agreed to teach me how to read Hebrew, on the condition that *Tatte* would never know about our surreptitious endeavor.

"I can read Hebrew," I ventured fearfully.

Never before had I admitted to this feat, and I wondered why I was sharing my most treasured secret with someone I barely knew. When Anna's eyes lit up, I knew that I had hit the mark.

"Wonderful!" she exclaimed. "I'll teach you English, in exchange for your Hebrew. Is it a deal?"

I nodded, suddenly overcome with misgiving. Did I really think it appropriate to teach a Christian girl the Hebrew language? It was...absurd! How could I share the holy letters of the *Alef Beis* with her?!

Anna didn't give me time to reconsider.

"My mother usually takes care of the laundry," she remarked. "This week I offered to take over, seeing that she's so preoccupied with my grandmother's illness.

"I think I'll make this a permanent change," she cheerfully continued. "Won't Mama be thrilled?!"

I nodded enthusiastically. Anna's presence would spell the end to my laundry-day ennui, and herald the expansion of my vistas. I could already picture myself spouting fluent English to the surprise and wonder of...of whom? I wouldn't dare reveal this secret to my friends, let alone my parents. It would have to remain between Anna and me.

Maria was already finishing up by the time I remembered to supervise her actions. Feeling slightly remorseful at my negligence, I bid Anna good-bye.

"Until next week, Esther," she reminded me.

Until next week.

Chapter Seven

*T*he path towards home was strewn with stones and pebbles, but I failed to complain about them as I did every week. Maria walked alongside me, balancing the heavy laundry basket in her arms. She looked at me strangely from time to time, no doubt wondering at my good spirits and cheerful humming. She must have appreciated the change from my usual dour post-laundry countenance.

This time was different. I had not spent the endless hours wallowing in a sea of boredom and self-pity. Instead, I had been treated to a scintillating conversation with someone who actually shared my thirst for knowledge. It was an invigorating experience.

What would Mamme say to this new friendship? I wouldn't dare find out. She would certainly comment on Anna's religion, and on her questionable upbringing. Then she would once again bemoan the fact that I display no interest in forming close bonds with my peers. 'What's wrong with Chaya Malka, the Rav's daughter?' she would ask. 'I'm sure you could find a lot to discuss with her.'

Anna was different. She understood me without my needing to explain everything in detail, and furthermore, she wasn't intimidated by my lineage. *Tatte's* position as

Plawo's elected *Rosh Hakahel* did not cast its shadow over our relationship and for that I was grateful.

Lebowitz's cow greeted us with a swish of its hairy tail, and I instinctively quickened my pace. Home was but a few steps away. Humming energetically, I rushed up the three wide stairs, waiting impatiently for Maria to get herself and the unwieldy basket through the entranceway.

As soon as I followed Maria through the door, I realized that today would be one of *those* days. A lone candle flickered in mournful splendor on the table, and *Mamme* sat immobile on a hard-backed chair, staring into its fathomless depths.

"Chaim Hershele," *Mamme* whispered. "*Mein kind*, Chaim Hershele."

Today was Chaim Hersh's *yahrtzeit*. He had been taken from us at the tender age of eight, when a severe bout of tuberculosis resisted the doctor's best efforts at eradication. I had been only two years old at the time of the tragedy, but I had lived in its shadow ever since.

Sometimes I felt as though *Mamme* expected me to display Chaim Hershele's outstanding brilliance, Miriam's golden-haired grace, and the innocence of two newborns who had died in childbirth. I was the one who carried the burden of my siblings' unfulfilled futures, and the responsibility weighed heavily upon my young shoulders.

I can't remain here, I thought with finality. *The house is saturated with grief; suffused with shattered hopes and slaughtered dreams. It would be best if I made myself scarce until nightfall.*

The remaining hours stretched before me, questioning my right to desert my mother during such a difficult time. Anna's pithy English description reverberated accusingly in my mind. *Spoiled Princess. Spoiled Princess.* Was this yet another display of my derided status? As an only daughter, shouldn't I remain near *Mamme* to offer solace with my mere presence?

I couldn't. *Mamme's* red-rimmed eyes frightened me and her gut-wrenching sobs tore my heart to shreds. It was too distressing to view my composed and gracious *Mamme* shuddering with grief at the memory of all she had lost.

I would go to Zalmen's house. Of my two older brothers, Zalmen was always my first address during moments of insecurity. He understood me better than I understood myself, and I sensed his genuine concern for his baby sister.

Menachem, on the other hand, was almost from a different generation. He had gotten married way before I was born, and his brood of lively boys had always overwhelmed me. To him, I was a curiosity. He had no girls of his own, and therefore didn't quite know how to deal with my quirks and concerns. Now that he had relocated to distant Krakow, our connection had fizzled out to a measly annual visit.

"Esther! What brings you to my humble abode?"

Zalmen stood on the side of the road and hailed me with a warm smile. He was clutching a large *Gemara* in one hand, and a stack of handwritten sheets in the other.

He must be going to deliver a shiur, I realized. *How could I have forgotten? As a newly-minted Maggid Shiur, Zalmen makes sure to be at his post at least an hour before the designated time.*

"Uh...Hello. I came just to visit," I stammered, suddenly ashamed of my cowardice. "What's so strange with an aunt visiting her adorable nieces and nephews?"

A raised eyebrow was the only response I got.

"Actually, I came to help Miri," I amended.

This declaration elicited a good-natured laugh from my brother.

"To help Miri?" Zalmen chortled. "How can my little

sister possibly help around the house?"

I was miffed. It was enough that a girl whom I had never seen before had titled me a spoiled princess. There was no reason why I should put up with that attitude from my own sibling!

"I'll have you know, R' Zalmen Hofert, that I am perfectly capable of holding little Shmuel and even playing with Chaya'la," I stated confidently. "You go ahead and give your *shiur* and rest assured that I'll keep the house running smoothly."

"So long as you hold Shmuel right side up," Zalmen cautioned, his eyes twinkling merrily. "At four weeks old, he's a bit too young for an aunt's experimentation."

I didn't even deign to reply. Waving farewell, I proceeded down the gravelly path that led directly to Zalmen's door. My hesitant knock was answered almost immediately by Miri, as calm and composed as ever. Despite the fact that her four-week-old Shmuel was gaining notoriety as a fussy baby, Miri managed to appear as though she were a newlywed instead of a mother to four little children.

"Esther! What a surprise!"

I flushed at her astonishment. An aunt was supposed to be a regular fixture in the homes of her nieces and nephews - especially if that aunt was a *spoiled princess* with no homemaking responsibilities. Miri's initial reaction was the most fitting confirmation of Anna's biting analysis. *Spoiled Princess.*

"Hello, Miri," I said, mustering the shreds of my self-confidence. "Is...is there anything I can help you with?"

The look on her face was one of such comical disbelief that I ditched my hurt in favor of amusement. Ten minutes previous, Zalmen had displayed the same reaction at my magnanimous offer.

"What happened?" she inquired worriedly. "You can

tell me, Esther. Is something going on at home?"

"No. Actually, yes. I came home with the laundress to find *Mamme* sitting at the table, near a lit candle."

Miri wordlessly pointed to the sideboard, where a small candle cast its flickering shadows upon the assorted knickknacks.

"Chaim Hersh," she said. "Do you remember him at all?"

I shook my head. No, I had no recollection of this wonder-child who had left his mark on my carefree childhood.

"I was a young girl of twelve when tragedy struck your family," Miri reminisced. "Since we lived just two houses down, I was privy to the goings-on that preceded that awful day. How your mother doted upon her *tzaddik'l*, her *ilui*. She sat at his bedside, feeding him spoonfuls of chicken soup. As soon as Chaim Hershele fell asleep, she started murmuring verses of Tehillim..."

Miri shuddered.

"I'll never forget the mournful sounds of her whispered pleas. Every time I stepped into the house to deliver a homemade meal, I was enveloped in that eerie existence where heaven and earth intermingle. There was a battle going on, and your *Mamme* was determined to be the victor."

"And where was I during those weeks?" I asked.

"You were in Zalmen's care continuously," Miri explained. "You followed him to *yeshiva*, to *beis medrash*... practically everywhere! It was a sight to see! Dressed in frilly pink dresses and adorned with the most charming socks and bows, you accompanied your tall, serious brother to his studies, day after day."

My sister-in-law fell silent, and I was afraid to push for details. No one had ever shared with me the events of that dreadful day, and I wasn't sure if I really wanted to hear about it.

"It was a beautiful summer morning when we heard frenzied screaming emanating from your home," Miri forged on. "My mother ran over to your house to hold your *Mamme*'s hand, but all was not over yet. Chaim Hershele was delirious with fever, and he was thrashing about in unbearable agony.

'I see the Angel of Death,' your *Mamme* screamed. 'He wants to snatch my baby's soul! NO! Chase him away!'

"It was so unlike your mother to create such a scene, but pain and panic can do that to the most self-controlled individuals. I followed my mother into the house, and the eerie screams seared my heart.

'He's coming closer!' she sobbed frantically. 'Can't someone save him?! Chaim Hershele, *gei nisht*! Don't go with him! Stay with me!'

"Mother held your *Mamme*'s hand, while I sponged down Chaim Hershele's flaming forehead. I didn't even notice your *Tatte* standing in the corner of the room and reciting the *Viduy* prayers. It was only when he approached the sickbed to enunciate the words of *Shema* that I grasped the enormity of the situation.

"Your parents were bidding their beloved son farewell. With love and devotion, they accompanied him on his final journey. Your father did it with acceptance, while your mother didn't let go until she realized that the decree could not be annulled. I was young, just twelve years old at the time, but I sensed the holiness in the room as your brother groaned for the last time.

'Chaim Hershele!' your *Mamme* sobbed. 'Go up there to our *Tatte in Himmel* and pray for us that we have the strength to go on. Your pure little *neshama'la* will surely adorn His crown for eternity.'

"My mother gently shepherded me out of the house, horrified that I had been present during those agonizing moments. We went home, but my heart remained in that little room, with your dear *Mamme*. Her pain had been so intense; so overwhelming - yet she had accepted Hashem's decree. I was awed by her strength, Esther."

Mamme! How did you do it? How did you muster the courage to forge on; to care for a rambunctious toddler with love and warmth? You gave me a carefree childhood, Mamme, despite the hardships.

At that moment, little Shmuel voiced his protest at the earnest discussion. His piercing cries were so alive; so healthy! I instinctively reached out to take him from Miri's arms, desperate to feel the warmth of his little body and the reassurance of his hurried heartbeat.

Miri watched my awkward movements with bemusement. Without a word of protest, she allowed me to try my hand at calming a fussy newborn. I held Shmuel over my shoulder, imitating the effortless pose of my experienced sisters-in-law. No luck. Shmuel's lungs were remarkably well-developed for a baby so small!

"I don't know how to do this," I finally conceded, handing the child back to his mother. "I guess I'm not much good at baby care."

"It comes with experience, Esther'ke," Miri reassured me. "Maybe Chaya'la would appreciate your company."

After Shmuel's cold reception, I wasn't sure about Chaya'la's level of interest but it was definitely worth a try. Zalmen would surely inquire after my aptitude with his beloved children, and there was no way I would give him the satisfaction of my failure.

"Chaya'la, sweetie," I called out in my gentlest voice. "Where are you? Come see what Aunt Esther wants to play with you!"

What does one play with a three-year-old child? She's not interested in hearing a story, nor will she want to play with her brothers' kugelach.

Chaya'la didn't even give me the option of choosing

a game. With a sniff of disinterest, she hurried to her mother's comforting presence and hid behind her flowing skirts. Two twinkling eyes peered out from the safety of Miri's embrace, gleefully mocking my attempts at assistance.

"Miri, I give up!" I exclaimed good-naturedly. "Children pick up on our insecurities, don't they?"

Miri nodded, pointing towards the window while trying to disentangle Chaya'la and soothe Shmuel.

I followed Miri's finger and noted the darkening skies. Evening had descended upon Plawo while I had been engrossed in conversation. Somehow, in Zalmen's home, time took on a will of its own. None of my grandiose plans had come to fruition, but at least I felt equipped to return home and face *Mamme*'s overwhelming anguish.

"Don't tell Zalmen about the time I wasted," I begged. "He won't let me hear the end of it."

"I have an idea!" she exclaimed. "You see these packages lined up by the door? They've been stationed there for nearly three days, waiting for someone to have pity and return them to your house."

I smiled in relief. Here was my great opportunity to assist Miri - albeit in a miniscule way.

"I'll take them, Miri. Let no one say that I'm a spoiled princess!"

Ignoring Miri's questioning look, I grabbed hold of the three small packages and resolutely turned to go.

"Bye, *kinderlach*!" I called out, waving to Chaya'la and blowing a kiss to Shmuel.

A hearty wail was the only response they felt I deserved. On my part, I didn't think they were so off the mark. Children are very perceptive. My aborted attempts at entertaining them did not fall off their radar, much as I wished it would!

Chapter Eight

*A*nna!"

Her long blond plait bobbed in the distance as she assiduously scrubbed a mound of shirts and sheets. Although we had met numerous times in the weeks since our first encounter, I still feared that Anna would disappear from my world as suddenly as she had put in an appearance.

By now, I didn't even pretend to supervise Maria's deft movements. Leaving her to her own devices, I hurried over to Anna, as quickly as my cumbersome skirts and the uneven ground would allow.

"Anna!"

She slowly turned around, and her welcoming grin assured me that I had read the signals correctly. Anna was as interested in my company as I was in hers. Maybe she also put up with too much meaningless chatter on her side of town, and she sought the stimulation our conversations provided.

"How have you been, my *Spoiled Princess*?"

She wouldn't let up! Coming from anyone else, the words would have seemed a tasteless insult. Somehow, Anna lent them a certain lilt that transformed the words into an endearment of sorts.

"Do you want me to help you?" I offered.

"Absolutely not! I wouldn't want you to sully your delicate hands with water and soap," Anna facetiously replied.

I breathed a sigh of relief. Had she accepted my offer, I would have been hard-pressed to carry through. What did I know of stains and creases? It was Maria's job to see to those annoying details, not mine!

"Your brethren seem more than ready to sully their hands with honest, backbreaking labor," she commented, after a short pause.

"My...who?"

"You know, the Jews."

"Well, of course. Throughout the generations, we've always earned our livelihoods through honest labor. Here in Plawo, most of the residents are shoemakers, tailors, soap-makers - "

Anna shook her head.

"I don't mean livelihood, Esther. I mean all those young people who want to go up to Palestine and cultivate the land."

Oh. The Zionists. What does this young Gentile know of our inner conflicts? Is everyone aware of the new movement that has been sweeping our town, as well as so many other cities in Europe?

"You know what I'm referring to, don't you?"

It was more of a statement than a question, and I reluctantly nodded in the affirmative.

"You mean the Zionists," I said.

Silence fell between us, but it was not a comfortable silence born of friendship and mutual understanding. No, this silence hummed and brewed like the hush before an explosive confrontation.

I thought about *Bais Yehuda*, the Zionist party that had been launched in nearby Rozvodov in 1907, when I was just eleven years old. A junior division, comprised of youngsters aged twelve to fourteen, had been annexed soon after, but I had never spared them a moment of my attention. *Tatte* had vociferously expressed his opposition to the movement, and I never dreamed of questioning his stand. The Hoferts did not subscribe to the *Tag-Blatt*. We did not read the newly-published Hebrew books, nor did we attend the various lectures from guest speakers who propagated the Zionist cause.

We just didn't do that.

"You're not joining them?"

The question jolted me out of my unpleasant ruminations.

"Joining them?!" I retorted hotly. "What do you take me for - a lowly good-for-nothing?!"

"Whoa! No need to get so uptight," Anna said. "Why do you think the young Zionists are loafers?"

"They're wrong! They're exchanging a rich and glorious heritage - for what?! For emptiness! For pipe dreams!"

Anna didn't even glance in my direction. Thoroughly involved in the task at hand, she could have fooled me into believing that the topic truly did not interest her. Her blazing eyes, however, disclosed her passionate take on the issue.

"Esther, what exactly do you call 'emptiness'? In my eyes, your life is as empty as one's life can get. All you do is sleep and eat and dress up in pretty clothes. Is that meaningful?!"

The words stung. They pounced upon me in quick succession, demanding a counter-attack. But I was struck dumb by their force. I couldn't string together two words in defense of my coddled existence. Anna didn't wait for me to gather my wits.

"In my opinion, these idealistic pioneers are taking their future into their own hands. They're not just going along the path that has been mapped out for them."

"Do you know anything about that path?" I countered. "How can you deride a way of life without knowing its virtues?"

She was stumped, and I reveled in my moment of victory.

"Take my family, for instance. Yes, we have been blessed with great wealth and we don't have to till the land with our own hands. But our life is far from empty!"

I paused to collect my thoughts, noting with satisfaction that Anna had dropped all pretenses and was listening avidly to my every word.

"We live for our Creator, Anna! When I do something, I know that it has meaning. I am perpetuating a legacy that traces its way back to Creation!"

Good job, Esther, I congratulated myself. *That was a solid point!*

Anna seemed to concur. Rinsing a large sheet in the water, she said not a word. Her mind was processing my words, ostensibly seeking a loophole to insert her skewed viewpoint.

"What makes you so sure that the Zionist ideology is not a part of that self-same legacy?" she finally asked. "Isn't Palestine supposed to be the land of the Jews?"

"But it's wrong!" I blurted. "They're going about it the wrong way."

"How do you know?"

"It's wrong," I stubbornly reiterated.

Anna was highly unimpressed with my feisty assertion. From our short encounters, I already knew that she needed logical proof for every belief. She wouldn't accept the wrongness of Zionist ideals based solely on my say-so.

"You're talking like a naive child," Anna stated. "You can't disparage an entire segment of society just because you think it's wrong. More accurately, because you *feel* it's wrong!"

I didn't respond. There was nothing to say to her valid rebuttal. I had no tools at my disposal to refute her words, and I felt powerless to defend the sanctity of my heritage.

"Bring me some logical proof, Esther!"

Anna goaded me on with her characteristic sharp tongue, and I fell for it. Suddenly, I also felt the need to obtain ironclad proof that the Zionist ideals were undermining my religion. I would gather facts and information and confront Anna with an irrefutable truism.

"By the time next week rolls around, Anna, I'll have you convinced!"

Anna merely smiled; a smile that concealed more than it revealed.

"I'll attend one of their accursed meetings if only to show you how twisted their theories are!"

Another smile; another wordless challenge.

"Don't look at me like that, Anna! I promise you - by this time next week, you'll be forced to concede that I'm correct."

"It would be my pleasure," Anna graciously replied. "So long as you supply logical arguments, I'm ready to agree with your viewpoint."

It was a challenge, and I jumped towards it with alacrity. Esther Hofert was going to defend *Yiddishkeit!* I would show Anna that our heritage was not to be tampered with.

Tatte would be proud of me. He would never allow someone to disparage our way of life, and he would certainly want me to take the initiative in defending our religion.

Somehow, that last thought niggled at my conscience as I traipsed back to town behind Maria. Would *Tatte* really want me to attend a Zionist meeting? True, I was attending with the sole aspiration to disprove all their misplaced ideals. And yet... *Tatte* might not see things in the same light as they appeared to me.

Maybe I should leave the thorny discussions for those who are more well-versed in these issues. I don't want to incur *Tatte*'s wrath over a matter as fleeting as Anna's friendship. She would understand.

A hum of staid conversation greeted me as I reached the center of town. Several of my peers were settled around the giant oak that graced the tax-collector's courtyard, and their existence suddenly seemed so appealing in its simplicity and integrity. I signaled to Maria that she could continue on her own, and joined the cluster of girls.

"Old Mrs. Feingold taught me a new stitch last week and I finally got the hang of it."

"Really? Which stitch is that?"

"It's the double leaf stitch. You know, the one where you have to loop the thread into itself to get a leaf-like outline."

I listened to Etta's detailed explanation, trying to maintain a facade of polite interest. As soon as Etta spied me sitting on the outskirts of the circle she fell silent, ceasing her chatter mid-stream.

"Oh, Esther!" Etta exclaimed, using that deferential tone that so irked me. "I didn't realize that you had joined us!"

"Don't mind me, Etta," I said. "Just continue describing your double leaf stitch. I am finding it very...uh...fascinating."

Etta exchanged a meaningful glance with Malka, who was sitting on her right. Their skeptical looks plainly told me that my assurances had not merited a shred of acceptance.

"That's alright," Malka said, with saccharine-coated tones. "It's always a pleasure when you join our conversations. We don't get to see you often enough."

Well, of course not! I wanted to retort, but wisely kept

my counsel. *When you discuss embroidery stitches, baking tips, and sibling rivalry, I have nothing to contribute!*

A strained silence engulfed us. Furrowed brows bore testimony to the efforts invested in finding an appropriate topic that would suit the sophisticated needs of Esther Hofert. After all, she couldn't be bothered with simple, everyday chatter. Her existence was on a different plane from that of the average Plawo teenager.

I smiled mirthlessly at my all-too-accurate perception of my friends' thoughts. Was it any wonder that I felt uncomfortable in their presence? They placed me in a glass cage, not allowing me to join their conversations while expecting me to provide them with glimpses of a life they envied.

"Where's Rechel?" Malka suddenly inquired. "I haven't seen her all day."

"Oh, Rechel!" Chava'la exclaimed, dramatically putting her hand on her heart. "Don't ask!"

This comment piqued our interest, as its speaker had intended. We leaned forward to hear the latest Plawo news tidbit. Somehow, Chava'la always managed to get hold of these snippets before any of us even suspected that anything was afoot.

"Rechel is sitting at home with her parents," Chava'la said. "The shutters are closed and the door is securely locked."

"You're giving me the creeps!" Etta complained. "Tell us what happened already!"

"I'm getting there! They're all sitting at home, and refusing to see any visitors. It's like a *shiva* house," Chava'la whispered. "As though they're mourning someone's death."

There was a sharp intake of breath - probably silent Devorah's contribution to the conversation. She took things terribly to heart and couldn't bear discussing anything remotely painful or difficult.

"In fact, they are mourning someone," Chava'la pronounced deliberately.

"What?! Who?!"

"Who passed away?"

"I heard her grandmother was ill..."

Chava'la held up her hand and everyone fell silent, dancing to the beat of the drama queen's drum.

"They're mourning someone, but not his death," she said.

"Could you just tell us what happened?" Malka asked in exasperation. "Don't make us pull out each measly detail by force!"

Chava'la looked in the other direction, focusing on her more compliant listeners, myself amongst them.

"Rechel's brother left with a Zionist youth group this morning."

Pandemonium broke loose in the cozy little circle. Devorah seemed on the verge of tears, while Etta stared at Chava'la with her mouth agape. I also tried to muster a semblance of horrified astonishment at the news, but my conversation with Anna had ruined my chances.

See how they're reacting to the news? I silently argued with a non-existent Anna. *It's obvious that Rechel's brother trespassed on forbidden ground. His family is mourning his spiritual demise, Anna! In their eyes, Zionism is death! Death!*

Chava'la was not done with her masterful storytelling. When she was certain that our attention was once again focused solely on her, she picked up the thread of her shocking revelations.

"Pinchus Kramer had been attending those awful meetings for quite some time. His parents, of course, didn't know about his nighttime activities. But Rechel... Rechel knew! She had discovered his dark secret and she concealed it from her parents."

"Why did she do that?!" Devorah blurted.

We all turned to look at her in surprise. Her face was a mottled red, as though the effort of actually speaking aloud had cost her dearly.

"Why she kept it a secret?" Chava'la repeated. "She wanted to protect her brother from her parents' wrath. Who knows what they would have done if they would have found out about his secular interests?!"

"But she could have saved Pinchus!" Etta argued. "If my brother would do something as ridiculous as that, I would waste no time in informing my parents!"

The girls laughed. Etta was one of ten sisters, and she always bemoaned the fact that she missed out on the excitement that having a brother entailed. Her house had never seen the joy of a *vacht nacht,* a *bris,* or an *upsherin.*

But her point was well-taken. Everyone was nodding in agreement, aside from me. I understood Rechel all too well. If one of my brothers would have gotten into serious trouble, I would have done my best to conceal the details from my parents. After all they had gone through, it was imperative that I protect them from further anguish.

Apparently, Rechel had felt the same way. Her decision, unfortunately, had exacted a bitter price.

"I can't believe he actually attended those meetings," Malka commented. "When Thursday night rolls around, I know to stay far away from old Gavriel's barn where the meetings are held."

So that's where the Zionists convene! Gavriel's barn is inconspicuous enough for their nefarious activities, and it's located at the outskirts of town.

Fradel leaned forward, and we instinctively inclined our heads to hear the confidence she seemed poised to share. Even Chava'la yielded her moment of glory in the sun to prim and proper Fradel, wondering what she could possibly contribute to a scandalous conversation of this sort.

"I once passed that barn late at night," Fradel recounted. "I heard wild cheering coming from within."

She looked around at her captive audience, and shivered at the memory of those spine-tingling moments.

"You cannot imagine how terrified I was! To reach Dr. Sportek's home, I had to pass right by that rollicking barn...and I couldn't dilly-dally. *Bubbe* was in desperate need of blood-letting, which couldn't wait until the following morning."

Nods of commiseration traveled domino-like down the line. We all knew about her *Bubbe*'s precarious condition, and we constantly prayed for her complete recovery.

"I tried to hide in the shadows while skirting around the little barn," Fradel continued.

A bubble of mirth gurgled in my throat as I pictured my staid friend acting the part of an undercover sleuth. For dignity's sake, I initiated a sudden coughing fit that successfully submerged my laughter in anonymity.

"When I walked past the cracked window on the left side, I couldn't resist peeking in," Fradel said. "I saw at least thirty young people gathered inside. They were all standing in a semi-circle around someone who looked like their leader and they were waving their hands like a bunch of lunatics. It was...scary!"

"Did you recognize any of the members?" Chava'la asked.

Fradel eyed her condescendingly.

"You don't really think I would list their names," she stated, awash in a wave of righteous indignation. "I mean, that's an absolute forbidden!"

That bubble of mirth tickled my innards once again, but I was embarrassed to erupt into another coughing attack. Fradel always made me want to laugh. Her extreme earnestness and placidity were in direct contrast to my exuberant nature, and I found it difficult to believe that we were two pegs in the same Plawo pegboard.

Chava'la appeared miffed by the implied insult, and she hurried to defend her thoughtless question.

"Of *course* not, Fradel! I would *never* expect you to gossip about others," she emphatically said. "All I asked was whether you recognized anyone. Did you?"

Fradel nodded in agreement and Chava'la wisely abandoned her line of questioning. The others breathed easier as the unpleasant feelings dissipated in the warm June sunshine. Verbal sparring was anathema to my peer-group. They preferred desultory conversations that taught nothing new while carefully steering clear of everyone's sensitive toes.

"Esther, you've been awfully quiet today," Malka suddenly remarked.

"I'm just...thinking," I replied.

I wished I could bite those words to dust as soon as they slipped out of my mouth. From the looks on the girls' faces, I realized that I had once again set myself apart. Why couldn't I just say that I was tired? I could have used the strenuous laundry expedition as an excuse for my lackadaisical appearance. But, no. Esther Hofert had to place her delicately-shod foot directly in her mouth and give her friends more of a reason to view her from a distance.

"Oh," Malka finally muttered. "That's...interesting."

"No, I mean I was just thinking about everything that Chava'la said," I said, hating my defensive tone of voice but too irritated to do anything about it. "I feel bad for Rechel and her parents."

And her brother, I thought but did not say. *He must have been so confused before he placed his faith in this foreign ideology. What would make a successful young To-*

rah scholar abandon his studies in favor of hand-to-hand combat in Palestine?!

My comment plunged the girls back into the topic Chava'la had introduced. I listened half-heartedly to the give-and-take that ensued, wondering how quickly I could make a polite disappearance.

When Fradel began repeating the details of her terrifying experience at the barn, I utilized the others' total absorption to make my getaway. Without so much as a 'goodbye', I left the girls to their intricate embroidery patterns and hurried home.

The Zionists hold their meetings in the barn, I repeated to myself. *Every Thursday night, they gather to propagate their ideological ideas. I suppose that's where I'll be headed tomorrow evening. For you, Anna - so that you acknowledge the fallacy of your beliefs!*

I pictured Fradel's horror if she would choose tomorrow evening to peek through the barn's window. Oh, how she would swoon at the sight of perfect Esther Hofert standing amidst the cheering throngs. Her astonishment would be so complete that I doubt she would be able to find her way home after the startling revelation.

Hashem, You know I'm doing this for Your honor. Don't let my ruse be discovered. Keep Tatte and Mamme in the dark until this entire charade blows over. I just have to show Anna that I'm correct, and then I'll go back to being the innocent, pure-as-gold Esther Hofert.

I knew that I was undertaking this endeavor with pure motives. After all, I had no interest in joining the coarse crowd in old Gavriel's barn! They were not my choice of company on a pleasant summer evening.

So why did I feel such a sense of...wrongness? Why was I plagued with a conscience that refused to be silenced despite my convincing rationale?

What would Zalmen say? I asked myself earnestly.

He would never join the Zionist movement, even on a lofty espionage mission!

But Zalmen is different, I refuted. *He doesn't need to prove to anyone that they're wrong. If I don't go tomorrow night, Anna will take it as proof that I agree with her viewpoint. I'll go just one time to gather the information that I need, and then I'll steer clear of that rickety barn.*

Just once.

How was I to know that 'once' was one time too many?

Chapter Nine

*I*t was musty and dark in old Gavriel's barn. Cobwebs hung from the ceiling, shimmering grotesquely in the reflection of the kerosene lamps. Stifling a scream, I watched an audacious spider skittering along the wall on my right. It seemed more at home in this dilapidated barn than I was, and I suddenly envied its anonymity.

What wouldn't I do to be a fly on the wall for the duration of the evening? I tried to meld into the shadowy corners of the shack, without sullying my frock with substances of questionable origin. It was a hopeless attempt.

"*Chaveirim!*"

The husky voice reverberated across the room. At last, something was happening! I thought the meeting would never get underway and I would be doomed to perpetual oblivion in my inconspicuous corner.

"Shalom!"

The attendees chorused this response, and it elicited a smile from the broad-shouldered leader standing in the center.

"Shalom to you all!" he exclaimed. "Who has spent the week dreaming of fruitful orange groves in our beloved land?!"

Enthusiastic applause. Whistles and cat-calls. Raised

hands waving in the air.

What am I doing here?! They're overstepping every boundary of decency and propriety! Is this what an ideological meeting is supposed to look like? Shouldn't it bear some tinge of solemnity; of discussion and deep thought?

I looked around at the flushed faces that surrounded me, and I was horrified to recognize some of my neighbors and acquaintances. Most of the members were teenage boys, but there was a sprinkling of young girls to diversify the mixture.

Miriam Grunster! She's Etta's younger sister! Why is she standing here, amongst these ruffians? She can't be more than fourteen years old.

I scrutinized Miriam's face, searching for the innocence and purity that had been stamped across it the last time I looked. Instead, I found passion and fervor. I found sparkling eyes and flushed cheeks that told her story of complete infatuation with the Zionist ideals.

Someone put her arm on Miriam's shoulder. It was Leah Dewick, an orphan being raised in the home of her elderly aunt. Leah whispered something in the younger girl's ear, and Miriam smiled in response.

She's not a newcomer to these meetings, I inferred. *Miriam appears more comfortable here, amongst strangers, than between her own troop of lovable sisters.*

I wanted to approach Miriam and shake this nonsense out of her tangled mind. Oh, how I wished I could make her aware of the red line she had crossed and urge her to return to the other side before the line became a permanent chasm. Her parents would never survive the shame and horror of Miriam's betrayal.

"*Chaveirim* and *chaveiros!*" the curly-haired leader proclaimed. "This is a momentous occasion! Ten of our most devoted members have departed yesterday for the shores of Eretz Yisroel!"

Pinchus, I thought. *He was one of the ten. His parents are almost sitting shivah for him, whilst his so-called friends are celebrating his achievement.*

"*L'chaim!*"

I swiveled around to see who had pronounced the age-old word of congratulations. It was someone who seemed vaguely familiar, but I couldn't place him by name or by face. Maybe he lived in a nearby town. I had heard that several youths traipsed over to the Plawo meetings every week, since their town did not yet boast its own.

A round of hearty congratulations followed, interspersed with curious questions about the travelers' planned itinerary.

"Why haven't you gone yet, Chanan?"

The leader, whose name I just pinned as Chanan, looked taken aback at the question, but he did not lose his composure.

"Do you really think I could fulfill my dream without nourishing yours?" he inquired rhetorically. "My most ardent wish is to find myself in the land of our forefathers, but I don't want to be there alone, *chevrah*! I want all of you to join me on my journey to a future of autonomy and freedom."

His impromptu speech was met by loud applause, and I dutifully clapped my hands to quell any questions from curious onlookers. In my opinion, these meetings were nothing more than opportunities to gather with friends. The Zionists were definitely fired up with their ideals, but I didn't hear any logical arguments that would convince a newcomer of the cause's rightness.

A youth started discussing the upcoming transport that would be departing within the next few months. He was interrupted time and again by boisterous cheering and whistling.

I had seen enough. There was no point in remaining

here to witness the youths' conduct. On my part, the subject was closed with finality. Zionism was a pipe dream, pulling young people who sought to expand their horizons. There was nothing uplifting or logical in their idealism, and Anna would simply have to accept that as a fact.

Conversation hummed around me in tidal waves, and I sought the shortest path to the entrance. Every avenue of escape was blockaded by a mass of excitable young people, but I couldn't wait until the meeting would wind to a close. I had to leave, and I had to leave *immediately*!

Looking neither right nor left, I lifted my head high and started walking straight ahead. My mumbled apologies went unnoticed, for the people I passed were all too involved in their leader's charismatic oratory.

"I'm sorry," I murmured. "Please, I have to pass. I must get through."

My hand rested on the barn's excuse for a door, and I exhaled a wordless thank-you to Hashem for bringing me thus far without mishap. The world outside beckoned with the warmth of familiarity and simple integrity, and I viewed the past hour as time well-spent for a just cause.

"Esther! Esther Hofert, the princess of Plawo!"

Should I turn around? Who spotted me at this most inauspicious time? Maybe I could make a run for it and pretend that this fiasco never occurred.

By the time I finished weighing my options, the decision had been made for me by others.

"What are *you* doing here, Esther?"

I was incensed. Did I ask any of these Zionists what *they* were doing in this ramshackle barn? Why did they feel justified in pelting me with their questions?

"Yeah," interrupted a tall, freckle-faced boy. "If I would be raised in the home of Shimon Hofert, I wouldn't dream of deserting my comfortable life for pioneering in Palestine."

"How can you say that?" Chanan hotly contended. "Zionism is not an escape route! It's a way of life; a higher calling."

Sure. Try to sell me another one, Chanan.

"If she decided to attend one of our meetings, she is one of ours," Chanan continued. "I think - "

"No, no!" I desperately blurted. "I am *not* one of you!"

From the horrified expressions blossoming around me, I realized that I had just transgressed one of the Zionists' unwritten codes. How was I to know that one may never interrupt a leader?!

"If you will excuse me," Chanan coldly said, "I don't think anyone brought you here by force. You can be honest with us. We're all here for the same reasons."

This time, I waited a beat to ensure that he had truly finished saying his piece.

"I am not here as a...a Zionist," I explained. "I came because I..."

My voice trailed off uncertainly. I couldn't tell them that I had come to spy in order to support my arguments against their faulty reasoning. They would be livid! But how could I allow them to believe that I truly wanted to join their ridiculous cause? Word would leak out in the Plawo streets, and my parents would never live down the shame and hurt.

"It's alright," freckle-face said. "We all come here with the assurance that our attendance will remain confidential. No one repeats whom he saw, what he heard, and what was planned during a meeting. So you can remain, Esther Hofert, without worrying about your oh-so-perfect reputation."

Who is this youth who dares to address me as though... as though I were truly one of his free-thinking peers?! I will not give him the satisfaction of a response. Nor will I defend myself in any way, for the leader will wipe my words into the dust. I will have to remain in my place until this awful gathering disperses.

"So we welcome a new member to our Plawo contingent," Chanan ceremoniously proclaimed. "Our ranks are swelling unbelievably, *chevrah*! Before long, every one of your friends and siblings will be begging to join us. You'll be at the forefront, *chevrah*, blazing the trail for those too cowardly or short-sighted to join us from the start!"

"I just want to clarify my presence here," I said hastily. "I am not a full-fledged member of your group, much as you all seem to believe I am. I came to...to see. That's all."

My words drew laughter from the crowd, and I felt their amusement morphing into beads of perspiration on my flushed face. I had gathered my courage to clarify my position, and all they could do was laugh at me?!

"They all say that," Chanan exclaimed with a wave of his hand. "Every newcomer introduces himself with the same speech. It doesn't take more than a week or two for him to regret his words and beg the *chevrah* to forget his previous insecurity."

"I will be the exception," I couldn't resist interjecting.

No one bothered to offer a response. In their silence, I read disbelief and mockery. Chanan's coal-black eyes seemed to pierce my convictions, but I kept myself in check by thinking about next week's exchange with Anna. She would certainly find the entire incident amusing, and she would be forced to admit that the Zionist ideals were balloons full of hot air that could be punctured with the slightest prick of holiness.

I was too proud to leave under the watchful gaze of my so-called *chaveirim*. Without so much as a glance at the starry sky beckoning me from beyond the door's splintered wood, I retraced my steps. Only when I reached the comfort of my cob-webbed corner, did I breathe easier.

How terrible could the ordeal possibly be? I would remain statue-like in my spot, without offering another word for or against the goings-on. As soon as the meeting would be adjourned, I would make my escape.

Home had never seemed so warm and enticing. Amidst a crowd of passionate youths who considered me a member - albeit an unwilling one, I felt lost.

"So, *chaveirim* and *chaveiros*," Chanan shouted above the din. "We have drawn up a list of eligible travelers. These are members who we believe are ready to undertake the dangerous journey to Palestine and strong enough to overcome the obstacles they will encounter."

A sudden hush descended upon the assemblage. Everyone watched in rapt attention as Chanan withdrew a crisp sheet of paper from his pocket. Deliberately, he unfolded it and smoothed its symmetrical creases.

"*Chaver* Yoav Gertner. *Chaver* Chaim Brolofski. *Chaveirah* Miriam Grunster."

Miriam?! Would she really abandon her family in pursuit of a dream?!

I looked at Miriam, expecting to see shock and fear smoldering in her eyes. Instead, I observed her embracing Leah and then raising her hands way above her head in a display of excitement. Leah appeared disappointed that her name hadn't been announced, but she was trying to squelch her disappointment in favor of Miriam's joy.

The exuberant display of congratulations made me sick to my stomach. While the others gleefully clapped their lucky comrades on the back, I battled an overwhelming urge to break down and cry.

'What about your parents?' I soundlessly screamed. 'How will they react when they wake up one sunny morning and find your bed empty and your drawers bare? Maybe you'll be considerate enough to leave a note explaining your disappearance, but even if not - they'll find out. They

will know and they will mourn!

'Miriam, your sisters will be devastated! Etta will be ashamed to show her face in the Plawo streets, and your dear mother will fall apart from the strain. You can't do this, Miriam. You CAN'T!'

But Miriam didn't hear me. She was too busy accepting congratulations and making empty promises about writing letters from her post in Eretz Yisroel. Interesting... why did she see blossoming orange groves where I saw arid desert plains? How did she perceive her future as a glimmering prism of promise when all I could discern was a display of desolation?

"Aren't you going to congratulate me?"

I blanched. Did Miriam really not understand my feelings on the topic? Her large blue eyes sparkled intensely, and I resisted the urge to look away.

"Congratulate you?" I repeated quietly, painfully aware of Leah's hovering presence. "That's actually the farthest thing from my mind right now."

"You have no idea how long I've been waiting for this day," the young girl continued fervently. "At long last, I can break free of my restrictive Plawo shackles. I can finally make a difference in the world!"

My silence seemed to feed into Miriam's need for justification. Without any prodding on my part, Etta's sister clarified her motives in abandoning tradition for sun-dappled shores.

"I'm just one of ten," Miriam said. "One of ten sisters who can do her share of mending, cooking and cleaning. Do *I* make a difference? Absolutely not! All they need are my hands; my output. They need me to help with household chores."

Leah put her arm around Miriam's shoulders in a protective stance.

"Here you make a difference, Miriam," Leah murmured. "We appreciate you for who you are - not just for what you do."

I wanted to refute her claims, but I knew that my words would fall into an abyss of static. Miriam was not interested in hearing about her queenly role as a Jewish daughter. Nor did she want to hear accolades about her wonderful parents and charming sisters. Here, in this miserable excuse for a conference room, she felt wanted and needed. This decrepit barn fed into her desire for freedom and idealism.

I remained silent. I, Esther Hofert of the golden tongue and rational mind, could not think of a single remark that would shake Miriam's staunch belief in the rightness of her path.

I'm sorry, Etta! I've failed you. Within several weeks, you'll be feeling much the same way Rechel must have felt today. There was nothing I could say to change her mind, Etta. Please - you must believe me!

But Etta would never know. When the news of the latest Zionist expedition would sully the Plawo streets, I would appear as shocked and horrified as all the others. I would shake my head in commiseration and murmur regretfully about innocent Miriam's luckless choice.

While Miriam turned towards Chanan who was offering his congratulations in a most grave and earnest tone, I slipped away. Ignoring the accusatory stares directed my way, I hurried to the door once again. There was no way I could wait around until the crowds dispersed. I had heard enough; way more than I had wanted to. In any case, *Mamme* would certainly be worried about me. Rarely did I venture out at night. The quiet streets of Plawo did not offer much of an incentive.

I looked up at the starry skies stretched like diamond-studded velvet above the universe. The stars were winking at me conspiratorially, reassuring me that they would never reveal my midnight wanderings. *Mamme* would never have to know the pain of bereavement that Rechel's mother was presently experiencing. She would never feel the piercing betrayal of a young daughter who chose to fight distant battles instead of combating her inner demons.

Softly, so that no one but I and the quivering stars should hear, I sang a song of gratitude to Hashem. The tension of the past few hours rode along the waves of music, dissipating in the warm air.

My secret was safe. No one would know that Esther Hofert had participated in a Zionist gathering. This was a one-time escapade that didn't bear repeating.

Or so I thought.

Chapter Ten

The days until I was slated to meet Anna crawled past with the alacrity of a tired turtle. I couldn't wait to share my impressions of the Zionist meeting, and to force Anna into grudging agreement.

Our conversation, however, didn't proceed as smoothly as I had envisioned.

"You're basing your conclusions on emotions, Esther," Anna sighed, speaking slowly as though she were conversing with a toddler. "Emotions aren't facts. Not by a wide margin!"

"You can't concede defeat, Anna. That's your problem."

Anna forcefully denied my claim, saying, "This has nothing to do with me! I don't care whether Zionism is correct or not. It's a Jewish thing, remember? I'm just trying to get you to provide *proof*, Esther. Logical *proof*."

The way she emphasized that word transformed it into something sacrosanct; something superior to mere speculation.

"I went, I saw and I understood," I insisted stubbornly. "It's very easy for you to comfortably lounge on the grass and refute everything I say. I went out and gathered first-hand evidence, Anna. It was a torturous experience, but I did it for the sake of upholding the truth."

Anna shrugged, and her silence spoke more eloquently than words. She was unimpressed with my efforts and didn't grant my conclusions a grain of significance. In her eyes, my sacrifice had been for naught.

"You know that won't convince me, Esther," she said. "Tell me the truth - does it have you convinced?"

"Yes. Absolutely."

"I didn't know you as one to be ruled by emotional drama."

Her disdain was palpable, and I rushed to defend my scraggly honor.

"You weren't there, Anna. You didn't observe the coarseness and wild laughter; the blind idealism and empty cheering," I contended. "Why don't you go and find out for yourself? I'm sure you'll react as strongly as I did."

Anna took me up on the challenge, and I berated myself for my impetuous suggestion. *What would Anna, a non-Jewish girl, find at a Zionist meeting? Even more disconcerting - how would the others react to a stranger in their midst?*

I pictured Chanan's reaction when Anna would inevitably offer one of her pointed remarks. His coal-black eyes would blister with fury and he would immediately discern that she was an imposter. After forcing her to identify herself, Chanan would do *something* extreme. I couldn't imagine what that *something* would be, but I was certain that it would be far from pleasant.

"It's not such a good idea, Anna," I said, hesitation marring the smoothness of my voice. "I don't think you should place yourself in such an...uncomfortable position."

Her laughter showed me just what she thought of my fatalistic attitude.

"You're chickening out on my account?" Anna grinned. "I'll be alright, Esther. I know how to fend for myself."

That's precisely what I was concerned about. Anna's strength of character would place her directly in the line of Chanan's fire, and she would be too proud to conceal her true intentions.

"Why don't we lay this argument to rest?" I offered plaintively.

"No chance of that!" Anna cheerfully replied. "I'll go to that meeting and either prove or disprove your claims. After that, we can bury the discussion and mark it a done deal."

Oh, there's no reasoning with this headstrong character, I thought. *I hope the situation won't blow up in her face when she arrives at Gavriel's barn Thursday night.*

"So tell me the details, Esther. Where and when do I make my appearance?"

"The meetings are held at old Gavriel's barn -"

"Where?" Anna interrupted.

"You know, the barn behind old Gavriel's house."

"Who precisely is old Gavriel?" she asked with mounting annoyance.

"He's the...the *gabbai* of the *shul*," I offered weakly.

"He's the *what* of the *what*?!"

I gave up. Anna was a member of a different community and she would never know the Plawo residents as I did.

"It's at the outskirts of town," I explained carefully. "You walk along this path leading away from the river, until you reach a small cabin. Turn right at the cabin and after a minute or two you should spot a dilapidated building that still has remnants of red paint clinging to its roof. And don't go to the front of the barn – that entrance is boarded up. There's a rickety door in the back that will lead you straight into their welcoming arms."

A tremor tripped its way up my spine, setting all my nerve endings on fire. I could almost hear the loud breathing of the hot-headed youths as they surveyed the spy who dared to infiltrate their domain. I saw the balled-up fists of those young idealists as they struggled to maintain control in the face of such open provocation.

But Anna did not see all that. All she saw was a debatable issue that her heroic endeavor would eventually resolve. She heard the call of adventure beckoning from afar, devoid of the danger and potential shame it involved. She saw my firm convictions which, according to her, were based on flimsy foundations.

Maria gestured to me from afar, flapping her hands in a desperate attempt to catch my attention. At her feet, the voluminous laundry basket was stacked high with pristine, soaking wet articles of clothing. Anna, on the other hand, had nothing to show for her extended stay at the riverside. The pile of laundry awaiting her attention loomed just as high as it had when I had arrived.

"Go, Esther," my enigmatic friend urged. "Maria is getting decidedly impatient."

I hesitated. This conversation had really been derailed, but there seemed no chance of it ever getting back on track. Wasn't Anna supposed to accept my personal testimony and join me in condemning this unfamiliar vermin that had insidiously invaded the minds of our youth? Wasn't I supposed to emerge as the heroic purveyor of truth, who spared no efforts in discovering its hidden seeds?

"Go on," she said with a smile. "I'll fill you in on all the details next week."

I smiled weakly in return.

"They meet only on Thursday evenings," I offered. "And it's best if you just keep quiet while you do your spying work."

"Don't worry about me. I can very well take care of myself."

That's precisely what I was worried about, but when Anna made a decision, it was apparently set in stone.

I turned to leave before another useless attempt at persuasion could slip out of my mouth. Anna would go to the meeting, she would make some sort of ruckus, and then she would report on her findings. We would agree that Zionist idealism was not for us, and then we would thankfully put the topic aside in favor of more interesting tidbits.

So why am I so anxious? I wondered morosely, as I made my way towards Maria. *Why do I feel as though something momentous is in the offing?*

"Your Mama not be happy," the laundress sniffed in her broken Polish. "She say you watch. You not watch. You talk."

"I watch and talk," I defensively replied. "I do two things together."

Maria merely shook her head in faint disapproval. "No. No good."

That's all I need! Maria is going to report on my new friendship and Mamme will want to know what it's all about. I can just see it. 'Oh, Mamme. Please meet my new friend, Anna. She's the daughter of Teacher Podolsky, over on Francisca Street.'

"This is my...secret friend," I whispered conspiratorially to the grim-faced washer-woman. "Special friend, see? No one knows about her – not even *Mamme!*"

No response.

"Only you know, Maria. I trust you."

This seemed to get through to her. Amazing how a compliment could dissolve the most righteous of indignations. My secret was safe.

*   *   *

It wasn't until the following morning that I realized just how unsafe my secret was. As the aroma of freshly-baked *challah* tickled my sleeping brain cells, a fuzzy warmth joined me under the feather blankets.

Thursday morning. Preparations for *Shabbos* were already in full swing, with *Mamme* presiding over her kitchen like a kindly monarch overseeing a grandiose endeavor. Every week, she attacked the mountain of *Shabbos* chores with vigor, as though it were the first time she was privileged to do it.

And I, little Esther? I usually inhaled the enticing scents and tried to stay out of her way. With an indulgent twinkle in her eyes, Mama would ply me with some freshly-baked goodies as soon as I made my belated appearance.

"*Ess*, Esther'ke," she would coax. "*Ess*."

I heard the unspoken plea behind those innocent words. Eat for the children who were but are no more. Eat for those precious souls who cannot taste their mother's food. Eat, and allow *Mamme* to nurture you in place of those she lost.

So I ate. I ate apple *streudel* and delicate, flaky pastries. I tasted new *kugels* and old-time favorites. Sitting at the kitchen table, I forced myself to clear the heaping bowl Mama placed before me, silently paying homage to Chaim Hersh and Miriam. Sometimes, I thought about the innocent newborns who had never merited the sensation of their mother's love, and I ate for them, too.

Mama's radiant smile made the ordeal worthwhile. She hovered over me with undisguised pleasure, reveling in my gargantuan appetite. I hadn't the heart to leave anything over, although my puny eating habits could barely tolerate the sudden onslaught of nourishment. After all, how many teenage girls could stomach a royal repast first thing in the morning? Even the most voracious eaters would be hard-pressed to mirror my weekly accomplishment. It was my sacrifice for Mama's happiness; my gift to the woman who loved me more than herself.

This particular morning, however, held none of the usual *Erev Shabbos* charm. Warm sunshine dappled my patchwork quilt, dancing over the folds with careless abandon. My fingers traced the outline of the sun's kiss, but my heart remained impervious to its whispered promises.

Anna.

She was probably dreaming about tonight's adventure, formulating the questions she would throw at the unsuspecting Zionist leaders. Much as I tried, I couldn't pinpoint the reason for my growing unease at the thought of my fearless friend taking on an entire slew of idealistic Plawo teenagers. Didn't I trust her ability to withstand their jeers and taunts? Couldn't she use her incisive intellect to shoot down all of their theories?

She could. Of that I was sure.

But what about me?!

The thought tickled my sleepy consciousness, rousing it awake without the usual allowance for morning sluggishness.

You're in danger, Esther, a little voice whispered. *Anna will never pretend that her ideals are in sync with theirs. She'll rant and rave, until Chanan will forcefully put a halt to her impassioned arguments. But Anna won't give up. When Chanan starts interrogating her, what will she say? Will she admit that I had put her up to this? Will she take our secret friendship and willfully toss it to the wolves?!*

The horror of such an unveiling was too awful to contemplate. How those youths would rejoice at the news that Esther Hofert, the haughty daughter of the famed *Rosh Hakahel*, had actually befriended the daughter of a Christian schoolteacher! They would waste no time in tearing my reputation to shreds and dragging it through the Plawo streets.

Impulsively, I threw the covers to the floor and leaped out of bed. I couldn't remain impassive while my future teetered on the blade of destruction. With frantic movements, I donned the frock that Maria had painstakingly pressed the night before. As I frenziedly plaited my long hair, I couldn't help marveling at the speed with which my morning routine had been completed. Panic has a curious way of obviating the need for languor and introspection.

When I entered the kitchen, I tried to lose myself in the hubbub of activity.

"Good, the *strudel* should be done," Mama mumbled. "I'll take it out and let it cool on the table."

Everything was as it should be. Mama puttered in the spacious kitchen, seasoning soups and kneading dough. She was utterly oblivious to the shadowy horror that was inching its way toward our doorstep. How would she react when she heard that her Esther, her beloved and innocent princess, had actually befriended a...Christian?! A non-Jewish girl?!

"Good morning, Esther'ke. You're up early today."

I stretched my lips into a contorted smile, mumbling something about the wonderful smells that had pulled me out of bed. In response, Mama prepared a plate that far surpassed the offerings she usually served.

"*Ess, mein kind.*"

I groaned. Who could eat an ordinary breakfast on such a day, let alone a gourmet five-course dinner enough to feed an entire family?

"*Mamme,* I - "

"*Ess,* Esther'ke. We'll talk later."

So Esther ate. The cosseted youngest daughter who would soon be revealed as a conniving spy ate to satisfy her mother's desires.

There was nothing I could do to prevent the inevitable. Anna had decided to attend the meeting despite my hesitation. Knowing her fiery nature, she wouldn't last more than ten minutes without disclosing her true identity. From there to my greatest moment of shame was but a small jump of horrific proportions.

I'm sorry, Mamme! I wasn't thinking! Anna's friendship means so much to me, but I'll give it up. I'll relinquish the spark of life it awakens in me in order to spare you further shame and grief.

Too little, too late. I knew that without anyone delineating the futility of my actions. If only I could prevent tonight's catastrophe, my family would be spared. If only...

Every bite was torturous, especially with my unsuspecting mother hovering over me with pride and pleasure. I persevered, shoveling the steaming food into my mouth with the fortitude of a gladiator. I would give *Mamme* this last pleasure, before her entire world crumbled to smithereens.

In Plawo, the improbability of a young Jewish girl teaming up with someone like Anna was so extreme that its occurrence was sure to make waves. I would be branded a wayward soul; an *apikorus*. And my parents – they would have to bear the burden of my tarnished reputation.

It was between the apple *strudel* and the chocolate *babke* that inspiration struck. I would not await my fate with the foolishness and despair of a sitting duck. No, not if I could help it.

I would also visit old Gavriel's barn tonight. That was my only viable option. Standing at Anna's side, I would ensure that she maintained her peace. I would forcibly clamp my hand over her mouth, if necessary, to prevent my secret from being exposed. With –

"Esther!"

Tatte's laughing eyes replaced Anna's piercing gaze,

obscuring my view of the evening's planned adventures.

"You're up early today," he commented, pointing at his *tefillin* bag for emphasis. "When do I have the privilege of greeting my only daughter after *davening*?"

Strange. I had never thought much about my sleeping habits, but my parents apparently paid great heed to this seemingly insignificant detail. Not that I could blame them, of course. My friends dragged themselves out of bed at the crack of dawn – at least according to their descriptions – to help their mothers with housework. I, on the other hand, lounged around in bed until boredom propelled me towards the kitchen.

"Good morning, *Tatte*."

Tatte patted me gently on the shoulder, and his fatherly warmth solidified my decision. I would face the taunts of the assembled Zionists to preserve my parents' honor and security.

The hours passed in an agony of suspense. I traipsed through the fields surrounding our home, picking at the sprouting weeds in an attempt to look useful. At times I wondered miserably whether the sun had decided to stand still, as it had done in the story of *Gidon* that Zalmen once told me.

On one of my forays through the town streets, I met Etta. She was gingerly carrying a wrapped package and goose-stepping towards her sister's home.

"Hello, Etta," I called out, desperate for some distraction from my racing thoughts.

"Esther! Uh, how are you?"

What is it about me that sets my friends on edge? They seem so...uncomfortable in my presence!

"I'm fine, *boruch Hashem*. What about you?"

"Uh, also fine. *Boruch Hashem*. I'm headed to Rivka right now."

"That's wonderful!" I exclaimed, completely misjudging the amount of false enthusiasm I exuded. "I'm actually headed in that direction."

If Etta looked less than thrilled at the prospect of my company, I didn't have to notice.

"Could I help you with that package?"

Etta shook her head.

"No, that's alright. My mother prepared supper for Rivka and her family and it has to be delivered before her boys come home from *cheder*."

I nodded in understanding. Rivka's newborn twins had made quite a commotion when they joined the family. All of Plawo had rejoiced in the double *simcha*.

"Couldn't Miriam deliver the package instead of you?"

It was a foolish comment, and it slipped out without asking my permission. I wanted to tell Etta about her sister's predicament, but my fumbled attempt didn't bode well.

"Miriam?! You mean, my sister?"

"Of course. How many other Miriam's would deliver packages to Rivka's house?"

As soon as the sarcasm wrapped itself around my words, I regretted its presence. Etta, however, seemed oblivious.

"My mother asked me to go, so I went," she finally said. "In any case, Miriam is best left alone. Her help is not worth the sour atmosphere it generates."

Etta clamped her mouth shut and busied herself with readjusting the perfectly adjusted package. She had said more than was deemed proper, and I sympathized with her discomfort.

"Oh, I...I was just wondering," I blurted. "I haven't seen her around lately. That's all."

Only at Gavriel's barn last week, I mentally amended. *There was no sourness enveloping her then!*

Etta shrugged her shoulders; the very same shoulders I wished to shake in an agony of warning. *Take care of your sister*, I wanted to say. *She's falling...falling...*

But I didn't say it. Call it cowardice; or call it self-preservation. I couldn't enter Etta's world with a sledgehammer and expect her to accept my words without question. If I chose to reveal Miriam's secret, I would inevitably reveal my own.

"Uh...goodbye," Etta said.

I waved half-heartedly and continued walking along the street, to allay Etta's suspicions. I had said I was headed in the same direction, hadn't I? How would it look if I turned around and immediately retraced my steps?

The sun draped its multi-hued farewell cape over my shoulders as I meandered disconsolately along the Plawo streets. I couldn't help envying Etta her uncomplicated existence. Ensconced in the warmth of family, she needed nothing more than her daily chores to provide her with the satisfaction she so justly deserved. True, her house had more people than beds, but it was so vibrant and inviting. Etta, I was sure, never grappled with the overwhelming feelings of emptiness that sucked the joy out of life's daily happenings.

And she didn't get herself into ridiculous scrapes involving Christian friends and Zionist gatherings, a little voice murmured insidiously. *She treads the straight and narrow while you, Esther Hofert, insist on trampling through the wilderness!*

These thoughts accompanied me throughout the ensuing hours, until they were finally quashed by sheer fright as I approached Gavriel's barn. A tentative push on the creaky door led me over the border from observer to participant.

"Welcome, *chaveirah!*"

Whom is he welcoming so ecstatically? And why is

he looking at me with such an all-knowing twinkle in his eyes?

Instinctively, I whirled around to see who had merited Chanan's effusive greeting. No one was standing behind me.

"Esther! I knew you would be back," Miriam exclaimed. "Your attitude last week reminded me of my own approach during the first meeting. I just knew we're cut from the same cloth."

"Not – uh, yes. That is, I hear what you're saying, Miriam," I stuttered. "I...I'm still just...looking."

I was acutely aware of the grand audience following our exchange with eagle-eyed interest. Apparently, my participation provided an approval of sorts. It gave them the stamp of authenticity that they so desperately craved.

Where is Anna? I hope she didn't arrive yet. No one seems overwrought or suspicious, so I suppose she couldn't have made her appearance. Yet.

"Come, Esther," Miriam urged. "Come stand near me. I want to share this experience with you!"

Her friendly demeanor repulsed me, although I couldn't pinpoint which aspect of it made me feel like a renegade. Gazing into her sparkling eyes, I saw only Etta. Etta walking towards her sister's house to deliver a package of nutritious food. Etta finding her niche amongst her siblings, and enjoying their company with unaffected innocence. Etta, who would be beyond horrified when Miriam departed in pursuit of gilded emptiness.

"Esther!" she insisted. "Over here!"

"I'd rather stay near the door," I responded quietly. "I...I want to enjoy the fresh air."

It was a ridiculous statement, considering the numerous cracks in the barn's walls that allowed every fresh breeze to intrude on our meeting. But the others remained silent. Chanan signaled Miriam with his eyes, directing her to desist.

"We were all like that, at first," he muttered. "Give her time. Just give her some time."

I clenched my fists angrily at his know-it-all demeanor. I would *not* change with time. I wanted to stay near the door because...because I needed to protect Anna from herself. Not because I felt uncomfortable, or unwanted!

"*Chaveirim* and *chaveiros*!"

Chanan's commanding voice sliced through the desultory conversations, bringing them all to a screeching halt.

"Tonight, our meeting will be graced by the presence of a celebrity. A Zionist celebrity from Lithuania."

A wild guessing game ensued, with each attendee catapulting possible names into the air, only to have them come crashing down with Chanan's smiling dismissal.

"Hertz!"

"Weiss!"

"Bar-Kochav!"

The names came thick and fast, but none hit the mark. I watched Chanan presiding grandly over the shouting match and I wondered how Anna would react to the scene. Would she be as repulsed as I was? Would she find it refreshingly informal, or would she detect the screaming emptiness begging for attention?

Where are you, Anna?! Did you lose your courage?

"You will have to remain in suspense just a bit longer," Chanan stated. "Our guest should be here momentarily. Until then - "

A collective groan emanated from the barn's dingy interior, but Chanan was unfazed. He treated the youths to a commanding glare, and their complaints died away like echoes of a long-forgotten song.

C-r-r-e-a-k.

The door gave way behind me and I caught my balance in the nick of time. Anna had better have a good explanation for her lateness! Why, she had nearly missed out on a mysterious guest speaker!

"Anna!" I stage-whispered. "Where *were* you?!"

Anna coughed; a decidedly masculine cough that resonated sharply in my ears.

Perhaps she's ill, I thought sympathetically. *That would explain her tardiness. She shouldn't have come tonight...although I'm sure glad she did.*

"Are you feeling alright?" I whispered, waiting impatiently for my friend to appear. "Venturing out like this is really not wise, Anna."

The door continued creaking open slowly. I resisted the urge to heave it wide open, allowing Anna the pleasure of making her grand entrance.

"Come on, Anna!" I urged impatiently. "There's a guest speaker coming soon. I'm glad you arrived in time!"

Another cough emanated from behind the quivering door and my heart contracted at its raspy sound.

"Excuse me?"

Her voice sounded queer. I glanced up sharply, peering through the widening crack...directly into a pair of smoldering, midnight-black eyes. Those eyes sat beneath a pair of graying eyebrows that presently waggled comically at my breach of conduct.

Oh, the shame! The flustering, blustering shame that colored my face and tingled along my spine! I gracelessly moved away from the open doorway, allowing others to catch a glimpse of the unknown visitor.

"Oh, Eliezer ben Yehuda!" Chanan called out deferentially.

It was the first time I had heard Chanan subjugate himself to anyone. This stranger must be highly accredited to intimidate our intractable group leader.

"*Chaveirim, Bruchim Habaim,*" the man proclaimed,

spreading his hands expansively to include the entire universe in his warm greeting.

His voice had a hypnotic quality, as did his fiery eyes. There was something about his carriage that bespoke nobility, yet his informal get-up seemed to convey quite the opposite. Dressed in shorts and a white, open-necked shirt, the man seemed to have been transported directly from Palestine to address our humble Plawo gathering.

The others were obviously taken by his striking presentation. They gaped at him in wordless wonder, awaiting the pearls of wisdom that would surely pour forth from his mouth.

Only I, Esther Hofert, couldn't concentrate on the enchanting goings-on. I stood sentinel at the doorway, hoping against hope that Anna would arrive before the meeting's adjournment. Would my guilt-laden sacrifice be for naught?

"I have come to share with you the wonders of our Land," he said. "I have come to teach you the secrets of our home."

Everyone leaned forward expectantly, and I couldn't help smiling at the air of suspense that pervaded the room. My smile, however, did not linger too much longer. As soon as Eliezer ben Yehuda began speaking in earnest, I found myself drawing closer to the breathless crowd, anxious to hear every word he so delicately strung onto chains of promise.

He was a riveting speaker. His words were not the empty banter of the Zionist youths. They rang with meaning and purpose, and they actually seemed logically sound. He had a single purpose in life and he would stop at nothing to bring it to realization. This former *Yeshiva* student had decided that our brethren in Eretz Yisroel must adopt Hebrew as their official language, and he had even compiled a complete dictionary for the cause. His efforts had borne fruit and Hebrew was gaining popularity in the growing settlements.

Anna! Where are you?!

The thought flitted through my mind time and again, until it eventually disappeared in the oblivion of Zionist idealism. Only when the lengthy discourse wound to a close, did I realize how late it had become.

Anna had never arrived to the meeting.

But I, Esther Hofert, had truly arrived. As I followed the others into the darkness of the Plawo night, I plotted next week's escapade. I had to attend another meeting, if only to assure myself that this was a fluke. Eliezer ben Yehuda had fired my imagination and set my soul aflame with passion for an ideal I had so recently rejected. Was it an illusion...or was there deep-seated truth concealed beneath the raucousness I so detested?

Chapter Eleven

Anna's absence extended far beyond her no-show at the Thursday night gathering. She wasn't at the San River the following Wednesday, nor the Wednesday thereafter. I couldn't understand it. Did something happen to her? Or was she avoiding me for some perceived injustice?

I spent those long Wednesday washing days dreaming about Eretz Yisroel. The meetings had become my lifeline to something more meaningful than my humdrum existence, and I held on to them with fortitude. Gavriel's barn captured my heart and set my imagination aflame.

Eretz Yisroel. My home.

I was ready to do anything for its future. Anything, that is, aside from the ultimate sacrifice – the relinquishment of my beloved family. How could I possibly leave *Tatte* and *Mamme*, to mourn their daughter while she was still alive? How could I disappoint Zalmen, who thought that I was the luckiest young girl to tread the streets of Plawo?

Chanan did not pressure any of the attendees for a commitment. He knew the art of gentle persuasion, and he used it with perception. If I ever expressed doubts at departing to that far-off land, he was quick to lay them to rest.

"No one is asking for an immediate decision," he once remarked. "For now, it's enough that Eretz Yisroel is alive in your heart and in your mind."

For now. Those were the key words. For now, I could continue juggling the disparate worlds I was attempting to straddle. For now, I could wear the mask of docile Esther Hofert, beloved only daughter of the esteemed *Rosh Hakahel.* For now, I could also appear like a dedicated Zionist group member. So long as I wasn't pressed to the wall, I could still maintain my balance.

The status quo wouldn't last forever, but I reveled in it nevertheless.

"Esther, I would never have believed that you have it in you," Miriam told me as we strolled home together from a meeting. "You seemed so...stand-offish when you first arrived. I was sure that you would keep your distance."

"I thought so, too," I admitted ruefully. "I didn't think that Zionism was a logical pursuit...until I heard Eliezer ben Yehuda speak. His depth...his clarity...it just made everything come together."

Miriam nodded.

"I know what you mean. I was hooked as soon as I heard Chanan describing the beautiful land and all that we could do to make it come alive once again. I don't need all those long-winded explanations," she admitted. "They bore me to tears."

"To each his own," I replied.

Miriam was reacting just as Anna had warned me not to. Her decisions were based on emotional drama, but I was different. I didn't allow myself to be swayed by baseless feelings. I had heard the truth in the Zionist ideal and I had embraced it wholeheartedly.

You would be proud of me, Anna, I thought. *You would admit that my conclusions are logical and that they have a solid foundation.*

A sunny Wednesday morning in mid-May proved me wrong on all counts.

I was sitting on the ground, watching Maria thumping a particularly stubborn set of bed-linens. Her exertions made me tired and the lack of activity on my part merely exacerbated my fatigue.

"So how's my friend, the Spoiled Princess? I heard your singing all the way to the other side of the river!"

I blinked.

Has boredom brought me to the border of insanity? Hallucination is one of the first symptoms, if I'm not mistaken.

"Well?! Aren't you going to greet your old friend?"

There was no mistaking Anna's jocular tone of voice. Struggling to sit up, I rubbed my eyes and self-consciously straightened my rumpled skirts.

"Anna!"

"So you're not just a dressed-up hunk of stone," she remarked. "I was beginning to wonder whether you'd stayed here to vegetate during the months that I was gone."

The familiar rush of laughter and annoyance bubbled up within me, and I felt myself being swept up by Anna's love of life.

"Vegetate?" I repeated. "No, far from it. Anna, you have no idea what's been happening while you were gone."

"I'm sure. Plawo was always the place for constant entertainment and exciting adventures."

Her sarcasm was not unfounded. Hadn't I complained often enough that nothing ever happened in my hometown? Why was I so bothered when Anna echoed my sentiments?

"Come on, Esther. Let's walk through the forest a bit. I have so much to tell you!"

I glanced at Maria for a moment, but Anna didn't allow my thoughts to travel that path.

"And don't tell me that you have to supervise the washer-woman," she admonished. "I know how well you do that task, Esther! Lying here with your eyes closed isn't doing much for society...or for the laundry!"

"What about your tasks?"

"You mean the laundry? Mamma did that yesterday, before I got back. Not that you seem interested in where I was these past six weeks."

I shook myself out of my reverie. Anna was right. Here she had finally reappeared, as suddenly as she had disappeared, and I hadn't even had the courtesy to ask for an explanation.

"I'm just shocked that you're here," I excused myself. "I waited for you, week after week, and you have no idea how many sob stories I created on your behalf."

Anna laughed, and the towering trees seemed to laugh along with her.

"Don't ask, Esther. Remember that last conversation we had, when I insisted on attending one of those Zionist meetings?"

As if I could ever forget, Anna. You have no idea what your insistence caused!

I nodded mutely, biting my lips to tame the deluge of words that wished to make themselves heard. Anna deserved the civility of a listening ear after such a lengthy absence. There would be ample time to discuss my recent discoveries and newly-awakened sentiments.

"I really planned on attending that meeting," she continued, "but my father's unplanned journey overrode my plans."

"Your father went somewhere?"

"Uh huh. Not just my father...and not just somewhere!"

The momentary silence was punctuated by lively

birdcalls and rustling movements in the underbrush. I inhaled deeply, relishing the sheer freedom of untamed beauty.

"Several town elders had unexpectedly offered my father a paid trip to Marienbad - "

"Mari-what?!"

"Don't tell me you never even heard the name!" Anna exclaimed with mock horror. "Marienbad is an upper-class resort town, where people go to relax and...well, and that's just about it."

"So your father went to that resort town," I said slowly, wondering how that explained her prolonged absence.

"I'm not done yet," Anna grinned. "The town elders are indebted to my father for building up our school system over the years. They wanted to pay for my parents' stay, but Mamma couldn't go. What with all the children and chores, she felt it would be irresponsible to just up and leave in the middle of everything."

"So you offered to run the household instead of her," I concluded with admiration.

Anna had the grace to blush as she denied my inference.

"Not quite, Esther. I offered to take Mamma's place in Marienbad."

A chortle of disbelief tickled my throat, but I held it firmly in place. Had the situation taken place in my home, I would never have had the audacity to make such an 'offer'.

"Papa was pleased that he would have someone to arrange the technicalities...food and everything. And I was thrilled with the chance to get out and see the world a little."

"But...but what about your mother? Didn't she want to go?"

"Oh, you don't know my Mamma," Anna said. "The

only place she really wants to be is at home. Travel, for her, is an excruciating experience and she would do anything to avoid it."

Anna tripped along beside me, enthusiastically describing every detail of her vacation. The sights she had seen and the places she had visited were exotic, at least to my untrained ears, and I couldn't help envying her.

"Marienbad is this sleepy little town, but there's so much to see there!" she said. "I wish we could go together someday."

Visions of a town infested with priests and cardinals flitted through my mind. Marienbad was probably highly suitable for my vivacious friend, but it wasn't for me.

My home was in Eretz Yisroel.

I said that out loud, much to Anna's amazement.

"Your home is…where?!"

"In Eretz Yisroel," I repeated slowly, savoring her astonishment. "You know, that's - "

"Palestine."

Anna was taken aback, but she wasn't ready to relinquish her hold on the conversation.

"Marienbad is not a home, Esther. It's a place to visit."

"Maybe for you," I replied shortly. "What would I do in such a place?"

"Well, if it's good enough for some of your most esteemed rabbis, I imagine it would be good enough for Your Highness, too."

Now it was my turn to be shocked. This was the first time I had heard the name Marienbad, and here Anna was insisting that it was populated by *rabbanim*. I felt like a first-class fool, drowning in waters way out of my depth.

"Er…I didn't know that," I finally admitted.

"You should have seen them," Anna enthusiastically continued. "They looked like…angels. Some had long white beards and such sharp eyes. Papa said that he had never had the privilege of conversing with such wise individuals.

"Enough about me," Anna said. "Let me hear what you've been doing while I was gone. Not that there is much to be done around these parts..."

"Actually, these past few weeks have been full of activity," I replied defensively. "I discovered a new world, Anna. A world full of promise and pride."

A raised eyebrow was the sum total of Anna's response, but I knew that my words would rouse her interest.

"You didn't attend that Zionist meeting Thursday night."

Anna nodded.

"I did."

"You did?! Why?! After the last botched attempt, you insisted that it was all just stuff and nonsense."

"Initially, I went to protect you from yourself. I knew that you were liable to come into the barn like a fireball, setting everything and everyone aflame."

Anna wanted to protest, but I held up my hand to stave off her indignant response.

"You never showed up, Anna. I stood near the door for the duration of the meeting, hoping that my sacrifice wouldn't be in vain."

"But it was," Anna sympathized.

"It wasn't. You didn't arrive, but someone else did. Eliezer ben Yehuda. He's a linguist from Lithuania, and he delivered a lecture that put the entire Zionist philosophy in a different light. I finally understood the *logic* behind it, Anna. I got the proof that you insisted I need."

Anna was struck dumb, and I gloated in my revelation. For once, I had stumped my friend, and the experience was truly gratifying.

"Esther..."

I grabbed hold of a low-hanging tree branch and snapped off a spindly twig. Life was good. The dreams of my Zionist ideals fueled my every breath, and now I even had the pleasure of using Anna as a sounding board. A sigh of contentment wafted in the air, as though the entire universe was rejoicing in my good fortune.

"Esther, I don't know what to tell you."

"Admit that I'm right, for once, and ask for details," I prompted.

Anna shook her head, hesitantly at first and then with mounting certainty.

"I told you that I was in Marienbad with my father," she slowly said. "And I also told you that we met many of your great rabbis there."

I nodded impatiently. None of this was news to me. Did Anna think that my short-term memory was so unreliable?

"When I saw the rabbis for the first time, I knew that they were the ones with the answers," Anna continued. "I asked Papa to unravel this issue for me – for us."

"For...for us?"

"Yes, for us. I wanted to know whether the rabbis backed this new movement, or if they thought it a danger to your nation. I mean, we had been heatedly arguing this point the last time we met, and I couldn't rest until I got answers. Solid answers."

I held my breath, watching as Anna crumbled some fresh green leaves between her fingers. Assiduously avoiding eye-contact, she continued mauling the innocent greenery as though that would make it easier to voice her thoughts.

"And?"

"And they answered my father, clearly and unequivocally. They said that Zionism, in and of itself, is a lofty ideal. The entire Jewish nation aspires to the time when the Redeemer will lead them back to their land."

Anna was speaking quickly, spewing the words out of her mouth in an attempt to get rid of them.

"But it's not the right time," she continued. "The rabbis said that the Zionist followers feel they must ditch age-old traditions in an effort to build a brighter tomorrow. They're wrong!"

"Wh-what are you talking about?" I asked.

"You know very well what they're referring to," Anna countered. "Didn't you tell me after that first meeting that the attendees were wild and unrefined?"

"Yes, but - "

"Don't try to whitewash their actions now! Esther, it's wrong."

I should have conceded defeat then and there, but my dreams were too precious to relinquish. I would not allow this young Christian girl to deride my Jewish pride and denigrate my staunch ideals.

"Easy for you to say, Anna," I coldly replied. "You never attended those meetings, for all your talk and bluster. You don't even know what it means to be a Jew, let alone a Zionist!"

Anna shrugged. "You're right. I'm not Jewish. But I've seen enough to convince me that you, Esther, are lucky. Yes, you're a Spoiled Princess - "

I smiled, despite myself.

"You might be coddled and lazy," Anna said with an answering grin, "but you're still a princess. Why would you throw that all away?"

"I'm not throwing anything away," I protested. "Eretz Yisroel is my home! Does it bother anyone that I dream of its rebuilding?"

"But that dream comes at the expense of your religion!" Anna cried in frustration. "Why don't you see that?"

"Just because you think so doesn't make it a fact, Anna."

"I'm not the one who pinpointed the problem," she countered quietly. "Your rabbis said so, Esther. *Your* rabbis!"

I shrugged, completely at a loss. I didn't know which *rabbanim* her father had spoken to, and I couldn't refute their words with knowledge I didn't possess. Somehow, the ideas I had been learning seemed so *right*...so uplifting! Anna was wrong. She had to be.

Silence settled between us, roaring like a raging river as it meandered over the rocks of our stormy conversation. We were firmly entrenched in our positions, unwilling to concede even an inch in the name of peace.

"This is ridiculous," Anna said. "Why are we fighting battles when we're as far from the battleground as one can get? This is something the rabbis and the Zionist leaders have to iron out. Not us."

I agreed wholeheartedly. Why would I discuss my beloved land with the a non-Jewish girl? What could she possibly understand of the deep-seated yearning that had gripped our nation since time immemorial? Could she ever fathom why Eretz Yisroel wasn't just a piece of land, like all others? In her eyes, Poland and Palestine were of equal significance.

"You know, I picked up some Hebrew words while we were vacationing," Anna proudly confided. "I'm way ahead of you in my lessons."

"All I know is what you taught me," I admitted. "Spoiled Princess."

Anna laughed, setting our world right-side-up with her tinkling joy.

"You've come a long way," she said. "Before I left, we even conducted a coherent English conversation. Remember?"

"Mmm..."

"Next time I'll bring along my English primer," she

promised. "On the condition that you bring me something in Hebrew."

We parted amicably, our argument lingering somewhere behind us without impinging on the newly-created truce. Much as I wished to prove my point, I couldn't relinquish the one friendship that allowed me to feel like an equal.

Anna, however, thought otherwise.

Chapter Twelve

I went to the barn the following evening, determined to quash Anna's arguments with a hefty dose of inspiration. Chanan would surely know how to counter the rabbis' words...although cowardice would probably strike me dumb as soon as I would be given the floor.

For a fleeting moment, I relished the thought of bringing Anna to one of these gatherings. I was certain that after one experience, she would accept my views as her own.

Little did I know that Anna had chosen another adventure for that night; an adventure that involved my unsuspecting parents and my ill-concealed secrets. From furtive comments and revealing remarks, I was able to piece together a fairly accurate account of what had transpired between my closest friend and my horrified parents.

*   *   *

Anna walked along the Plawo streets, staring in wonder at the comings and goings. Black-hatted men strode purposefully towards the main square, greeting each other heartily in the darkening gloom. Young mothers called in their children for the night and shuttered their windows with finality.

The day was done.

She breathed deeply, enjoying the scent of innocence and purity that pervaded the little town. There was something so...clean...about this life. It wasn't cleanliness in a physical sense, but in a spiritual realm. There was a definite undercurrent of purpose that tied these people to each other and to their Creator.

Esther! Why are you doing this to yourself? You have everything a girl could wish for – loving parents, financial security, adoring brothers...and deep, religious convictions. Why are you stepping into a minefield with your eyes closed?

The thoughts churned through her mind as she carefully followed the instructions she had obtained from Maria. The washerwoman had eagerly described the home of her employers, detailing its luxury and spaciousness. When Anna had asked her where it was located, she matter-of-factly stated that Main Street was the only location such a prestigious family could possibly choose to reside.

Here it is! The Hofert residence.

A bearded young man hurried past her, waving in farewell to a woman standing in the doorway.

That can't be Esther's father, Anna thought. *It must be one of her brothers. I wonder if it's the older one, or... or...what was his name again? Zalmen. I don't think it was Zalmen. He looked too serious and introverted.*

Then again, Esther said that Zalmen is a rabbi now. And the older brother recently moved to Krakow.

Stop procrastinating, Anna. Do what you have to do.

Anna climbed the three wide steps leading to the entranceway, and furtively glanced around. No one was in the vicinity. No one would be able to gossip about the stranger who had visited the Hofert home late Thursday evening.

A tentative knock on the door brought no immediate

results. Anna took a deep breath before pounding on the paneled wood in a burst of impatience.

I have to do this, Esther. Your parents will be livid and you'll feel betrayed...but I have no choice. I –

"Good evening."

Anna glanced up quickly. The woman she had previously glimpsed in the doorway now stood before her with question marks dancing in her kindly eyes.

"Uh...good evening, Mrs. Hofert. How...how are you?"

The woman looked at her in surprise. Was the girl lost? She didn't seem in the least bit familiar. Why would a young girl be wandering about Plawo as day morphed into night?

Anna shuffled her feet, feeling the woman's suspicions escalating with every passing moment.

"Can...can I please come in?" she ventured.

Please, let me come in and say my piece, she pleaded silently. *I can't stay here much longer! Who knows when Esther will come home?!*

Dina Hofert felt a surge of pity for this homeless waif. She must have fallen on hard times and begun wandering from town to town in search of food and shelter.

"It's just for a few minutes," Anna said. "I just...want to tell you something."

Mrs. Hofert moved aside, motioning for the young girl to enter. There was something striking about this stranger...a spark of refinement that lent her charm.

"Please have a seat," the woman graciously suggested, pointing to one of the armchairs in the spacious living room.

She has such a melodious voice, Anna marveled. *It's markedly similar to Esther's.*

"Mrs. Hofert, I...I...Is Esther home?"

If she was surprised that this stranger was acquainted with her daughter, Mrs. Hofert made no sign of it.

"Yes. She's probably in her room upstairs."

Anna swallowed a sigh. This was going to be much more difficult than she had envisioned.

"Could you...could you ask her to come down for a minute?"

"You know my Esther'ke."

The words were a statement, and Anna merely nodded, offering nothing in return.

Regally, Mrs. Hofert ascended the winding staircase and swiftly approached Esther's room. Maybe her daughter would be able to shed light upon this mysterious visitor. There was so much yet to be done on this Thursday evening. The last thing she needed was for a young intruder to disrupt her Shabbos preparations.

"Esther?"

Her soft voice reached Anna's ears, and she tensed in expectation. If Esther had decided not to go to the meeting, she would have a lot of explaining to do.

"Esther'ke? Can I come in?"

She's not there, Mrs. Hofert, Anna wanted to shout. *She's at old Gavriel's barn. Don't waste your time on calling a young bird that has prematurely flown its nest!*

A door creaked open and Anna pictured the middle-aged woman peeking into her daughter's empty room.

"Esther! Where are you?!"

Hurried footsteps tripped daintily down the steps, and Anna tensed. The moment of truth had all but arrived.

"I'm sorry. Esther is not home," Mrs. Hofert said with a worried frown. "I cannot imagine where she would be so late at night. Maybe she was delayed at her brother's house..."

Anna shook her head, causing Mrs. Hofert to start in surprise.

"You...you know where she is?"

A note of vulnerability had crept into the woman's voice, and Anna shuddered at the thought of what was yet to come.

"Esther is...somewhere else. She...she is at the...the barn."

"The barn?! What barn?!"

She has no idea! The poor woman doesn't even know what the barn portends!

"Old Gavriel's barn," Anna said slowly.

Mrs. Hofert held up her hand, as though she wished to stem the tide of shocking revelations by sheer force of will.

"Explain, please," she begged. "Why would Esther be traipsing around in the overgrown weed patches near Old Gavriel's barn? And so late at night..."

"Esther is in the barn because...because she...she joined them."

"Joined them?! Who? The cows?"

"No, no," Anna sighed. "Mrs. Hofert, the Zionist youth meetings are conducted in Gavriel's barn every Thursday evening."

It was awful to witness the change that overcame the gracious hostess. Anna prudently looked away, giving Mrs. Hofert a chance to rearrange her features and regain her equilibrium.

"You mean to say that my Esther, my beautiful Esther'ke - "

A strangled sound cut off her words and Mrs. Hofert coughed, once and again.

"Shimon," she weakly called out. "Shimon!"

Oh, no! She must be summoning her husband, Esther's father. Will I have to repeat the news to him as well?

"Yes, Dina?"

The voice emanated from somewhere far off, but Mrs. Hofert didn't respond. She stood in the center of the room, staring out of the large picture window. Was she hoping her daughter would appear and wave away these baseless accusations?

"Dina? Did you call me?"

Mrs. Hofert whirled around. She pointed wordlessly at the young girl cowering in the corner, and Shimon glanced at her in bewilderment.

"Er...welcome to our home," he said. "Are you looking for something?"

"Mr. Hofert, I just came to tell you where Esther is."

His bewilderment increased tenfold.

"Where...Esther...is..."

"She's at old Gavriel's barn."

This time, her words elicited a prompt response. Mr. Hofert's horror was impossible to miss, but within moments it had morphed into a frightening degree of fury.

"You – you will not come in here and besmirch my daughter's name," he thundered. "Esther would never attend a meeting of those...those wild Zionists."

"You knew that they met in Gavriel's barn?" Mrs. Hofert asked.

Her question went unanswered. Shimon Hofert dug his hands into his trouser pockets and started pacing the room like one possessed. With a snort of disbelief, he finally sat down on a hard-backed wooden chair and signaled the quaking young girl to sit down on an armchair.

"I'm sorry," he apologized, once again the genial gentleman all of Plawo admired. "Your words shocked me, but I can assure you that they are baseless. They are unfounded."

Anna looked down at the gleaming floor and wished she would be doing anything other than sitting in her friend's elegant home. She would even exchange this experience for two days of laundry washing!

"Who are you?"

"Anna," she replied simply.

Two pairs of questioning eyes demanded a more complete answer, and Anna was struck by her second flash of astonishment that evening.

They never even heard my name! Did Esther keep our relationship a secret? She must have been afraid that her parents would disapprove.

"I'll start from the beginning," she said. "Approximately three months ago, I went down to the river on a Wednesday morning to wash our family's laundry. As you know, Esther and the washerwoman are there every Wednesday as well."

Mrs. Hofert nodded her head, while her husband looked to her for confirmation.

"I didn't know who Esther was, but after a short time we got acquainted. Not just acquainted," she amended. "We became friends."

"Who are you?" Mr. Hofert asked again, with more urgency.

"My name is Anna Podolsky, and I live on the other side of the river."

"Podolsky," Mr. Hofert repeated. "You mean, your father is Paul Podolsky, the school teacher."

Anna nodded, cringing at the looks of horror directed her way. It wasn't her fault that she was born into a different religion, was it?

"Esther'ke! How could you?!" Mrs. Hofert groaned.

"I'm sorry," Anna earnestly apologized, although she knew that apologies were useless at this point. "I had no inkling that Esther was keeping this a secret. I didn't realize that you would...disapprove."

They looked at her with ghost-like countenances.

"I'm sorry."

It was such a poor statement; so paltry in comparison to the havoc it was meant to rectify.

"Go on," Mr. Hofert requested.

"At a certain point, we took to discussing the Zionist movement," Anna continued. "Esther firmly contended that it was wrong, from the bottom up. She was brought up well, your Esther."

They nodded miserably, knowing that the story was far from over.

This is going to hurt, Anna. Strengthen yourself. Don't try to protect your image...Esther's future is hanging in the balance!

"I told Esther that she can't voice an opinion without providing proof. Logical proof..."

How ridiculous my claims sound when they bounce around in this solemn living room. I thought logic was the answer to everything, but look where it took my trusting friend!

"Esther said that...that she would gather proof," Anna admitted. "She would go to one of their meetings and convince me that they were absolutely wrong."

"She went," Mrs. Hofert murmured.

"Yes, Esther went. She went one Thursday evening and reported the next week that the members were wild and unruly. She said that their ideals had no foundation; no meaning."

An audible sigh of relief resonated in the room, but Anna didn't pay it any heed.

"I didn't let her convince me," she shamefacedly admitted. "I contended that her views were based on emotion. I said that *I* would attend a meeting and then we would know where we stand.

"Apparently, Esther was afraid that I would reveal our secret friendship. Or maybe she feared for my safety. I'll never know what caused her to attend a second meeting; the meeting I was supposed to attend but never did."

Anna fell silent, but no one came to her assistance.

The blame and guilt multiplied a thousand-fold in the silence that followed, and she knew that the burden was hers alone.

"There was a dynamic speaker at that meeting who convinced Esther that Zionism is a dream worth pursuing," she hurriedly concluded. "Since then Esther has become an ardent follower. She attends their gatherings every week..."

They didn't want to believe her. Shimon Hofert toyed with his pocket watch, fumbling with its silver chain. He, who was never at a loss for words, now found himself searching for an appropriate remark to set things right.

"I came to tell you before it would be too late," Anna quietly concluded. "I felt that I had played a part in this terrible development, and I...I didn't know what to do."

"You did right, my child," Mrs. Hofert murmured, her maternal warmth awakened by the child's obvious discomfort. "It must have been difficult to...do this, but it was the right decision."

Tears of remorse gathered in Anna's eyes and she angrily swiped them away.

Why am I crying? Now, after all I've inflicted upon these suffering parents – only now can I cry? Where were my feelings until now? I should have realized that I was leading Esther, innocent Esther, into danger.

"Yes, thank you," Mr. Hofert stiffly concurred. "And now, if you will please allow us to discuss this..."

Anna nodded, accepting the curt dismissal with understanding. She gathered the torn shreds of her dignity from beneath the armchair cushions and hastily walked towards the door.

"I'm sorry," she whispered to the listening walls. "I'm sorry."

* * *

When I came home from the meeting, my parents were still sitting in the living room. I was surprised to see them at this late hour, and feverishly conjured up several different excuses to allay their suspicions.

"Esther," *Tatte* said warmly. "You're home."

I nodded dumbly. Why weren't they asking me about my midnight wanderings? Didn't it arouse their concern?

"Tell me, Esther'ke," *Tatte* continued. "Just tell me why you went."

I stared at him, unsure of his intentions. *Mamme* avoided my gaze, twisting her embroidered handkerchief into a neat little ball.

"Why I went," I repeated dumbly.

"Esther'ke, why? What are you looking for in that old barn?"

So they knew. Somehow, they had discovered my dark secret. I figured that it would come to light sooner or later, but I had hoped that matters would have resolved themselves before then. How anything could be resolved to our mutual satisfaction was beyond me, but I had held onto those ambiguous hopes.

"I...*Tatte*, I can explain."

They looked at me silently, expectantly. The people dearest to me in the entire world gazed at me with hopeful eyes, begging me to set their world right again. What could I say? I couldn't insist that it was all a fabrication. They had obviously gotten their information from a reliable source.

"*Tatte, Mamme*...I'm still Esther. Your little Esther'ke. Nothing has changed."

"Oh, *mein kind*," *Tatte* moaned. "How I wish I could take your words at face value. These ideas...they have a power. They eat away at our hearts and consume our minds..."

Mamme looked at him then, a look that spoke volumes. *Don't go that way,* she seemed to tell him. *Let's look to the future.*

I cringed. How had I, the cosseted only daughter, inflicted such pain upon my dear parents? All my life, I had been aware of their need for protection. I played the role they created for me to perfection...until now.

"Esther'ke, *Mamme* and I have discussed our options. It would be best if you go away for a while...far, far away."

Instinctively, I recoiled. *Tatte* held up his hand in a sad gesture of authority.

"I'm sorry, *tuchter.* Your freedom to make decisions has proven itself misplaced. Now you will have to leave the decisions to us."

I bowed my head in surrender.

It was a difficult conversation; a conversation fraught with accusation and tears. It was a night that would always be marked by an onslaught of remorse and the conclusion of carefree childhood. It was the night I entered the world of adulthood, burdened by guilt that would accompany me forever more.

As the first streaks of dawn dabbled playfully with *Mamme's* teary eyes, the decision was made. I should have been delirious with joy at the journey my parents offered me, but the circumstances painted it a dull shade of gray.

"Maybe...maybe I could go with one of my friends?" I ventured, in a last-ditch attempt to make the trip somewhat palatable.

"Which one of your peers would be willing to leave their families for such an extended period of time?" *Tatte* asked. "How many mothers can manage without the assistance of their daughters?"

My mother could, I muttered to myself. *Who needs me here? No one, that's who. At least in the barn I felt like I was making a difference...but see where it has led me.*

Straight into the arms of this unknown Titanic.

"There's a girl my age who might be able to make the trip," I foolishly persisted. "She...she's not like the rest of us."

Mamme's eyes blazed with uncharacteristic anger. She turned to me, her beloved daughter, and treated me to a glare usually reserved for recalcitrant servants.

"Don't even say her name, Esther! Isn't it enough that she tarnished your soul and tainted your mind?! Do you want to take her along with you so that she can inflict further damage?!"

They know about Anna! Who told them?!

"*Mamme* will accompany you," *Tatte* said. "The ship is departing on April 10th. That leaves you...two weeks to get ready."

"But...but Pesach," I mumbled. "How could we leave on Yom Tov?"

"The ship departs on *Isru Chag*," *Tatte* clarified. "We will have to travel to England on *Chol Hamoed* and remain there until the Titanic departs a day after Yom Tov."

His words were unequivocal and brooked no argument. At this point, I didn't have the strength to formulate an opinion. I had hurt my parents...and now I was being given an opportunity to make amends.

Tatte pleaded with me silently to accept his words and I nodded miserably. I would go on this luxurious liner with *Mamme* and we would even enjoy it. After all, who wouldn't be thrilled at the opportunity to board such a ship on its maiden voyage? I should be thanking my parents profusely, instead of accepting my fate like one sentenced to the guillotine. *Tatte* said that the ship would dock on American shores, and we would remain in bustling New York City for a week to see the sights. After that, we would return home on a European-bound steamer.

The month of separation from everything familiar

would be enough to wipe these newfangled ideas from my mind. That's what *Tatte* insisted. He offered me a one-time opportunity to travel on this monumental luxury liner. I should have been grateful.

But I couldn't bring myself to smile. *Mamme*'s red-rimmed eyes followed me to my bedroom, smoldering in the dark with pained disappointment. That was the last thing I saw before I fell asleep in the dawning light of a new day, and it was the first thing that greeted me in the land of sleep. *Mamme*'s eyes.

Chapter Thirteen

*I*t was a confusing time; a time of sky-rocketing enthusiasm and deep-diving mortification. Anna couldn't get over my good fortune, and constantly pestered me with questions about the planned journey.

"Where is the ship leaving from?"

"Anna, I told you already!" I said with exasperation. "It's leaving from a port in Southampton, England."

"Don't become all uppity with me just because you're one of those privileged luxury travelers," Anna warned, the twinkle in her eyes reassuring me that she wasn't all that worried.

"April 10 is the departure date," I continued.

"That's in two weeks, Esther."

I nodded. I had made the calculations so many times, that I could practically recite the exact amount of hours and minutes remaining until we boarded the RMS Titanic.

"*Titanic*," Anna whispered dramatically, rolling the unfamiliar word on her tongue. "What sort of name is that for the largest passenger ship ever created?"

"Not our decision, is it?" I remarked. "Those people at White Star Line own the ship so they get the privilege of naming her."

I looked up at the clear blue sky, savoring these moments of togetherness before Maria summoned me to accompany her homeward. Anna, for some reason, had come empty-handed this Wednesday morning, but the lack of laundry didn't seem to set her at ease. Quite the contrary, in fact.

"You're excited, Esther," she stated, with a hint of a question prompting me to respond.

"Of course I am! Wouldn't you be thrilled at the prospect of joining this historical journey?!"

Anna shook her head in confirmation but her sparkling blue eyes were focused elsewhere. Anywhere, that is, but in my direction.

She must be jealous, I realized with a start. *The daughter of a struggling school teacher would never merit such a high-priced experience. And here I am prattling endlessly about the details of my luxurious cruise.*

"Why did your parents offer you this trip?" she asked, gazing into the distance as though something of great interest was transpiring at the horizon.

"Why?" I repeated, stalling for time. "That's a good question. Why would my parents want to treat their beloved only daughter to a once-in-a-lifetime opportunity? Considering that money need not be an issue, why should they not offer me this trip?"

Please, don't delve any deeper, Anna. There's no way that I could tell you how horrified they are with our relationship. How disgusted they are with my Zionist leanings...How desperate they are to separate me from all that I hold dear.

Don't ask me anything, Anna. You would never understand.

Anna scrutinized my face carefully, and I held my breath. Would she accept my words at face value?

"Lucky girl," she finally pronounced. "Spoiled Princess, in fact."

I laughed aloud, enjoying the sound of my own merriment.

"Never mind, Anna. Those lessons you gave me will definitely come in handy. After all, the ship is traveling to New York City. I'm sure that most of the travelers consider English their primary language."

Anna dramatically patted herself on the back, and I laughed once again. What a pity that I couldn't enjoy her company during a trip that promised to provide me with memories for a lifetime. She would know how to make the most of every experience.

"So, if I go to Southampton now I'll be able to catch a glimpse of this beauty?" Anna asked playfully.

"No," I replied. "You would have to go down to Belfast for that."

Once again, I enjoyed the look of surprise on my friend's smiling face.

"Belfast? Where's that?"

"In Ireland. That's where the Titanic was built."

Anna shook her head, uncomfortable with the sudden reversal of our roles. She had always been the all-knowing leader who dispensed information with the graciousness of a reigning monarch. For once, I had achieved that coveted status but it didn't sit right on my shoulders.

"If you'd be traveling on the Titanic, you would make sure to find out the name of every construction worker, captain and crew member," I said in jest. "I'm so excited that I pounce upon every bit of information my father manages to unearth."

Good job, Esther, I congratulated myself. *No use in lording your good fortune over your closest friend.*

"Right you are," Anna said. "Well, you'll have to work really hard on this trip, Esther. I expect to hear every detail when you get back!"

"I'm not going yet!" I protested. "Didn't we just agree

that there are two full weeks remaining?"

"And did you forget about your holiday next week? And didn't you tell me about seventy-three times that you have to visit the seamstress to get an entire wardrobe sewn up? After all, your *Mamme* insists that you're already a...a *kallah* maid."

Our laughter mingled comfortably in the stillness of this spring afternoon.

"*Kallah moid,*" I managed to gasp between giggles of hysteria. "*Mamme* says that I have to look presentable. Some of my friends are actually counting down the days to their marriage!"

Anna looked at me in disbelief, but wisely refrained from comment. In her circles, matches were certainly not even suggested at such a young age. My sisters-in-law, on the other hand, had both cradled newborns in their arms by the time they hit the ripe old age of seventeen. With my seventeenth birthday looming on the horizon, *Mamme* was understandably feeling pressured by the community matchmakers.

"Whatever," Anna said, as she gestured to Maria waiting impatiently behind us. "You'll be a busy *kallah* thing these next two weeks, and then you'll be off, leaving me all by my lonesome self."

"It's not forever, Anna," I hastened to reassure her.

"I know, I know. That's just my jealousy speaking."

Anna. How do you always know what to say to diffuse the most uncomfortable situations?

My friends were struck dumb when they heard the news of my impending journey. Unlike Anna, they didn't pester me with questions or pelt me with last-minute instructions. Instead, they waited in silent awe for Esther Hofert to share some of her glorious plans with them.

Interestingly enough, I lost most of my enthusiasm

when faced with their admiring silence. In Anna's company, I barely restrained my words to enable her a word in edgewise. Now, however, I found myself groping for fascinating tidbits about the famed Titanic.

"The ship could hold a lot of passengers," I told them. "Three and a half thousand!"

They gasped, as I had done upon hearing the astronomical number. I envisioned a city on the ocean, traveling into the setting sun as myriads of passengers lined its decks.

"And not everyone is being put up in the same quarters. There's first-class, second-class and then very simple accommodations for third-class travelers."

"How are you traveling, Esther?"

I looked at Etta in surprise. Since Miriam's sudden disappearance, she hadn't shown her face much in public. The shame of her sister's defection deeply wounded her gentle soul, and her anguished eyes were but a reflection of her mother's agony.

"Uh, Etta! I didn't see you!"

I've been avoiding you, Etta, though you wouldn't know it. I can't face your pain. The guilt is strangling me, Etta! I could have said something...I could have saved your sister from herself!

"Are you traveling first class?" she repeated, looking straight at me with renewed interest.

I shook my head forcefully.

"No, of course not! You would never believe the price of a first-class ticket!"

The girls leaned forward in eager anticipation.

"It's 875 pounds! You know what that means? Think of the crisp dollar bills some of us get from relatives in America. You would need 4,375 of those dollar bills to secure passage in a first-class suite!"

I knew that some single berth tickets in first-class

could be purchased for just 30 pounds, but I enjoyed the looks of awe that greeted my dramatic statement. There was no way I would ruin that impression by informing them that my second-class ticket had cost merely 13 pounds.

Not that thirteen pounds was something to sneeze at. With that sum, one could feed a family of twelve for a full month!

"Wow!" Malka exclaimed. "So you must be traveling second-class."

I nodded.

The girls fell silent, mulling over my words.

"I wonder if you'll be back in time for my wedding," Brenda said.

"Of course I will! Aren't you getting married after *Shavuos*?"

Brenda nodded, and the others sighed in happy anticipation. They crowded closer together, pestering her with questions about her preparations. Names of dressmakers were thrown about, as were the intricate design titles given to some of her embroidered tablecloths.

Brenda was a *kallah*...and I, Esther Hofert, was planning a trip on the Titanic. It was incongruity at its best.

When I informed my friends at Gavriel's barn that I would be away for a short while, they congratulated me enthusiastically. I had begged *Mamme* for one last chance to bid my friends farewell, and she reluctantly gave her consent.

"Don't tell *Tatte*," she warned me. "He would never understand."

But *Mamme* understood. She knew that I couldn't cut off contact without giving notice. Little did she suspect that I wouldn't muster the courage to inform the Zionist youths that I was departing from their midst...forever.

I just told them that I would be traveling on the famous luxury liner that White Star Line was launching on its maiden voyage. There would be ample time to worry about their reaction to my defection when I got back.

Chanan stared at me mockingly.

"So the princess of Plawo wants to rebuild Eretz Yisroel, doesn't she?"

I flinched. What had I done to ignite his sarcasm? Why was he belittling me in front of the others?

"Only the best for the *Rosh Hakahel*'s daughter. A cruise on the Titanic, huh?"

"Chanan, let her be," a voice called out from one of the corners. "She's going on a pleasure trip and when she comes back, she'll be a seasoned traveler."

"Sure," Chanan snorted. "You'll sit on a plush armchair and watch the sunset every night, and when you get back you'll be ready to embrace the wilderness of Eretz Yisroel."

I shrugged noncommittally. No one had to know that this was my final fling. The dream of pioneering our holy land had bowed its head in deference to my parents' anguish. Never would I repeat my foolish mistakes. Upon my return, I would be a model daughter. Of that I was certain.

"*Chaveirim*," Chanan called out. "*Chaveiros*! Where do our hearts belong?"

I tuned out his flaming rhetoric, relieved to be relegated to the shadows for the duration of the meeting. Leah winked at me several times and I allowed myself to smile in return. Without Miriam at her side, she looked like a mother bird bereft of her young.

"Enjoy your trip," Leah wished me warmly as we walked out together. "Don't bother yourself with Chanan. He simply cannot understand how someone could wallow in luxury when the poor of Eretz Yisroel are desperate for assistance."

If that comment was supposed to make me feel better, it sure did a poor job. I felt like a spoiled youngster who grabbed everything for herself, without considering the needs of others.

I'm doing this for Tatte, I reminded myself. *Tatte wants me to go, to 'clear my head of these foolish ideas', as he says. That's not to say that I'm not thrilled with the idea, but...it's not like they make it out to be. I'm not that selfish.*

Leah patted me warmly on the shoulder, and I watched as she ambled towards the most decrepit shack in all of Plawo. The cool night air slithered under my thin clothing. It was time to return home, to the frenzied preparations and excited plans.

Yes, it was time to close this painful chapter of my youth and assume a more mature outlook on my future.

It was funny how fickle passion could be. Once I was told that Zionism was an absolute forbidden – in my home, at least – I was forced to give it up. And it didn't even hurt as much as one would imagine.

I suppose Tatte is right. The Titanic trip definitely sweetens the blow and makes it almost palatable.

Dear, brilliant *Tatte.* He always knew which keys to use in opening our hearts.

Part III:
Aboard the Titanic
April 1912

Chapter Fourteen

G o in peace and return in peace, *mein kind.*"

Tatte's hands trembled slightly and I couldn't meet his eyes. I knew that my illustrious father was not referring to a physical sense of peace, but rather to an inner serenity which he perceived I was lacking.

"*Tuchter'l...*"

How could so much love and concern be compressed into one solitary word?

"I...I will come back the Esther you always knew," I promised, gulping down the salty moisture that threatened to drown us in regret. "*Tatte,* you don't have to worry."

"A father worries, Esther'ke..."

He stared into the distance, looking for *Mamme* who had made herself scarce as soon as he placed his fatherly hands on my head.

Mamme stood near the loading dock to ensure that our luggage was taken directly to our reserved suite. With nary a tremor in her voice, she graciously pantomimed that the porters handle her precious bundles with extreme care.

How do you remain so composed, Mamme? While I'm dissolving in a heap of tears, you manage to maintain your grace and poise...I suppose you're not grappling with the guilt and shame that insist on accompanying me on our journey.

Satisfied that our belongings had been taken care of, *Mamme* returned to our little family circle. She cast a worried glance at *Tatte* and received a reassuring nod in return. Everything was alright. The dreaded farewells would soon be drowned out by the ship's ceremonious foghorn.

"Nu, Esther'ke," *Tatte* jovially called out. "What do you say to this beauty?"

"It's...it's...enormous!"

Tatte laughed, dispelling the previous tension in a gust of good humor.

"Enormous is right, Esther. Much as I tried to envision the Titanic, my imagination never even came close to its reality."

"The entire Plawo would be able to fit onto this ship," I mused. "It's wondrous how such a monstrosity could possibly stay afloat."

"And not just stay afloat," *Mamme* interjected, "but take us all the way across the ocean..."

Tatte glanced at his pocket-watch. It was getting late, and he still had to make the long trip back to Poland. Urgent community matters that had been postponed until after Pesach now required immediate attention, and he couldn't waste an entire precious day at the Southampton docks.

"There's Captain Smith!" he exclaimed, pointing at a middle-aged man standing imperiously on the Titanic's deck. He cut an imposing figure in his crisply-starched uniform, with his right arm outstretched to signal a recalcitrant crew-member.

A bugle sounded, reminding me of the *shofar*'s insistent calls. A shiver of apprehension sidled up alongside me. The trip was nearly underway. I, Esther Hofert of small-town Plawo, was actually joining the most esteemed travelers on the Titanic's maiden voyage.

Mamme squeezed my hand warmly to let me know that she was with me in my turmoil. Much as we desired to set out on our journey, it was difficult to take that final leap into the vast unknown. How many times in the past sixteen years had I ventured out of Plawo's protected confines? Not much, and not too far. The Titanic was planning to take me to a different world; an unfamiliar universe!

With a smile of genuine enthusiasm, *Tatte* shepherded us towards the boarding dock. His eyes roved continuously, taking in the sights and sounds that overwhelmed even one as travel-weary as he.

As I placed my foot on the gangplank, *Tatte* bent closer to me and whispered into my ear.

"Esther...*mein* Esther. Hold your head high and represent our nation. And remember – your *Tatte* is waiting impatiently to hear every detail of your trip!"

I smiled at him, not trusting my voice to speak.

Why does every trip have to be preceded by a farewell?! It's so difficult to leave...yet so impossible to stay.

Tatte! You'll be proud of me! When I come back, I'll agree to everything you suggest and advise...I'll be the model child, like Menachem, I vowed mutely, then reconsidered for the sake of truth. *Well, almost like Menachem.*

I walked on ahead, giving my parents a moment of privacy before the ship's departure would leave us on two separate sides of a watery divide.

Mamme's kerchief playfully danced in the breeze as she waved a final goodbye and followed me into the teeming mass of passengers and crew members.

What a commotion! The crew was inundated with requests for directions and assistance, but they maintained their composure. *Mamme* and I stood off to the side, waiting for the chaos to subside. We couldn't possibly find our rooms when so many people were desperate to do the same.

"Good afternoon, ma'am."

I looked up in surprise. Who was addressing me amidst all the tumult? The young man, dressed in uniform, appeared neither threatening nor intimidating.

"My name is George Barlow, ma'am," he continued, glancing pointedly at *Mamme*. "I am a second-class bedroom steward and the name on your ticket lists you as one of my charges. Please, follow me downstairs to your accommodations."

I nearly laughed aloud at his pompous speech. *Mamme* hadn't an inkling as to what he was trying to say, while I barely got the gist of his lengthy introduction.

"Mr. Barlow," I said hesitantly. "My mother...ah...no speak English. Polish."

"I see. You don't understand English," he told *Mamme* who gave him the same uncomprehending stare as before.

Mr. George Barlow scratched his head and appeared befuddled. "Uh, ma'am, I...I..."

His voice trailed off as he turned to see his colleagues efficiently shepherding passengers to their destinations.

"Come, follow me," he said, waiting while I translated his concise commands for *Mamme*.

Anna, you have no idea how much you've helped me! Those English lessons are more important than either of us imagined!

"Let me carry your luggage, ma'am," Barlow intoned courteously, reaching down for *Mamme*'s handbag.

Mamme clutched it to herself indignantly and fixed the steward with a penetrating glare. Barlow immediately withdrew, throwing up his arms in defeat. Crooking his finger, he signaled that we follow him to the far right.

"Come, *Mamme*," I urged impatiently. "That man is going to show us to our rooms."

"You're sure, Esther?" *Mamme* hesitated. "I think we'd better keep our distance from that *ganav*. He wanted to steal my bag right in front of my eyes! Did you see that?!"

"Oh, *Mamme*! He wanted to help you! Come, I can barely see him in this crowd!"

I pulled my mother after me, murmuring apologetically to all the people we elbowed out of our way.

"Ma'am, please enter," Mr. Barlow ceremoniously declared as soon as we approached.

I gaped at the yawning chasm staring back at me, wondering where precisely this was going to lead. It was a dark, small cavern that seemed highly unstable.

Mamme, however, had no qualms about the matter. As soon as I had explained that Mr. Barlow was employed to service us, she willingly followed his unintelligible directions. With poise and confidence, she swept past the steward and gestured to me impatiently that I follow her inside.

Gingerly, I placed one foot in front of the other. The cavern swayed slightly, but righted itself in the nick of time. With a flourish, Mr. Barlow entered behind us and pressed a small button. The doors creaked closed, and a sudden *whoosh* threw me against the wall.

"Wh-what was that?!"

George Barlow chuckled, politely covering his mouth to hide his amusement. Apparently, laughter had been crossed off the list of stewards' acceptable behavior while on board the Titanic.

"This - " he choked out, between explosions of mirth. "Elevator."

"Elevator," I repeated.

"Go up," he pointed to the ceiling. "Go down," he said, pointing at the floor.

"Right," I interjected, pointing at the right side, extremely proud of the English directions I had recently mastered. "Left."

"No, no!" Barlow chortled. "Up, down. Finish."

So this cavern went up and down and it was called an elevator. I had never seen such a contraption nor heard of its creation. It was an interesting concept. One stepped into a small cavern and pressed a button to make it fly. Who would have believed it possible?

Thud.

The cavern, or elevator as Mr. Barlow had termed it, shuddered slightly and then stood still. With a loud creak, the door opened up and a shaft of bright light illuminated the dim interior.

"After me, ma'am," the steward called, stepping out of the elevator with confidence.

"Come, *Mamme*. We're nearly there."

Mamme's pallor was an exact portrayal of her feelings. She swayed slightly, grasping her precious handbag for added security. Together, we exited that shuddering, heaving contraption and followed Mr. Barlow down a well-lit corridor.

"Dining room," he stated, pointing his thumb in the direction of a large, stately room. Tables and chairs were strategically arranged, creating an elegant atmosphere.

"This is where the meals are served," I whispered to *Mamme*.

"I wonder if we'll feel comfortable bringing our own food here," she replied. "Maybe we should eat in our rooms."

I shrugged. It seemed ridiculous to pass up on this one-time opportunity of eating in such marvelous surroundings, but *Mamme* was right. If we sat down at one of the elegant tables and started unwrapping our homemade food packages, the other travelers would be sure to notice and comment. It had the potential of being highly uncomfortable.

"Smoking room."

The room was completely empty, but I had no time to ponder its purpose.

"Lending library," our self-appointed tour guide continued.

I peeked inside. Rows upon rows of books stood sentinel on wooden bookshelves. I wondered what language they were written in, and then immediately quashed that question. Those books were certainly not for me.

"Here we go!"

Mr. Barlow stopped short and opened the door of yet another room. This time, it was a beautiful bedroom that greeted us with warmth. *Mamme* breathed a sigh of relief and placed her handbag on the closest chair.

She gestured her thanks to the waiting steward, but Mr. Barlow didn't seem inclined to leave.

"This is your suite, ma'am. If you'd like to relax or just walk around, there's an enclosed promenade over there," he said, pointing further down the corridor. "And if you need anything, feel free to ask me for assistance. George Barlow."

He tipped his hat and strode out of the room, closing the door behind him. While I tried to make sense of his flowing words, *Mamme* wasted no time in acquainting herself with our room.

"Beautiful," she murmured, opening one cupboard after another. "So fresh and clean...We could put our clothing directly on the shelves without worrying about any dust."

From my fastidious mother, that was the ultimate compliment. I was certain that her handbag contained a pile of *shmattes* and cleaning solutions, but they would apparently remain untouched. The Titanic had passed

Mamme's initial inspection.

"One…two…three…four…good, the suitcases are all here."

I stared out of the round window that afforded us a view of the endless ocean waters. It was almost frightening to see the blue expanse stretching, stretching further than the eye could see. What were we, if not a mere speck in this gargantuan body of water?

I was aware of *Mamme* puttering around behind me, murmuring to herself while she placed each article of clothing in its proper place. Her quick movements seemed incongruous with the serenity flowing along outside my little porthole.

A shrill whistle pierced the air. We were finally off!

"*Mamme*! We're moving!"

"So we are," *Mamme* replied matter-of-factly. "The journey has begun."

She continued sorting our packaged foods, completely oblivious to the drama taking place outside. Calm and punctilious as ever, *Mamme* wouldn't be able to relax until every last item found its place.

"I'm going out to see," I said. "I think there's a…a promenade where we can see what's going on."

Good, Esther! I congratulated myself. *You're learning the language. Promenade. That's what Mr. Barlow said.*

"Go ahead," *Mamme* agreed. "I'll join you when I'm done here."

I quickly turned the golden doorknob and made my escape, before *Mamme* could insist that I help her with some of the unpacking. Standing in the corridor, I felt the grandiosity of the moment settle about my shoulders like a voluminous cape. Here I was, a young sixteen-year-old Jewish girl, making history. The Titanic had been hailed as one of the world's greatest wonders, and I was actually standing on board as it set out upon its maiden voyage.

A slight heave brought me back to my senses. The ship was moving, and I was missing out on the view! I hurried towards the enclosed promenade that Mr. Barlow had so graciously pointed out, expecting to see it crowded by curious onlookers.

The deck was empty, save for a young, dark-skinned girl who was wheeling a toddler in a carriage bearing the symbol of White Star Line. Apparently, the shipping company had thought of every detail, down to the babies' mode of transportation while on board.

"Hello," I said cheerily. "How's the view?"

The girl looked at me with that befuddled expression that labeled her a non-English speaking individual.

"Oh, no English?" I asked.

She shook her head in negation and I sighed. Here I had thought that Anna's expert teaching skills would open the doors of communication on all fronts, but my first encounter had proven me wrong.

I meandered over to the large glass panes lining the walls and looked out at the whirl of activity. The Titanic had been detached from its moorings and was gracefully pulling out of its niche at the port.

Oh, no! A hulking vessel was approaching our ship, as though intent on wreaking havoc. Why wasn't anyone doing anything?! The unknown ship, titled proudly "*SS New York*", couldn't have been more than four feet away from us. Instinctively, I moved away from the window and shielded my face with both hands.

G-r-r-r-r.

The grating noises didn't sound too calamitous. Holding my breath tucked inside my chest, I opened my eyes and dared to glimpse at the accident in the making. A closer look showed me that the boat was not at fault. It had been pulled away from its moorings in the Titanic's powerful wake, and had been dragged into dangerous proximity. Before I could fully process the imminent catastrophe, it was averted. A small tugboat was attached to the *SS New York*, and it was pulled away in the nick of time.

Behind me, I heard someone exhaling raggedly. The young girl with straight dark hair had participated in this dramatic foreplay as well.

I put my hand on my heart to describe my fear, and she smiled in understanding. Pointing at herself, the girl said, "Ruth Becker".

"Esther Hofert," I replied, extending my hand for a polite handshake.

Ruth looked at my outstretched hand in wonder and I flushed. Didn't she know what a welcoming greeting was supposed to look like? I had thought that this was a language everyone understood.

Once again, she pointed at herself and stated, "Guntur".

Guntur? What's that supposed to mean? It can't be her name. She told me that already.

"Ah...Guntur, India," she slowly enunciated.

"India!" That sounded familiar. "You live in India."

The girl nodded enthusiastically.

"I...Poland."

Ruth nodded again, and then smiled at the young toddler.

"Richard," she said.

I smiled at the cherubic face looking up at me and resisted the urge to chuck him under the chin. If a handshake had been a foreign custom for this Indian-born girl, who knows what she would say to a child-friendly gesture? His dark-brown eyes scanned my face before he finally gave me a toothless grin. Esther Hofert had passed muster, in his humble opinion.

The Titanic was moving swiftly now, cutting through

the waters like a scythe unleashed in an overgrown wheat field. I gazed out of the window, completely enraptured. Ruth Becker tapped me on the shoulder and waved goodbye, then left me to my ruminations. Once she had stepped out of the enclosed promenade, I felt a delirious sense of freedom skipping in to keep me company. It was just me, the Titanic, and a fathomless body of water.

"Ki B'simcha..."

For with joy you shall depart, and in peace you shall return...

Ensconced in a bubble of pristine beauty, the song meant so much more than it signified on land. I took pleasure in the sensation of giving myself over to music's magnetism, especially in the absence of any listeners. With every word that wafted into the air, I felt *Tatte's* presence coming ever closer. This was his blessing for me, his only daughter, when we parted and this was the blessing I chose to unleash on the Titanic's shining floors and glass-paned walls.

But it wasn't only the Titanic that was privy to my emotional outburst. As I regretfully listened to the echoes fading away, a hurried tap-tapping of feminine heels dispelled the magic of the last few moments.

"Oh, my goodness! That was unbelievable! Simply marvelous!"

The woman standing before me was a sight to see. Her elegant get-up bespoke wealth and power, and her carefully made-up face gave her the appearance of a dressed-up mannequin, like the ones I'd seen at Bella the seamstress.

"Unreal, my girl! Absolutely stupendous," she ranted.

She was speaking so quickly and excitedly, making it impossible for me to distinguish a single understandable word. It seemed that my singing had disturbed her, or maybe rubbed her the wrong way.

"I'm sorry," I said slowly, trying to recall the words for apology that Anna had painstakingly taught me. "Excuse me."

"Sorry?! What are you talking about, child?!"

I spread out my hands in the classic gesture of miscomprehension, and she finally realized that her harangue had been bouncing off a brick wall.

"Ah...You don't understand English," she said.

"A little," I told her. "Speak slow."

The woman inhaled sharply, adjusting the exquisite shawl expertly flung over her shoulders.

"Hello, dear. My name is Melinda Bonair."

I shook her outstretched hand, murmuring, "Esther Hofert."

"Esther, I must tell you how impressed I am by your singing."

My heart nearly galloped away on the wings of horror. This outrageous apparition had actually listened in on my most private moments. I felt exposed.

"I am an expert on these things, Esther," she continued. "See, I am a musical director at The Opera House in Manhattan."

Her words swam together in one amorphous glob of high-brow English. My consternation must have been written all over my face, for Madame Bonair immediately backtracked.

"I'm sorry, dear. Let's try again. I am in the...theater. Yes, theater?"

I nodded. Although Plawo didn't boast a theater of its own, I was well-aware of its entertainment capacity...and its inherent dangers.

"I do...ah...music."

She pantomimed playing a piano, while I nodded enthusiastically.

"You - " she said, pointing imperiously in my direction, "sing beautiful! Amazing!"

I blushed at the effusive compliment, looking down at her high-heeled shoes for distraction.

"When you strike a high note, your voice remains so sweet and clear, like a...like a bell."

Melinda Bonair patted my arm, managing to instill even this friendly gesture with a hint of authority.

"I'm traveling first class, of course," she commented, "with my husband, Bill. I was just exploring the lower levels to satisfy my curiosity."

"I'm second-class," I offered.

She nodded, as though she had already surmised as much on her own. With a disdainful sniff, she slung her brightly-patterned shawl over her right shoulder.

"I'm going back to my suite, Esther. I'm sure we'll see a lot of each other in the coming days."

I nodded, though I wasn't so sure and not half as enthusiastic as this outspoken American.

"Hang around with me, child," she said, leaning over as though she were imparting a message of untold wisdom. "Your English will improve dramatically, and even your posture will be transformed."

This time, I didn't even bother responding, knowing that Madame Bonair did not expect a reply. Her magnanimous offer was a gift that I ought to treasure and appreciate.

"Goodbye, dearie!" she called from the exit. "Nice meeting you!"

She finally left, in a swirl of shawls, jewelry and heavily scented perfume. Her departure gave me back the solitude I had so enjoyed, but its magic was gone...trampled under the heels of an all-knowing matron who had impinged on my privacy.

It was high time I return to our room, where *Mamme* had remained with the task of unpacking. I wondered what was taking so long, considering that we had a total of only four suitcases between us and two overstuffed handbags.

Maybe she had fallen asleep on one of the comfortable beds. After all, these past few days had been a marathon of Pesach cooking, serving, clearing away, packing and finally, traveling. It couldn't have been easy to set out on a journey a mere few hours after Pesach had bid us a fond farewell.

I'll make it up to you, Mamme. You'll be surprised at how enjoyable this trip will turn out to be.

I glanced around wistfully at the deserted promenade. A slight scent of perfume still clung to its environs, and I sighed. Madame Bonair had definitely left her glamorous stamp on the first day of my journey.

Tatte suddenly seemed very far away.

Chapter Fifteen

*I*t was awful.

Mamme lay listlessly in bed day after day, attempting to paste a smile on her face every time I entered the room. I pretended to revel in her cheerful mien, though her greenish complexion and vanished appetite were about as antithetical to happiness as one could get.

Seasickness had struck with a vengeance. When the ocean rolled and roiled, *Mamme* heaved along with it. And when the waters calmed down, *Mamme* fell back against her pillow and concentrated on breathing deeply before the next attack overwhelmed her.

Those were grueling days. I watched *Mamme* suffering, and I felt guilty at every speck of enjoyment I eked out of our Titanic experience. How could I explore the fascinating gymnasium open to the first class when *Mamme* was retching violently yet again? How could I enjoy peeking in at *Café Parisian* whilst the first-class passengers dined, when *Mamme* couldn't stomach the mere mention of food?

Melinda Bonair, however, thought otherwise.

"Your Mom is seasick and there's nothing you can do about it, Esther," she told me Sunday morning. "More than half the journey is gone and all you've done is mope around."

I shrugged.

"Don't do that, dearie," Melinda continued. "Come with me to the upper deck. I wouldn't mind some company to sweeten my daily sunbathing session."

Since our chance encounter on Wednesday afternoon, Melinda had been hounding me. She invited me to her suite and gave me guided tours of the first-class department.

Once, while we were headed to the tennis court to ascertain whether Bill Bonair was still playing there, we nearly collided with a young couple strolling languidly along the deck.

"I – I'm so, so sorry," Melinda said. "I didn't notice you coming. Please forgive me. I apologize."

I was astonished at her sudden transformation, from proud-as-a-peacock benefactor to subservient bystander. Why, the young woman didn't seem any different than Melinda herself. She also carried herself with that affected poise and haughty air that characterized most of the first-class travelers. And her shawls weren't half as ostentatious as those of my self-proclaimed friend.

"Apologize, Esther!" Melinda whispered forcefully.

What's the big deal? We didn't even collide with them!

"I'm sorry, sir," I blurted.

The young man waved a be-ringed hand in our direction, dismissing our apologies as well as our bothersome presence. His wife offered a small smile to soften his abruptness, and they quickly left us behind in a cloud of pompous glory.

"Esther!" Melinda breathed, as soon as the couple rounded the bend. "Do you know who that was?"

"No."

"Colonel John Jacob Astor IV and his wife, Madeleine!"

"That's nice."

"Nice?!" Melinda bellowed. "Is that all it is – just nice?! The Colonel is a multi-millionaire; one of America's social elite!"

I processed that piece of information. Apparently, the bejeweled young man was extremely rich.

"Er...Melinda, I get the impression that you aren't that poor yourself."

Melinda's bark of laughter was so unexpected as to nearly throw me off-balance. She clutched her purse while waves of rollicking mirth incapacitated her for the better part of five minutes.

"No, no, Esther," she finally managed to say. "There's rich and there's rich. Oh, your innocence is just so delicious and refreshing!"

She must have noticed my complete bewilderment, for she immediately launched into a detailed explanation.

"The Astors are not just rich, Esther. They're millionaires. You have no idea how much power they hold and how they're looked up to. I mean, compared to them, Bill and I are just little ants scrabbling at the base of a towering mountain."

I nodded compliantly, although the concept didn't make much sense to me. Since when did money give one the status of a hero? Why would a few million dollars grant one the status of an icon for the entire American society?

"And speaking about millionaires," Melinda continued, "take a look at who just emerged from the kennels where our pets are being held. That's Ida Straus."

I groaned. Another name; another dazzling fortune.

"Her name should evoke your interest, Esther. You know, her husband Isidor is the owner of Macy's department store."

"Macy's?"

Melinda's exasperation was comical to observe.

"You mean, there is no Macy's back where you come from? What sort of city can get by without one?!"

My poor little Plawo. With one derogatory comment, Melinda Bonair had relegated it to the backwater territory where primitivism reigned supreme. What did she know of the beautiful sunsets and wildlife we were privileged to enjoy? She would never comprehend the closeness and warmth that enveloped our community and the security upon which we thrived.

It was nothing like this cutthroat existence that I was viewing first-hand aboard the Titanic. Wherever we went, I noticed people counting each other's maids and assessing their competitors' wardrobes. I could almost see the numbers adding up in their minds as they noted with satisfaction that their presentation definitely stood head and shoulders above the rest.

It was sickening.

Melinda vehemently disagreed.

"With a voice like yours, Esther, you could also ride the waves of upper society. Believe me, your voice can take you places."

Why does she insist on mentioning that one-time singing fiasco? I had no intention of providing a free performance, yet Madame Bonair seems intent on an encore.

"Don't look at me with those puppy eyes, Esther. You would be silly to throw away such unbelievable talent. And the speed with which you're picking up English is... astounding. I've never seen anything like it."

"I – I have to go downstairs," I stammered. "*Mamme* is probably fretting about my lengthy absence."

Melinda nodded graciously.

"Send your Mom my best regards and tell her how much I'm enjoying her daughter's company," she said. "Oh, there's Bill! Run along, dear. I'll see you after dinner."

Mamme was still lying supine in bed when I returned, after my lengthy morning hiatus. Her eyes lit up when I entered the room, evoking the familiar surge of guilt that was my constant companion.

"Esther'ke! Where were you?"

No secrets, Esther. Remember where secrets have led you in the past. You don't want to go that route again.

"I was spending time with Madame Bonair, *Mamme*," I answered carefully. "She showed me some more rooms that I hadn't seen before. Just imagine – the Titanic has a dark room especially for photographers so that they can develop their pictures while on board!"

Mamme looked duly impressed.

"Ah, that nice Jewish woman who's been taking care of you while I was ill...What did you say her name is?"

"Madame Melinda Bonair."

"Right. Bonair. Interesting name for a Jewish family, but in America they surely do things differently than back in Europe," *Mamme* commented. "I'm glad that you found such good, Jewish company...considering that I'm certainly out of commission."

"Oh, *Mamme*! I would exchange her company for yours any day! I wish you would get over this seasickness already so that we can begin enjoying our trip."

I felt my cheeks warming uncomfortably as *Mamme* continued extolling the unknown woman's virtues. To her, the word 'Jewish' connoted 'frum'. She was probably envisioning a refined woman, wearing a modest head-covering and simple clothing. Bill Bonair had probably been cast as a *Talmud Chochom*, or at least an honest Shomer Shabbos laborer.

What would she say when she laid eyes upon the flamboyant couple? Would the tennis-playing Bill and his frivolous wife pass muster? They were certainly Jewish; Melinda had assured me as much. But that was as far as their religious convictions went. It stalled at the border of identification, with the title mostly concealed in deference to America's hedonistic existence.

"Maybe you want to go on a short walk, *Mamme*?"

"No, not now, *mein kind*," *Mamme* regretfully declined. "I hope I'll feel better by tomorrow, and then you'll be able to show me around a little."

"But tomorrow's already Monday! Captain Smith says that we're more than halfway through the journey," I contended.

"I know, Esther. I know. What can I do?"

I immediately regretted my outburst. *Mamme* was weak and in pain. I couldn't expect her to go gallivanting about the Titanic promenades, when all she really wanted was a place to rest her aching head.

"Here, *Mamme*. I'll serve you some *kichen* and preserves for breakfast. Consider it the most upgraded maid service aboard the Titanic."

Mamme smiled weakly but turned her head away.

"Not now, Esther'ke. I think I'll go to sleep for a little bit, until the queasiness eases up."

I stood at the porthole, holding my measly offering in disappointment. *Mamme* didn't eat. *Mamme* didn't drink. And it was all my fault. If I hadn't gotten swept up by the Zionist winds, we would all be reveling in the spring buds that were surely appearing right out our kitchen window.

Instead, *Mamme* was lying weakly in bed and I was spending my time with a questionable character who seemed intent on getting me to sing in public. It was a pathetic situation.

"I'll go see how Ruth Becker is faring," I ventured. "Remember, *Mamme*? She's that twelve-year-old girl from India who is always babysitting her younger brother, Richard."

No response.

"That toddler is so adorable! He smiles at me with childish innocence, and he doesn't seem to care where I come from and what accent I am branded with."

Still no response.

"I...I want to see how she is, *Mamme*. And while I'm at it, maybe I'll check up on the Sage family. They're traveling third-class, *Mamme*. The entire family! Can you imagine – traveling with nine children to a new land?!"

I turned around to survey *Mamme*'s reaction. My prattling usually disturbed her, but this time...

Mamme was fast asleep. Her even breathing told me that this would be a lengthy nap. Oh, well. I placed the *kichen* on a small table near her bed and hurried out of the room in search of Ruth Becker.

On my way to the enclosed promenade, I peeked into the alluring library room. The room was deserted, save for an individual who seemed to have set up residence there. Ruth had told me that his name was Lawrence Beesley, and her hand gestures signified that he was a schoolteacher by profession. He was peering intently at a large textbook, with at least a dozen other books scattered about in haphazard abandon.

What a waste of a luxury trip, Mr. Beesley, I thought. *You could read all you want at home!*

He wasn't asking my opinion and I wouldn't offer it unsolicited. Melinda, on the other hand, would surely have put him in place already.

"Esther!"

The delighted cry warmed my heart. At least there was someone on board who was truly interested in my company. Ruth waved to me from the entrance to the promenade, urging me to join her.

"Hello, Richard," I crooned, leaning over the White Star Line carriage. "Are you having fun with your big sister?"

He gurgled happily, and I instinctively leaned over to smooth his unruly dark curls.

Zalmen would be mightily surprised at my sudden interest in little ones. At home, he could barely get me to hold my own nieces and nephews.

We sat in companionable silence, watching as day morphed toward dusk and then slowly meandered into the dark alleyways of night. The language barrier made communication stilted and unsatisfying, but there was something very comfortable about sitting together and observing nature's wondrous transformation.

"Ma-ma!" Richard chanted. "Ma-ma! Ma-ma!"

A string of gibberish emanated from Ruth's mouth and I wondered lazily whether I could get her to teach me the language. Wouldn't it be nice to come home with a solid English foundation as well as a smattering of whatever they spoke in far-off India? Anna would be flabbergasted!

"Go Mama," she told me carefully.

"You go Mama," I confirmed. "Good night! And good night to you, little one! Sleep well!"

Richard smiled, and the duo departed. I heard him chanting his ubiquitous "Ma-ma" as he was being wheeled through the long corridor. His voice faded away, leaving me alone with my thoughts.

It must be about 8:00 already. I should really see how Mamme is faring. But this is the time when the band plays! Melinda invited me to keep her company after dinner...and I wouldn't want to miss the nightly performance.

I walked towards the stairwell, firmly trampling my conscience underfoot.

I'll check up on Mamme as soon as the band departs, I promised myself.

"A ride up in the elevator, Ma'am?"

That voice sounded remotely familiar.

"This way, ma'am!"

Mr. George Barlow! I hadn't seen him the since the day of departure, and here he was, as pompous and ceremonious as ever! He was standing at the door of the elevator, playing self-importantly with some sort of contraption that probably controlled its movements.

"Uh...no. That's alright. I take the stairs," I mumbled.

The twinkle in Mr. Barlow's eyes assured me that he hadn't forgotten my terror during that first elevator ride.

"As you wish, ma'am."

He had the grace to turn away and hide his smile until I passed. When I turned to look back, however, his cheerful grin couldn't be more pronounced.

Maybe by journey's end, I'll venture another ride, I thought doubtfully. *Maybe.*

When I stepped into the first-class dining area, I was surprised to note that the band's performance was already well underway. It must have been much later than I had assumed.

All eight band members were aligned on a small stage, and they wielded their instruments with confidence. Wallace Hartley, the conductor, was at his best. I could tell from the absolute silence that reigned in the dining room that this performance far surpassed the others.

Most of the musicians seemed vaguely familiar, since they were all traveling second-class. In my comings and goings, I had spotted many of them sitting with their instruments, fine-tuning them or simply playing for sport.

The ambience was magnetic. Clinking cutlery and murmured exclamations of pleasure served as a perfect backdrop to the classical music wafting throughout the cavernous room. I inched closer to the bandstand, trying to remain inconspicuous. Had someone asked me to explain my fascination with the goings-on, I would have been hard-pressed to offer a suitable reply. There was something about this heavenly music that pulled at my heartstrings and rendered me incapable of logical reasoning.

Back home, I had always been captivated by music. While my friends tapped their feet impatiently during their fathers' *zemiros* renditions, I closed my eyes and willed it to continue forever. Zalmen knew that he could procure my cooperation by offering to teach me a new tune or piece of harmony.

This, however, was different. The band's polished playing was in a league all its own, and it left Plawo's *koppela* biting the dust. I was undeniably smitten by its presentation.

"Esther!"

The sharp whisper startled me from my dreamy state, and the arm around my shoulders brought me back to the here and now.

"Esther, I was wondering where you are," Melinda whispered.

I smiled. It was nice to be noticed, even by someone as bothersome as Melinda.

"Isn't the performance outstanding?"

A new piece was being introduced. I put my finger to my lips, hoping she wouldn't be insulted. I needn't have worried. Madame Bonair didn't take offense at my gesture. She simply took no notice of it.

"I asked Wallace Hartley if someone could sing along as a soloist," she continued. "He refused, stating that it wasn't in his contract. But he's being a fool, Esther, isn't he? If you would get up there and sing just one song, the audience would be ecstatic! You would have it made, my dear!"

"M-me?!"

"Well, of course! You didn't think I would be standing up there and offering my mediocre voice to the public! It's your talent that I'm after!"

The band was forgotten momentarily, as I sought to put this woman in her place.

"Melinda, there's no way I would have agreed to that!"

"And why ever not, dearie? Don't you know that one performance would give you a ticket to the greatest opera houses in existence?!"

I shook my head forcefully. How could I get her to understand?

"Because...because there are men in the audience."

That should do it. Even someone as determined as Melinda Bonair can't refute my obvious claim.

"And therefore?"

"Wh-what do you mean? I can't sing in front of men."

Melinda looked at me strangely.

"I don't understand you, Esther," she said. "I caught you singing once, and I'll catch you doing it again. If you can sing for the water and the walls, why can't you sing for men?"

This was too much. Melinda was deliberately being obtuse to cow me into submission, but for once I was determined to stand my ground.

"It's *halacha*, Melinda. I mean, Jewish law."

"You mean, Jewish law doesn't let you sing?"

"It lets me sing," I corrected her. "But not within the earshot of men."

Melinda finally caught on.

"You don't say," she said. "I've never heard of such a strange stipulation, Esther."

"You are Jewish, aren't you?"

"Yes. But it never stopped *me* from singing in public."

I shrugged. This was not up for discussion and the sooner Melinda accepted that, the better off we'd be.

"So Jewish law would rather you throw your talent into the garbage bin," she commented sarcastically.

"Singing is my personal pleasure," I said. "It has nothing to do with anyone else."

Melinda bit her lips and stared straight ahead. I had never seen the self-assured woman battling with her temper, but I was pretty sure that these were telltale signs. Her shawl was coming undone, yet she made no move to fling it artfully over her shoulders. Madame Bonair was definitely unnerved.

"Well," she said after a long pause. "There's no use arguing about it. Hartley didn't agree to my proposal."

Thank goodness.

"Let's forget our little spat, Esther," she continued. "It was silly of me to force you into a corner, and even sillier of you to resist."

Her appraisal was way off the mark, but I was glad to put this uncomfortable conversation behind us. With the band winding up its lengthy performance, I wanted to grab the last few moments of bliss before returning to our suite for the night.

"Thank you for listening, ladies and gentlemen," Wallace Hartley proclaimed.

His words were greeted by an enthusiastic round of applause.

"It would have been ever more beautiful with your singing," Melinda couldn't resist whispering.

I ignored her remark, concentrating instead on the musicians as they lovingly packed away their gleaming instruments. It was interesting that I had never expressed an interest in learning to play a musical instrument until I saw these maestros in action.

"Come, Esther," Melinda said. "I want to go up to the deck for a few minutes and Bill is deep in conversation with Major Archibald Butt. You do know who that is, don't you?"

I shook my head tiredly. No, I didn't know and I truly had no interest in finding out.

"He's the president's military aide. President Taft, right?"

Right. Whatever you say, Madame Bonair.

"Bill finds him a fascinating conversationalist and he won't be up anytime soon. Be a dear and keep me company."

So I was a dear and I trudged after Melinda as she ascended the stairs to the upper deck. The grittiness beneath my eyelids told me that it was getting late, but the indefatigable Melinda still had stores of energy to expend.

"You look tired, my girl," she said solicitously. "Let's see. It's 11:30 p.m. right now. I'll make sure that you turn in by midnight. Agreed?"

Midnight sounded just about right. I was sure that the cool night air would awaken me from my sudden lethargy, giving me a second wind until Melinda kindly dismissed me for the evening.

Why do I feel bound to this strange woman? She's been generous with her time and explanations...but does that obligate me to run after her like a marionette on a string?

We stood on deck, shivering in the surprisingly frigid temperatures. The sea was absolutely calm, appearing like an unmarred sheet of glass stretching to eternity.

"O-o-o-h, it's cold," Melinda chattered. "Who would believe that mid-April temperatures could fall so -"

A bell clanged sharply three times, interrupting her mid-sentence. I looked up to the watchtower, from where the sounds emanated.

"It's just one of the lookout's signals," Melinda said. "They're constantly signaling each other for one reason or another. Boredom, if you ask me."

My curiosity had been awakened by the bell's call, and I wondered how the lookout post was set up. Were people stationed there at all times? Did they really keep watch for pirates, as Zalmen had once tried to convince me?

"You think Captain Smith will let me see the inside of that room?"

Melinda laughed.

"Don't set your heart on it, dear. Why would you want to waste your time on a simple lookout tower, anyway? You still haven't seen the Turkish baths and the saltwater pools."

I strained my eyes to see through the darkness, but all I could make out were the frenzied gestures of two men. They seemed agitated about something, in their perch way up high.

A sudden jolt drew my attention to the right.

"What was that?!"

Melinda hadn't felt anything. She was staring out at the calm expanse, clutching her shawl in search of warmth.

A hulking shadow appeared out of nowhere at the right side of the deck, and a scream of terror shot up my throat. A second gentle jolt made it die on my lips. This time, I noticed, Melinda had also felt the movement.

"You felt that bump?"

I nodded.

"We must both be tired," she said lightly. "These little jolts never bother me during the day."

A third, more insistent, nudge pushed me toward the railing and I ventured a glance at my middle-aged bene-factor. She was afraid.

Chapter Sixteen

*E*dith!" Melinda called out upon spotting her friend, Edith Louise Russel. "What's going on?"

"I don't know," she confessed. "I felt these strange jolts as I was entering my room...Officer! What's going on here? Why are there ice particles falling all over the deck?"

I turned to see the little ice shavings she was referring too. They looked like glistening diamonds littering the floor, and I resisted the urge to pick them up.

"Oh, nothing, Madam," he hurried to assure her. "Nothing at all. Just a mere nothing. We hit an iceberg, that's all."

Edith smiled in relief.

"You heard what that nice officer said? It's nothing. We just hit an iceberg."

Edith bent down and picked up some of the ice particles scattered at her feet. With a whimsical smile, she started throwing them overboard.

"Isn't this exciting, Melinda? Lighten up! The officer said there's nothing to worry about."

Melinda nodded gravely, and Edith sighed in resignation.

"Do as you wish. I'm turning in for the night."

She gracefully went down the stairs, her exaggerated hairdo bobbing with each step.

"Edith is right," Melinda conceded. "Time to call it a night."

I couldn't agree more. The day had been crowded with new sights and sounds, and I craved the stability of *Mamme*'s presence. Sleep would do wonders to the wild workings of my mind and imagination.

"Hard-a-starboard!"

The hoarse command sounded panicky, and it sent the ship swerving suddenly to the left. I held onto Melinda's arm in fright, but she was as unsteady as a twig whipped by the wind.

"Where is Hutchinson? Where is he, that carpenter?" Captain Smith bellowed, appearing on deck without his usual pomp and splendor. "Thomas Andrews! Get down here and assess the damage!"

Officers scurried to and fro, getting in each others' way and accomplishing nothing in the sudden fray. I wondered why the captain had become so unhinged by the events. After all, hadn't the officer said it was nothing? The jolts probably signified a few scrapes on the ship's gleaming exterior. Was that a reason to cause such a hullaballoo?

"Uncover the lifeboats!" the captain ordered.

I was afraid to look at Melinda. I didn't want to see my terror reflected in her eyes, for that would make the threatened tragedy all too real. Maybe the captain was just being cautious. Maybe he wanted the lifeboats uncovered because...because...

"Swing 'em out!"

Captain Smith's voice held a note of hysteria. The officers didn't dare tarry any longer. They raced up to the boat deck to reach the sixteen lifeboats anchored in the davits. There were another four canvas-sided collapsibles stowed on the roof of the officers' quarters that I had noticed upon passing earlier that day. Would the officers remember to swing those out as well?

"That's Charles Lightoller," Melinda whispered. "He's the Second Officer."

"Hadn't we better get the women and children into the boats, sir?" Charles asked.

Captain Smith nodded, unable to utter a single word. I saw the Second Officer hesitating for a fraction of a second, obviously shocked by the severity of the situation. He then swung into action, racing across the deck as though it were burning under his feet.

I didn't feel anything. The Titanic seemed steady enough, and I wondered whether all this commotion was just a precaution. Would we all be thrust into the lifeboats' flimsy confines for naught?

At that moment, I heard some officers murmuring worriedly about several third-class cabins that had begun flooding.

Oh no! Not the Goodwins! Hashem, watch over that large family! They want to build a new life for themselves somewhere in Florida...Don't let them perish here, in the middle of nowhere!

They were flustered, those crisply-uniformed officers. Captain Smith gave the order to load the lifeboats, and within moments total chaos ensued.

Hurried footsteps pounded up towards the boat deck, and I watched Melinda's made-up face crumbling in the face of distress.

"Oh, what do we do? What do we do? Bill! Where are you? Bill!!"

Her cries, so uncharacteristic and so helpless, pierced my heart. Without considering the propriety of my actions, I reached out to take her trembling hands in my own.

"Melinda, stay calm. Everything will be alright, with Hashem's help."

She stared at me, her large blue eyes portraying a deep emptiness, as though she saw things that I couldn't fathom.

"No, no," she cried, shaking her head. "Bill!"

An officer stopped near us, carrying a child in his arms.

"Don't stand here, ladies! Go up! Get into a lifeboat before we all drown!"

"Bill!" Melinda screamed hysterically.

"Forget Bill," the officer urged. "He'll follow you in another lifeboat. Women and children first."

We followed the young officer up the stairs and towards a small lifeboat.

"Get inside!" he ordered frantically.

Melinda followed directions, like a docile youngster listening to her teacher. Her eyes darted around, from one face to the next, and I knew that she was searching for her husband.

"Come, Esther," she said.

I put one foot over the side of Lifeboat #8, when I was struck by sudden horror.

Mamme! Mamme was downstairs, in our suite! She was probably sleeping, or retching violently due to the sudden movements.

Mamme!

"Esther, quick! The lifeboat is nearly full to capacity!"

Melinda's desperate scream was drowned out by the hordes of crying children and panicked women. I felt suffocated by the crowds and wanted to get away...just away. I had to find *Mamme.*

I turned around, pushing at the human wall that had closed in around me. I had to go downstairs, to the second-class cabins. *Mamme* was there.

Melinda caught the hem of my dress and forcefully pulled.

"Leave me alone!" I screamed. "I must get *Mamme!*"

"Get inside," Melinda shouted with equal desperation. "Your *Mamme* will come on her own. Don't-"

"She can't! *Mamme* is ill and weak! She – she's waiting for me!"

Melinda pulled harder, but I was determined. Our dispute did not go unnoticed, and within moments a sour-faced officer appeared at my side.

"Don't be silly, young woman," he ordered. "Get into the boat. This is your only hope for survival!"

"But my mother!" I gasped. "She's downsta-

"Forget your mother!" he said coldly. "You'll never make it down. The water level is rising as we speak."

I listened to his words in horror and Melinda made use of my momentary weakness. She pulled me inside the lifeboat mere seconds before it was lowered into the freezing, deceptively calm waters.

"*Mamme!*" I screamed. "*Mamme*, I'm coming! I'm coming to save you!"

I sobbed violently, my shoulders heaving to the tune of my inner tempest.

"She is certainly on another boat," Melinda reassured me. "The officers evacuated the rooms, Esther. You hear me? Your *Mamme* is safe and sound. You'll meet up with her in the morning."

Melinda put her arms around me, forcing me to subside. The wracking sobs refused to relinquish their hold on my shivering frame, as I pictured *Mamme* lying in bed and wondering what the shouts were all about.

She's probably waiting for me to come and explain, I berated myself. *Mamme is too weak to venture out on her own. And...and if someone comes to rescue her, she won't even understand!*

I gasped as the enormity of the situation hit me.

Mamme doesn't know a word of English! How will the officers be able to evacuate her?!

They'll lift her up and put her in a lifeboat, I assured myself. *They won't leave her there. They'll make sure of that.*

The night was dark. Stars twinkled down at us but on this day, the 27th day of Nissan, there was no moon to be found. Not even a sliver could be spotted, as though it were hiding its face from our immense tragedy.

"Melinda," I stammered.

"Yes, Esther?"

I marveled at her composure. She had left the Titanic without knowing the whereabouts of her husband, yet her poise remained unaffected.

"Melinda, you think *Mamme* would follow the officers even if she doesn't understand a word they're saying?"

Madame Bonair looked at me with compassion,

"Certainly, my dear. They wouldn't leave her there to die."

To die. To die. They wouldn't leave Mamme to die. Hashem! You see my Mamme! Take her out of the room and put her on a lifeboat! Only You can save her.

I'll never visit those Zionists again. I promise!

"I promise!" I cried out.

My scream was lost amidst the hysterical crying on board. Women and children huddled in their seats, bemoaning the family members they had left behind. The lifeboat was large, but only half-filled with passengers. Along its sides, several men tried to steer us to safety but they were obviously unschooled in the art of rowing. Their movements were rough and uncoordinated, jerking us to and fro like pendulums.

Mamme could have been here. If only I had been tending to her instead of standing at Melinda's beck and call.

I saw Ruth Becker sitting next to her mother, and I envied her. Why did she get to escape together with her mother, when *Mamme* was not here at my side? Little Richard was crying inconsolably, and I tried to soothe him by stretching my lips in the semblance of a smile.

He wasn't impressed.

"Ruth!" I cried. "Ruth, *Mamme* no."

I wanted some commiseration, maybe another assurance that everything would be alright. But Ruth looked straight ahead, grasping her brother's hands as though that alone could keep her safe. Her glassy-eyed stare frightened me, and I averted my eyes.

"Look," someone called out. "It's going under!"

The Titanic was tilted at a sickening angle, with barely ten feet of the deck showing above surface. From the distance, we spotted a number of dogs racing frenziedly across the deck. Someone had obviously unlocked the kennel to allow them at least a miniscule chance at survival.

It was 2:18 a.m. when the lights on board the Titanic went out. The electricity had gone, as had all hope for the remaining people on board. I watched in horror as the boat split down the middle, with one section gracelessly falling into the murky depths.

The stern rose to an unbelievable height, and I was able to see some people holding on for dear life. With a heart-wrenching plunge, it splashed into the water and disappeared from view. The Titanic was no more.

Chapter Seventeen

*A*ll I remembered from those long hours drifting in the merciless ocean waters was the silky feel of Melinda's evening dress. I rested my aching head on her broad shoulders, not caring an iota whether she would view this as a lack of classiness.

Gradually, the wails and screams subsided and a restless silence reigned supreme. Eyes that had seen life pulled out from beneath their privileged feet now stared out at the dark vastness, searching vainly for surviving family members. I, too, kept my eyes trained on the bobbing heads and waving arms that gradually dwindled in number as the night progressed. Was *Mamme* treading water, clinging onto a plank of wood like so many others? Had she made it into one of the lifeboats or...or was she saved some other way?

Three agonizing hours crawled past, disappearing beneath the ocean's glassy surface. I sat motionless, hugging my knees close to my chest in an attempt to garner any bit of warmth my body could offer.

Dawn blushed lightly at the horizon, and we all watched in silent awe as that blush deepened and assumed a multi-hued appearance. A new day was being rolled over yesterday's catastrophic events. A new page was being turned in our lives; a page that might contain fewer characters than the previous one had listed.

Mamme! Do you see it? Do you see the sun rising, ever so slowly, amidst a retinue of pastel-colored bridesmaids? Do you see the hope and promise that I'm trying to discern?

"Good morning, Esther," Melinda whispered. "Good morning to all the hardy Titanic survivors."

Her voice tolled gravely, so unlike the affected tones she usually preferred. Apparently, her flamboyance and youthfulness had found temporary lodgings in the newly-buried Titanic.

While I contemplated the drawn faces turned towards the rising sun, a large hulking ship loomed up before us with the name *Carpathia* emblazoned across its hull.

"There's another one!" a sailor called out from his perch at the lookout.

The ship's motors were stilled and curious faces peeked over the edge at our miserable group. Within moments, we were being hauled on board by able-bodied seamen who shinnied up and down rope ladders with amazing alacrity.

"That's twenty-eight, sir," an officer said. "Twenty-eight passengers on Lifeboat #8. Pity they didn't fill 'er up to capacity. This boat could have held at least double that amount!"

"Quit the philosophizing, mate," the captain retorted. "Jot down the figures and let's move on. We're still missing some of the boats."

"Aye, sir."

We lay scattered on the deck like so many dandelions pulled out by their roots. Our water-soaked clothing clung to our shivering bodies much the same way horrific memories clung tenaciously to our feverish minds.

"Bill," Melinda whispered, rubbing her eyes tiredly. "Must find Bill."

She stood up unsteadily and starting walking towards the other side of the deck. I, too, gathered my strength and paced to and fro amidst the Titanic survivors.

"*Mamme*. It's me, your Esther'ke. Please, *Mamme*. You must be here. *Mamme*?!"

My cries went unanswered. I scrutinized every face, but the blank eyes gazing back at me were not the warm, loving eyes I desperately needed to see. They were haunted eyes; eyes that had seen images that could never be forgotten.

"*Mamme*! Where are you?!"

I cried. I pleaded desperately with mute bystanders who saw my pain but could do nothing to ease it. Choking on my words, I repeated them like a mantra, hoping that maybe this time they would produce the longed-for results.

"Another boat, men!"

The triumphant call sent me scurrying to the dangling rope ladder. Maybe this boat would be the one carrying my beloved *Mamme*. Maybe this discovery would be the answer to my prayers.

One after another, the survivors were pulled up. Two of them were carrying their precious pets in their arms, cuddling the dogs as though they were children.

How could you?! How could you take those dogs when Mamme desperately needed that space?!

I was being unreasonable, and I had enough presence of my mind to understand that. But there was nothing I could do about it. *Mamme* wasn't here yet, but these dogs were. It made no sense.

From afar, I saw Melinda slumped in a dark corner. Her once-proud shoulders were rounded, and her bejeweled fingers were clasped tightly on her lap. Bill was nowhere to be seen.

"Ma-ma!" Richard Becker suddenly squealed from his

comfortable perch in Ruth's arms. "Ma-ma! Ma-ma!"

Oh, how I wanted to cry along with him. How I wished I too could see my mother and call to her with the trust and guilelessness this toddler possessed. But my *Mamme* wasn't here. She wouldn't hear me, no matter how long and how loud I called out to her.

"What time is it, mate?" the captain called out to a passing officer.

"08:50, sir."

"Time to get a move on," said the captain. "We've done all we can here."

"No!" I cried, balling my fists in helpless agony. "You can't do that! Don't leave my *Mamme* here! *Mamme*! She must be found!"

The captain didn't hear my frenzied screams, but Melinda did. She stood near me in a protective stance, bravely biting her lips to stem her own tears.

"Shh...Esther, they've done all they can. I'm sure there are other boats in the area that will continue the rescue work."

I vehemently shook my head.

"I left my *Mamme* once, back on the boat," I sobbed. "I'm not making that mistake again. No!"

Melinda held my hands firmly and looked directly into my eyes.

"Esther, the *Carpathia* is traveling to New York City. That was the Titanic's original destination, remember?"

I nodded, soothed by her take-charge attitude.

"Your *Mamme* knows that we're going in that direction. When she reaches dry land, she'll find some way to contact you."

"You...you really think so?" I asked tremulously. *If only...if only that would be true.*

"I know so, my dear. Have you ever known me as a liar?"

No. But can I trust you with...my Mamme?

Melinda put her thumb under my chin and lifted my face so that I was looking directly into her red-rimmed eyes.

"I'm worried about Bill," she admitted, "but I know that we'll be reunited. Staying here and making a scene won't do him any good. I'd rather spend the time recouping my strength so that I can pick up the pieces of my life and put this nightmare behind me. Behind us."

"B...but *Tatte* won't know what happened," I rambled. "He's waiting to hear from us. How...how will I let him know?"

"Don't you worry, darling. The world will know about this catastrophe. Who can ignore the sinking of the unsinkable? Who can overlook the fall of the mighty?"

It was true. The luxurious Titanic, touted as queen of the seas and as utterly invincible, had sunk to the bottomless depths of the Atlantic Ocean. All of its high-flying passengers had been reduced to mere shells of their formerly glamorous selves.

Hashem was sending us a message...but what was I supposed to take from this? I truly regretted the foolhardy adventures I had set out upon back in Plawo. The experience had matured me, to some extent, wiping off the last carefree shades of childhood.

Just give me a chance to prove it! Hashem, I promise that I'll make You proud. If only Mamme would be found already.

"Sir!" a red-haired crew member called out.

"Sir! Captain Rostron!"

The captain turned towards the excitable young seaman, annoyance stamping his features.

"We haven't got 'em all! They say there were sixteen lifeboats and four collapsibles. We - "

"Do you think I don't know that, Henry?" Captain

Rostron retorted. "We cannot remain here indefinitely. We've got our survivors to worry about. Others have been sent to finish up the rescue work."

"But ain't it a pity, Sir?" the redhead persisted. "We're here already. We could just scout around a bit..."

"Scout around?!" bellowed the captain. "Do you call our concerted rescue efforts just 'scouting around'?!"

Henry's recalcitrant expression was priceless. He bobbed his head mechanically, retreating from the scene with the grace of an overstuffed, waddling duck.

I was ecstatic. Here was the proof I had needed to support my most fervent hopes.

"Melinda!" I urged, shaking her awake.

"Mmmm?"

"Melinda, you must wake up! I have important news to share with you!"

"Hmmm..."

She looked at me through half-closed lids, and I wasted no time in sharing my excitement.

"Some of the lifeboats haven't been found yet," I said. "*Mamme* must be on one of those still at sea!"

Melinda nodded, still half comatose.

"And Bill is probably there, too," I added, as a charitable afterthought.

She drifted off to sleep despite my announcement, but the drawn look on her face had been replaced by something akin to serenity. Hope was a potent force that worked wonders, its intangibility notwithstanding.

While Melinda slept, I took myself on a tour of the *Carpathia*. Wherever I went, tragedy dug its gruesome fangs into my heart. There was so much pain; such palpable fear and sorrow. How could one ship contain all the tears, shed and unshed, that were but a sign of what was yet to come?

The young woman who had huddled silently in the far

corner of our lifeboat was still cowering in that self-same position. Her moaning reached epic proportions, then died down to a keening whimper that eerily reverberated in my mind.

"My dear Ida!" she cried, time and again. "Master Straus!"

Something about the names triggered my memory and I approached her cautiously.

"Why did you go?" she whimpered. "Why? Oh, why couldn't I have gone in your place?"

"Er...Excuse me, ma'am," I said in my careful English. "Who...who are you?"

Green eyes framed by long, black lashes looked at me vacantly. This woman must have lost her entire family, I thought with compassion.

"What's your name?" I tried again.

"Ellen," she said. "Ellen Bird."

Hadn't she been mourning the disappearance of Master Straus? What could possibly be their connection?

"I am Ida's maid," she continued woodenly. "That is, I was her maid until...until now."

"Don't say that," I soothed, drawing upon my freshly-born hope to strengthen her, as well. "Some of the lifeboats haven't been recovered yet. Your master and mistress may be coasting along the ocean in one of those."

Ellen shook her head vehemently. She didn't want my hopes or promises.

"They're not," she insisted.

"I heard the captain saying that some lifeboats are - "

"But Ida and Isidor Straus are not on any of the missing lifeboats," she interrupted. "They're here, on the *Carpathia*."

This was getting mighty strange. Why would Ellen mourn her mistress if she had already been rescued?! Was she mourning their lost belongings?

"So…what exactly are you crying about?" I asked, with a touch of impatience.

How dare she mourn something insignificant while my *Mamme* still hadn't been found! It was downright… inconsiderate!

"They're on the boat," Ellen said, "in body-bags."

"In…in what?"

"Body-bags," she cried, a note of hysteria coloring her words. "They're dead!"

Oh. Dead.

The glamorous Madeleine Astor was sitting on a cushion several paces away. She looked compassionately at the distressed young maid, and then turned her innocent eyes in my direction.

"Never mind her," she said softly. "The Straus residence is the only home she has ever known. Without her mistress, she's orphaned. Alone."

Alone. Orphaned. Will those horrible words describe me, as well?

"At least she knows," the wealthy woman sighed. "She can begin dealing with her loss, while the rest of us are waiting in limbo. Waiting and hoping for a signal of life."

"Your husband…" I hesitantly queried.

She shook her head sadly, yet with such ladylike perfection as to make it seem a most graceful movement.

"I don't know. John Jacob is…somewhere. He wouldn't go down without a fight."

The nurse sitting at her right patted her arm comfortingly.

"Now, now," she crooned. "It wouldn't do for the mistress to fret."

Madeleine Astor looked up at me ruefully.

"They don't even let me worry," she whispered. "But you tell me – is there anything else I can do now for my poor husband?"

"Pray," I instinctively replied. "Pray, as I've been pray-ing for my mother."

"Your...mother?" she asked, furrowing her forehead in confusion. "I thought I saw Melinda before. Weren't you sitting together?"

"Yes, we were. But my mother hasn't been found yet."

"Your...your mother," Madeleine repeated. "You mean, Melinda Bonair is not your Mom?"

I forcefully shook my head. The horror of being so closely associated with a woman I had barely learned to tolerate was indescribable.

"Melinda is most definitely not my mother," I clari-fied. "She's just...a...friend."

"Hmm...a family friend," Madeleine said. "I always wondered at the disparity between the two of you. And your accent...I just couldn't place it. Well, thank good-ness she's here to help you through these difficult times."

Yes. Thank goodness. Had she not pulled me into the lifeboat against my will, I would have been together with Mamme now...in life or in death.

"Be strong, little girl," Madeleine said in parting. "I hope your mother will be found. She deserves to raise you as much as you deserve her love and devotion."

I nodded, blinking back the tears that had inexpli-cably gathered in my eyes. Madeleine Astor's words had touched a raw, exposed nerve. *Mamme* deserved to raise me; that much was obvious. But did I deserve her love? Her devotion? After the misery I had inflicted upon her and *Tatte*, was I maybe being dealt anguish in return?

Don't think that way, Esther, I berated myself, echo-ing *Tatte's* favorite lines. *Hashem is good and all He does is good.*

Madeleine looked after me with large, sorrowful eyes and I wondered whether she was thinking about herself or about me. Fate had tied us together in the most improbable of circumstances...for the time being.

On my way back to the cabin we had been assigned, I saw Lawrence Beesley reclining on a burlap sack. The school teacher who had spent his every waking moment in the Titanic's spacious library now seemed strangely bereft. Without mounds of books surrounding him, he looked like a lost child.

The two children sitting near him seemed comfortable in his presence. I recognized them as Michel and Edmond Navratil, two little French boys traveling with their doting father. They were barely out of babyhood, yet they sat like little mannequins in a dress shop, focusing on some indeterminable point in the distance.

The school teacher paid them no heed, but they seemed to take comfort in his silent company. In a world gone upside-down, any form of stability was a blessing, even if that stability was named Lawrence Beesley and he couldn't be bothered with two little children.

I felt a strange sort of kinship with these round-faced little boys. They, too, had been traveling with one parent and they were also forging ahead without knowing what awaited them.

That's where the similarities ended. I was certain that these two innocents weren't weighted down by guilt and regret. They merely waited with utmost confidence for their father to reclaim them so that life could revert to its usual patterns.

It was only many days later that I discovered the truth behind their innocent family façade. Their father, a French tailor, had traveled under the alias Louis M. Hoffman. He had smuggled these two cherubic toddlers out of Europe, hoping to rebuild his shattered life in America.

An unsighted iceberg had overturned his carefully-constructed plans. It had claimed his life and orphaned his sons, who couldn't be identified by the names they had assumed for the journey. Their pictures were circulated internationally until distraught family members recognized them and reclaimed the traumatized children.

But glancing at Michel and Edmond, I knew none of this. I sighed, averting my eyes from the children's innocent trust. They knew with certainty granted only to children that their Papa would return.

And what do you know, Esther Hofert from Plawo?

I *davened* during those interminable days aboard the *Carpathia*. I poured my worries and fears into the words of *tefillah*, and sent them up to my Father who could fulfill my deepest desires. This was the only thing I knew with certainty.

Chapter Eighteen

We finally arrived, on the night of the 18th day of April. Cunard Line Pier was abuzz with activity, as law-enforcement officers tried to keep the crowd of ten thousand onlookers under control. They had been waiting for more than two hours in the drizzling rain for news of their friends or relatives. Now that the ship had arrived, they were impatient to begin their searches and queries.

New York City was everything I had imagined, only *more*. There were more people, more buildings, more noise, more crowding...It made Plawo seem like a little pocket in nature, tucked away amongst the trees for posterity.

"Welcome to New York, Esther," Melinda pompously declared. "Let's get registered and then we can go home."

Home. Tatte and Mamme. Our house standing amidst flowering blooms and blossoming trees. Oh, how long will it take until I see it all again?

"Uh, Melinda?"

She didn't hear me. With the grace and confidence I remembered from a lifetime ago, Melinda was making her way towards an officer sitting somberly at a small desk.

"Melinda?"

"Come, run along," she called over her shoulder. "I don't want to spend even one extra minute in this chicken coop."

"But...but I also want to go home," I said. "Whom should I speak to?"

"Don't be silly, my girl," Melinda forcefully replied. "You're coming home. With me."

"But I - "

"Don't worry about a thing, dear. Do you think Poland is just a hop and a skip away from New York?"

"No, but - "

"A trip back home has to be arranged carefully, Esther. We have to find out when a European ship sets sail, where it docks...And wouldn't it be wiser to wait for your mother to show up so that you can travel together?"

Melinda didn't wait for a reply. She strode over to the desk and pompously offered her name.

"Melinda Bonair. Write that down, sir."

The officer blinked in surprise. Most of the survivors had stood nervously before him, trying to reclaim their lost identities. High-profile American elite had been reduced to parodies of their proud selves, and the officer gave them the courtesy of preferential treatment to restore some of their self-confidence.

"You heard me? My name is Melinda Bonair, and I was rescued by the *Carpathia* in lifeboat #8. Here's Esther," she added as an afterthought.

"Just a moment, Madame. Let me put this down on the proper list. Organization is crucial when it comes to these concerted rescue efforts."

"Yes, yes," Melinda impatiently agreed. "Get on with your work."

"Alright. We have Madame Melinda Bonair - "

"That's Bon-air, sir. Not Bo-nair."

"As you wish. And then we have Estelle."

"Who?" Melinda asked sharply.

"Didn't you say that young woman's name is Estelle?"

Melinda snorted. "Not quite. But you can put her down as Estelle, if you wish. First step to Americanization, my dear."

I looked up at Melinda, who smiled gleefully in return.

"I just renamed you, my dear. How does the name Estelle suit your fancy?"

"Wh-what's wrong with Esther?" I asked, confused.

"Nothing at all. But here in New York, I think Estelle will go over better. Problem?"

I shook my head. No, no problem. Esther, Estelle – what did it matter? The chaos was giving me a severe headache, and I wanted to leave this churning maelstrom of humanity as soon as possible.

"Alright, Madame Bonair," the officer proclaimed. "We have it all down. Melinda Bonair, Estelle Bonair - both saved by the *Carpathia* and brought to New York City on April 18th."

"Good. Anything else you need?"

"Your address, please."

"1021 Park Avenue, New York City," Melinda rattled off. "You heard? 1021 Park Avenue."

The officer nodded and waved us away to allow the next survivors to step forward. I followed Melinda outside, to a scene that far surpassed anything I had tried to imagine back in my sleepy little hometown.

The first thing that assailed my senses and nearly bowled me over was the noise; the sheer volume of human and mechanical voices was beyond description. Everyone was running and a nearly identical expression of purpose and stress stamped every face rushing by me.

"Don't stand there gaping," Melinda reprimanded me. "You don't have to advertise the fact that you're a foreigner."

I was too wrapped up in my observations to make much of her stinging remark. While I gawked at the passerby, Melinda imperiously raised her right hand. She stood at my side with her hand in the air, neither waving it frantically nor showing any signs of impatience.

To my amazement, a yellow vehicle pulled up near us and a round-faced driver peered at Melinda deferentially.

"Where to, ma'am?" he asked.

Melinda tapped the car hood meaningfully, and the driver obviously got her gist. Without so much as a sigh, he scrambled out and opened the passenger door. His gracious, exaggerated bow brought me to the brink of unladylike laughter, but a glare from my guardian ensured that I remained within the realms of decency.

"Where to, ma'am?" the driver repeated, once we were safely ensconced inside.

"1021 Park Avenue. And make it snappy – my husband must be wondering where I am."

Turning to me, Melinda explained, "I'm sure Bill is home already. He was never one to lose a battle when the slightest chance of victory existed."

The driver grunted in something akin to admiration but Melinda ignored his attempt at ingratiation. Only she and I knew that her elegant display was a sham, covering up a heart that beat with trepidation and a soul that bore scars no human being should ever be forced to carry.

"Ain't it just terrible?" the driver murmured. "You ladies heard about that terrible accident way out in the Atlantic?"

Silence was all he got for his valiant stab at conversation.

"Don't tell me you missed the headlines!" he continued. "It's a tragedy like never before. A...a catastrophe! They say many people died...many, many people. No exact numbers, of course, but for sure more than a thousand."

"Well, Bill isn't one of them," Melinda countered.

"Bill? Bill who?"

"Bill Bonair, you dimwit!"

The driver swiveled around in shock, but a honk from a passing vehicle brought him back to his senses.

"Keep your eyes on the road, sir," she ordered, once again the consummate noblewoman. "It would be a shame to survive the Titanic and then lose my life in the streets of New York."

"S-survive the Ti-Titanic?"

"Isn't that what I just said?" Melinda coldly replied.

I felt bad for the poor man who could barely keep up with his passenger's quick wit. He scratched his head and tapped the steering wheel before offering his intelligent take on the revelation.

"You don't say, Ma'am. You're one of those lucky survivors. I would never have thunk."

"Thought, sir. You would never have thought."

Her poise was unbelievable. Instead of falling prey to his burning curiosity, Melinda merely corrected his grammar and then lapsed into a brooding silence. I was desperate to hear more details; details that had been released to the public in the wake of the disaster I had experienced. Following Melinda's lead, however, I too maintained a pact of silence.

"Here we are, ma'am," came the driver's subdued announcement.

Without being asked, he graciously opened the passenger doors on either side and bowed as we exited. I felt like an actress who had forgotten her lines at a crucial moment in the grand performance. Here I was being treated like a dame in the bustling New York streets, while inwardly I was still little Esther Hofert, a pampered Plawo youngster who barely knew what her neighbors' gardens looked like.

"Just a moment, sir," Melinda said, a flush creeping up her neck and coloring her cheeks. "I...I don't have your fare at the moment."

"Yes, yes," the cabbie interjected, eager to regain favor in the madam's eyes. "I see."

"You don't see at all," Melinda retorted. "Your fare is sitting somewhere on the ocean floor, for all the fish to feed upon. Wait here while I rustle up some more."

The cabbie jerked his head up and down, fingering his battered cap as it bobbed along with his nervous movements. Following Melinda's lead, I traipsed up the broad, marble steps and entered a room that was larger than Etta Grunster's entire house.

"Come on, Estelle," Melinda called. "Don't stay out there in the hallway like a guest. You're part of the Bonair family."

"For now," I said, brushing aside my annoyance at the name she had dumped upon my shrunken identity.

Until Mamme comes back. Until we book our return tickets to Plawo, I'll stay here. It's not like I have much of a choice in the matter.

"You're still standing in the hallway?"

I looked around at the mirrored walls and large expanse of empty floor space. Hallway, indeed. A family of ten could have divided up this unused territory into a kitchen and two bedrooms, and they would have been considered pretty well-off according to Plawo standards.

Don't say it, I cautioned my runaway tongue. *Don't turn yourself into more of a country bumpkin than you already are.*

I smiled shamefacedly when Melinda reappeared, acutely aware of the lack of sophistication she saw in me. Her gaze softened as she noticed my discomfiture, and she patted my arm in passing.

"Poor little foundling," she murmured.

The word didn't mean anything to me. Much as I had mastered the English language, its finer nuances still left me stymied. I waited impatiently for Melinda to finish her business with the awkward cabbie so that we could map out some sort of plan for the near future.

"Sure put that one in his place," she proudly asserted. "Some people are just too big for their shoes. Now, let's see. Katherine should be back already. I told her to resume her duties by August 15th so that we wouldn't come home to a layer of grime and dust. Charlotte, on the other hand, won't be back until tomorrow. Pity. She would have prepared a sumptuous welcome-home dinner for us."

My head was whirling from the sudden onslaught of information. Charlotte was obviously the cook in this great mansion, and Katherine...What did Katherine do here? Probably the cleaning, I figured.

"Katherine! Katherine, I'm home," Melinda announced, making her way into the gargantuan depths of the place she called home.

A young, bright-eyed teenager who couldn't be much older than myself came tripping into the kitchen. The starched white cap perched on her head was slightly askew, as was the frilly apron tied snugly around her waist.

"Oh, Madame Bonair!" she cried. "I heard about that awful accident and I was so, so worried. I couldn't sleep thinking of all your luggage gone into the Atlantic Ocean! And - "

"That's enough, Katherine," Melinda interrupted. "As you see, I'm here, hale and hearty. As for the luggage – it's gone."

"And how's the Master? I haven't seen - "

"I haven't seen him yet, either. He should be here shortly."

I heard the prayer in those confident words and I winced.

"Oh!" Katherine exclaimed. "And who is this?!"

"This is Estelle," Melinda quickly explained. "Estelle Bonair, for now. Put her up in the larger guest room on the second floor. I trust that it's been aired out recently."

"Yes, certainly! Just last night, in fact."

"Good. Estelle, follow Katherine to your room. I think it best we both rest up a bit before we discuss any serious plans."

I nodded dumbly, too entranced by the black-and-white tiles and gleaming countertops to say much of anything. Katherine stared at me curiously and then motioned for me to follow her up the winding staircase.

"Come," she said. "Madame Bonair is giving you her favorite guest suite. I guess you're really someone special."

Special? Yes, I suppose you could describe me as such. But I sure hope this specialness fades to boring in the very near future, Katherine. I can't stand much more of this pretend life.

"Here you go, Estelle," the maid said, opening an imposing mahogany door. "This is your room. That's where you'll put your clothes, in that walk-in closet and the rest of your belongings could be stored here, in this chest of drawers."

I ruefully glanced at the rows of empty shelves and rods in the spacious closet, thinking of the many gowns that had gone down with the Titanic. Apparently catching her mistake, Katherine covered her mouth with her hands and gasped audibly.

"Oh, I'm so sorry, miss! I didn't mean to rub salt on your wounds. You came here with nothing, right? Absolutely nothing. Wow, that must be awful."

I shrugged. My belongings were just things, for goodness' sake. Did Katherine realize that I had lost my *mother* somewhere in the midst of that gargantuan Atlantic Ocean?!

"Well, I guess that whenever you get some...uh... things, you'll put them where I showed you," she stammered. "And here's the bathroom, on your left, and a desk and chair for...well, for whatever you might need it for."

I nodded mutely.

"Er...Can you talk, miss?" Katherine asked, obviously gathering her courage in a last-ditch attempt to make conversation.

"Yes, Katherine," I said, slowly. "I can talk, but not right now. I'm awfully tired."

"Of course, of course!" she said, once again covering her mouth in mortification. "You were just saved from the Titanic! I mean, how could I forget?! You have to rest! Don't listen to me, Estelle. I have this horrid habit of talking non-stop, but I'm trying to get rid of it. At least when Madame Bonair is around."

This time, my smile did not feel forced. I was actually beginning to enjoy the girl's endless prattle. She was so charmingly innocent and well-meaning, that one couldn't remain annoyed with her for too long.

"I enjoy your chatter," I said honestly. "It takes my mind off other things."

Katherine smiled uncertainly, and quickly turned to leave.

"So you heard everything I said, right? About the closet and the drawers and the bathroom and the desk..."

"Yes," I replied. "And if I forget any of the details, I'll make sure to ask you."

I heard Katherine clattering down the stairs, and then Melinda reprimanding her for her noisy descent. With a sigh of relief, I sat down on an overstuffed maroon armchair strategically positioned beneath a large, oval-shaped window. It was nice to just sit, for a change, instead of running frantically after Melinda from one place to another.

The pleasure of rest was not destined to last more than a half hour. A sharp rap on my door pulled me out of my reverie.

"Estelle, come on down," Melinda called. "We have much to discuss."

I sighed in frustration. Couldn't this dreaded conversation wait until tomorrow? There was no way I could concentrate on anything, in the discombobulated state my mind was in!

"Estelle!"

"I'm coming," I grumbled to my reflection in the gold-rimmed mirror.

Remembering the verbal thrashing Katherine had received earlier, I sedately made my way down the varnished, spiral staircase. I spotted Melinda sitting on a high-backed wooden chair in what could only have been a grand living room, and I hesitantly approached her.

"Oh, Estelle! There you are!"

She motioned for me to sit down, and I did so gingerly. These chairs with their intricate engravings were not conducive to comfort or informality, I decided. They must be reserved for conversations such as these which bore fateful ramifications and which made all involved parties decidedly uncomfortable.

"I've been very busy while you were resting," Melinda said importantly. "I made inquiries."

It sounded so official. Melinda had made inquiries. She must have some information about *Mamme*.

"I discovered that the best place for you to be educated would be at the Beverly School for Young Ladies. It's an elite institution, where only the upper crust of society could afford to send their daughters. Obviously, Bill and I wouldn't dream of giving you anything less than the best, my dear."

"Wh-what did you say?"

"Estelle, you must listen carefully when spoken to," Melinda sighed. "I did a lot of research on your behalf and this is the most satisfactory solution I came up with."

"But...but why...Why a school?"

"Estelle! You don't want to remain an uneducated Polish immigrant all your life, do you?!"

"I...If...I mean, when I go back to Plawo, I'll have no need for an American education," I said. "When *Mamme* is found, we're going to head back home as soon as we can find berths on a ship."

"Oh, my poor darling," Melinda crooned. "Of course we'll wait for your mother! It's not as though I'm giving up on her!"

She seemed hurt by my implied accusations, but I was still confused by the shocking turn the conversation had taken.

"So why were you researching schools for me?"

"It's...It's a back-up plan," she stammered. "See, if your mother won't be found – and I'm saying if, Estelle. You hear? Let's say, in the worst-case scenario, you hear that your *Mamme* is not...not coming back, then what will you do?"

She looked at me expectantly. I didn't understand the question. Wasn't it obvious that I would return to Plawo on my own, if *Mamme* would...not be able to come with me?

"Well, what will you do then, Estelle?"

"I guess I'll have to travel on my own," I said quietly, afraid to voice the thought out loud.

"And who will pay for your return ticket?" Melinda persisted.

"I...I didn't think of that," I admitted.

"I'll tell you the truth," Melinda said. "I would gladly pay for your return ticket and everything else you might need. But...with Bill still not accounted for, I can't be too careful. I...I don't know where our finances stand and I have to start worrying about retirement and all that."

I stared at her, not understanding a word of her long-winded explanation.

"So you would have to earn the money on your own," she concluded, staring above my head as though purposely avoiding my gaze.

"Uh...how would I do that?"

"Your voice, Estelle," Melinda said quickly.

"My...my voice?"

"Now you understand why you have to go to school, my dear," she explained. "You need to become a polished young woman before you can appear on stage. Once you begin performing, you'll earn the money you need in no time at all. I guarantee it, Estelle.

"And of course, if your *Mamme* is found, there will be no discussion of schools or performances. You'll rest up here in my home and then head back to your small town, together."

I smiled wistfully. For some inexplicable reason, I was beginning to feel that a journey home with *Mamme* was just a dream...a wish that would remain in the realm of all other unrealized wishes I had ever harbored.

Melinda flipped through a small, leather-bound notebook.

"Here's the name and address of the school I told you about," she said. "I'll send Katherine over with all the necessary documents and information, and we'll have you registered before the day is out."

Hashem! Help me! Don't let Melinda throw me out for my audacity because I have nowhere else to go...But I can't go to this school where everyone will laugh at my ac-

cent and my ignorance. I...I want to go home.

"Melinda, I truly appreciate everything you're doing for me," I started, stumbling over my carefully-chosen words. "But maybe this can wait a bit? I...I don't want to go to school. I don't want to perform. I just...I just want to go home."

To my utter mortification, the words morphed into tears. Big, salty tears dripped onto my hands, scalding them with the heat of emotion. I sat in that straight-backed, wooden chair and I cried for the childhood that was being wrested out of my arms. I cried for my parents, who were losing their innocent Esther to the machinations of an unknown woman. And I cried for Melinda who wanted to help me, but didn't know how.

She stood over me in a protective stance, awkwardly rubbing my shoulders and stroking my plaited hair.

"Shhh...Estelle, it's alright. You know I won't make you do anything you don't want to do. I'm doing this for your future, Estelle, so that you won't remain separated from your family forever. Trust me, darling."

Oh, how I wished I could accept her words at face value. How wonderful it would be to place my trust in this caring woman who accepted me, for all intents and purposes, as her own.

But I couldn't. I felt that I was missing something. A crucial piece of the puzzle lay just beyond my grasp; a piece that would clarify Melinda's motives and shed light upon my inexplicable resistance to her warm overtures.

"We'll have you registered by nightfall, Estelle," Melinda soothingly continued. "But you don't have to attend. Do you hear me, darling? You don't have to go to Beverly School until you're ready and willing."

I nodded, sniffling into a handkerchief that had been placed into my trembling hands.

"And if your *Mamme* is found, Estelle, no one will be

happier than I," Melinda murmured. "You know that."

I rested my head on my arms, allowing Melinda to lull me into a false sense of security. The cherubic faces of the Navratil orphans flashed before my eyes. They were truly alone in the great big world. They didn't even have the comfort of a self-proclaimed guardian who could look out for their needs and see to their immediate future.

Stop moaning, Esther, I told myself sternly. *Melinda is trying to help you. As soon as Mamme arrives, we'll be able to leave this awful, noisy New York and return to Tatte. You heard what Melinda said. You don't have to go to school unless you want to.*

I heard Melinda rustling papers and then going off in search of Katherine. The gathering shadows caressed my face, willing me to relax on my first night on American soil.

'It won't be long,' those lengthening shadows whispered. 'You'll soon find yourself in the warm embrace of family. Until then, Estelle Bonair, just grin and bear it. Show the world what a Plawo immigrant can do.'

Chapter Nineteen

When the telegram arrived, only Katherine and I were home. She motioned for me to sign on the dotted line, but I shamefacedly admitted that this simple task was beyond my capabilities.

I really should go to school to spare myself these embarrassing incidents. If only Mamme would come back already, so that I could leave this all behind.

"It's from the Titanic rescue efforts!" Katherine exclaimed. "Look, here's their name on the right-hand side."

I looked and nodded my head, assuming that the unidentifiable scrawl was truly what Katherine thought it to be.

"Oh, this must be news about the master! I thought we would never hear from him!"

And maybe it's about Mamme, a little voice whispered into the thoroughfares of my heart. *Maybe it's the news you've been awaiting.*

Katherine put her finger to her lips and with twinkling eyes, she held the small envelope up to the window. The streaming sunshine made it possible to see an outline of letters and shapes...but not much more than that.

"Oh, bother," she muttered. "Trust this to be the day when Melinda will decide to have tea with her friends.

Those affairs usually stretch until late afternoon."

Until late afternoon! How would I survive the suspense? Short of opening the telegram and risking Melinda's wrath, there was nothing I could do but wait. I closeted myself in the beautiful room I had learned to call my own, and gave myself over to the joys of imagination.

In my mind's eye, I saw *Mamme* walking up the broad, marble steps of Melinda's home and nervously tapping on the door. I heard my silent footfalls descending the spiral staircase and felt the rush of warm air as I opened the door.

Mamme.

With a start, I shook myself out of my reverie and turned to the One Who carried the keys to my future.

"Hashem, I cannot hold on much longer here," I said aloud, hoping that Katherine was doing her duties downstairs as she had promised her exacting mistress. "The pressure to conform is growing stronger, but I must remain strong for *Tatte* and *Mamme*. Bring her home already, *Tatte in Himmel*! Give me the strength to endure the wait.

"And if...if the happy ending will not come to be... Hashem, give me the strength to hold on tight...to hold onto Your hand."

The main door whooshed open, announcing to all and sundry that the mistress of 1021 Park Avenue had returned. Contrary to Katherine's predictions, Melinda had returned before the sun even reached its noontime zenith.

"Oh, Madame Bonair!"

I heard Katherine's breathless greeting, and rushed out of my room.

"You have no idea what arrived while you were out!"

"Out with it, girl," Melinda said cheerfully.

"A telegram for you! From the Titanic rescue committees."

I stood at the head of the stairs, seeing without being seen.

"So Bill finally let himself be found," she said brightly. "I suppose he didn't want to forfeit his welcome-home dinner!"

The words were cheery and full of fluff, but the tense set of her shoulders belied her inner turmoil. Katherine fluttered around her, eagerly awaiting the good news.

"So what does it say, Madame?" she asked. "When is he coming home? I must tell Charlotte!"

I clearly heard the envelope being ripped open, followed by a short pause and a sharp intake of breath. There was no excited exclamation, nor was there a surge of disappointment. There was silence; a thick, graveyard silence that wrapped itself around my throat and sat heavily upon my heart.

"He's not coming back," Melinda said, her voice thick and slow. "Not now, and not ever."

I watched her stumble towards the outdoor patio, and then raced down the stairs. Much as I commiserated with her tragic loss, I couldn't lose sight of my own future. Maybe the telegram had also contained news about *Mamme*. Katherine would have to clue me in.

Bill was gone.

His body had been recovered on the night of the accident, but it hadn't been identified until three weeks later.

Bill Bonair, host and gentleman extraordinaire, was no more.

As for *Mamme* – there was no mention of her. No sign of life...nor of death. It was as though she had been swallowed up by the Atlantic on that dreadful night, leaving no trace.

Those were difficult days at the Bonair residence. Melinda didn't scream or cry, as I had expected. Instead, she maintained a stoic silence that spread itself like a woolen blanket over the entire household. I wished she would vent her feelings, so that we could all expel the breaths we were holding, but Melinda held onto her privacy with both hands. She had lost her husband to the jaws of the Atlantic, but she wouldn't give it the satisfaction of swallowing up her dignity and composure.

Thus, when Melinda approached me five days after the telegram had punctured her future, I was ready to do anything for her.

"Estelle, my dear," she said. "I've been thinking."

There wasn't much else you could have been doing, closeted in your room these past few days, I thought sympathetically.

"My life, as I know it, has changed irrevocably. I'm a widow, Estelle. No husband, no children."

She looked at me searchingly, but I didn't know how to respond.

"At least I have you, Estelle. You're like…like the daughter I never had."

I recoiled. The last thing I had expected was a discussion about myself. I had geared myself to offer my sincerest condolences, but Melinda was not looking for that.

"Let's be practical, dear. Your *Mamme* has not been found yet. It's been a month since the Titanic sank, but her body has not been recovered. What does that tell you?"

"I…I don't know," I whispered. "Maybe *Mamme* is alive and well somewhere, searching for me in the foreign streets of America."

"Estelle, darling, your *Mamme* would have to be registered on some sort of list if she were found alive."

I nodded.

"You know how many times I've contacted the rescue committees on your behalf. The name Dina Hofert never showed up."

I nodded again, mute horror taking control of my voice-box.

"There's only one explanation for that, little one. Your *Mamme*...she went to the same place as fifteen hundred other victims. The same place that Bill was sent to."

I shook my head forcefully, although I knew that her words couldn't be contested. Four long weeks of waiting and hoping had worn down my optimistic tendencies, and I had slowly come to accept the inevitable.

Mamme had gone down with the Titanic.

And it was my fault.

My defenses were down and Melinda knew it. Warmly, yet ever so cleverly, she obtained my concession that I would begin attending school the very next morning. I would do as she saw fit, if only to bring a smile to her face and some gladness to her battered heart.

"You won't regret it, Estelle," Melinda warmly concluded. "I need to know that I'm giving to someone...that my life still has some meaning. If you become the educated, poised young woman I know you can be, I'll feel fulfilled."

"I'll do it, Melinda," I said heavily. "Until I arrange my return trip to Plawo, I'll attend the school you chose for me."

Melinda suddenly appeared uncomfortable in her own skin.

"Uh, Estelle, about the return tickets...It's not so simple," she mumbled, looking up at the ornately carved ceiling with absolute fascination. "Remember I told you about how I would need every penny I own for retirement, now that Bill cannot provide for us anymore?"

I saw where she was going with this line of reasoning, but I could do nothing to stop her in her tracks.

"You'll have to earn the money on your own, darling," she said sorrowfully. "I wish I could do more for you, but my hands are tied."

Earn the money on my own? How much does a ticket

cost? And how will I go about earning money in this voracious American melting pot?

"Your voice, Estelle," she said, echoing words I had heard a lifetime ago. "Believe me, as soon as you enter the opera scene, you'll be flooded with offers and performances. You'll be back in Plawo before you know it."

Back in Plawo. Tatte, I'll have to do this in order to come home. It will be just one or two performances, but it will spare me a lifetime of wasting away here in New York. I don't have a choice, Tatte, do I?

I didn't think of asking Melinda how she could fund my schooling if the price of a ticket was beyond her means. Nor did I question her ability to purchase an exquisite wardrobe that outstripped my glamorous Plawo clothes by far. No, these discrepancies didn't penetrate my sorrow-filled mind. All I could see was the promised return trip dangling before my eyes, and I was ready to do anything to make that a reality.

"I must write to *Tatte* to tell him that I am alive and well," I told Melinda. "Do you think he knows what happened to *Mamme*?"

"I'm sure he does, dear," Melinda said.

She was all smiles, now that I had agreed to her suggestion. As soon as I left the room, she ordered Katherine to starch one of my new gowns in preparation for tomorrow's debut at the Beverly School for Young Ladies.

I trudged up the stairs to my private domain. It was time to pen the letter I had been postponing for want of good news to include. There was no use waiting any longer. My most fervent wishes wouldn't bring *Mamme* up from the depths. At least I still had my warm and loving *Tatte* who must be worried sick about my lack of communication.

The letter sprawled out on three elegant, cream-colored pages bearing the Bonair family emblem on top. I labored over each word, trying to inject it with the youthful charm and innocence that *Tatte* knew and recognized.

Tatte, I'm coming home. Maybe you know when a European-bound ship will be departing from American shores. I need to earn money for a ticket, but my guardian insists that it won't take too long.

Esther is coming home, Tatte. Your dear, beloved Esther is returning to Plawo at last.

Tell Zalmen that I have grown up a lot since the last time we spoke. I am not the little sister he always knew. No, Tatte. These past few weeks have matured me.

Would *Tatte* understand what I was referring to? Would he realize that *Mamme*'s disappearance had wrought a change in his cosseted only daughter?

I cannot bear the wait until we are reunited, Tatte. Until then, I will remember what you've always told me. Hashem is good and all He does is good.

I signed off, intentionally allowing my tears to blur my signature. It was important to me that *Tatte* should notice the pain and anguish we shared, despite the miles that separated us. I had purposely refrained from mentioning my luxurious surroundings and pampered existence so that he shouldn't imagine that I was wrapping *Mamme*'s loss in comfortable, gilded tissue paper.

Without daring to reread the impetuous lines I had scrawled, I slid the papers into their elegant envelope and wrote *Tatte*'s name on the outside, in bold black print.

R' Shimon Hofert
36 Main Street
Plawo

As the return address, I put my name and Melinda's home address, laboring over the alphabet I had only recently mastered. The letter was ready to be mailed. The envelope had already been sealed. For some reason that I couldn't fathom, I found myself faltering at the last stage of this crucial venture.

Just send it out, Esther, I told myself sternly. *You want Tatte to hear from you, his only consolation now that Mamme is…gone. Katherine would be more than thrilled to deliver it to wherever such kinds of correspondence are processed.*

I splashed cold water on my tear-streaked face and hurried to find Katherine before my courage deserted me. On my way down the stairs, I met Melinda coming up, a satisfied smile adorning her face.

"Your things are ready for the big day," she said.

Big day?! What is she talking about?

"You'll be the star of the school, Estelle. Mark my words!"

Oh. The Beverly School for Young Ladies. I promised to go tomorrow…but it shan't be for long. Tatte will make sure of that.

Confident in my father's speedy response, I found the strength to smile at Melinda and play the part of the docile schoolgirl. She took the envelope from my hand and gave it a cursory glance. An inscrutable expression flitted across her face, disappearing into oblivion before I could analyze its implications.

"Give that to Katherine," Melinda ordered. "She's the one entrusted with our incoming and outgoing correspondence."

Holding the envelope aloft like a victor's flag, I meandered through the mansion's lower level until I found Katherine engrossed in the painstaking job of linen-folding.

"Katherine!"

The girl jumped up, sending the linens cascading around her in a cloud of white and lavender.

"Oh!" she exclaimed, holding her hand theatrically on her heart. "You scared me, Estelle!"

"I'm sorry. I just...I wanted to give you this envelope to take care of. Melinda said you'll know what to do with it."

Katherine took the cream-colored envelope from my hand and perused it curiously.

"So you're writing letters, Estelle, are you? I was wondering what you do up there in your room all day. Can't say I recognize the name...or the address...but it's none of my business."

Right you are, Katherine. I don't really care to enlighten you.

"I'll post it for you, Estelle. And mind, next time you could call my name a bit more quietly."

"Sure, Katherine. I'm sorry," I murmured, turning to leave the small laundry room.

"Plawo," I heard Katherine reading out loud. "Now, what sort of name is that? Can't be any respectable town or village around these parts. I would've heard about it."

I giggled to myself, enjoying her bewilderment. Why would she think that I was corresponding with someone in far-off Poland? Did she even know that the country existed somewhere on the European continent?

In the days that followed, I hounded the postman mercilessly. Every morning, before I went to school, I waited for him at the doorstep and asked whether something had come for Esther Hofert. His polite "No, ma'am" accompanied me all the way to school, where it was slowly drowned out by the teachers' strident voices and the girls' mindless chatter.

Melinda was decidedly unimpressed with my impatience. She explained that it takes several weeks for letters to crisscross over the Atlantic, and it was unseemly for a young woman to converse with a simple mailman. I would have none of it. Melinda did not have a bereaved father sitting at home and wondering where his only daughter had disappeared to. She didn't have to carry her mother's death on her own shoulders, and she would never feel the pain of orphanhood as I did.

No, she couldn't understand. The mailman was the first person I had to speak to every morning. Only after hearing his unequivocal negative response could I resume my daily routine. It was enough that I had agreed to attend school in her merit. I didn't have to sacrifice every other desire that dared to contradict her own.

Chapter Twenty

*H*ad I known that the long-awaited response would not arrive before the passage of two months, I may have despaired. However, when my daily question was finally met with an answering smile, the lengthy eight weeks disappeared as though they'd never been.

"Here you go, ma'am," the mailman said somberly. "I don't think this is quite what you're expecting, but it's all I've got."

He gave me a thick, cream-colored envelope that was covered in colored markings and indecipherable encodings. Beneath the scrawled messages and postmarks, the envelope seemed awfully familiar.

It was mine. It was the envelope I had sent out so lovingly eight weeks previous, to my dear *Tatte*. It was the envelope that was supposed to transport me back home. And it had come back...unopened.

Pressing my fingers into the corners of my eyes to hold those treacherous tears inside, I rushed back into the house. Melinda was standing before one of the foyer mirrors, fixing her hair with utmost precision.

"Estelle!" she cried. "Why are you still here? School begins - "

"I'm not going," I muttered. "Not today, and not ever."

Melinda stared at me, allowing her eyes to explore the contours of my face, my rigid shoulders and then the envelope clutched firmly in my hands.

"You...You received a reply from Europe?" she asked.

"No. I mean, yes. It's..."

My voice betrayed me. Without another word, I thrust the envelope into her hands and rushed towards the stairs. Let Melinda deal with the incomprehensible stamps and postmarks. I wanted to stew in my disappointment just a bit longer before she cajoled me back into the role of gracious Estelle Bonair, up-and-coming young star in American society.

The reprieve didn't last long. On silent feet, Melinda entered my room and sat down near me on the freshly made-up bed. She put her arm around my shoulders and allowed me to vent my frustration without expressing even a twinge of annoyance.

"Estelle, darling," she crooned. "I understand how painful this must be for you."

You understand, Melinda?! What do you know of my home; of my warm and loving Tatte who awaits me back in Plawo? What do you know of my former life, where innocence and purity were allowed to reign undisturbed?!

"Is there any reason why your father would...refuse your correspondence?"

I stared at her in horror. The thought had never even crossed my mind. Was it possible that my letter had reached our home in Plawo and that *Tatte* had sent it back unopened? Did he...could he possibly sever contact?

"Estelle, talk to me," Melinda pleaded. "Can you think of any reason why that would happen? Is your father upset with you?"

Tatte, are you still upset about my youthful folly? Do you, too, blame me for Mamme's death?!

"I...I really don't know," I hiccupped. "It's...possible."

Melinda looked down at the envelope on her lap and sighed.

"Listen to me, Estelle. Mistakes do happen. The letter might have been delivered to the wrong address, for all we know. Or maybe it got lost in transit and somehow found its way back home."

She fell silent, and I knew that she was considering the improbability of such a grievous error.

"Then again, it's highly possible that your father sent the letter back from whence it came."

Her eyes bored into mine with an intensity impossible to resist.

"Tell me, Estelle," she said slowly. "Does your father blame you for anything?"

I trembled uncontrollably. There was something so powerful about Melinda's gaze that my regular defenses simply crumbled to dust before her.

"Melinda, I...I killed my mother," I whispered.

"Don't be ridiculous! Estelle, I was with you when we escaped from the sinking Titanic! There was nothing you could - "

"It was my fault that *Mamme* was on the Titanic," I interrupted. "My foolish mistakes forced her to take me on a trip...a trip that would end in disaster. Is it any wonder that *Tatte* wants nothing to do with me?!"

Melinda's blue eyes were staring into mine, and I felt the ties on my emotions slowly unraveling.

"I can't go back home like this," I cried. "I can't! *Tatte* is obviously heartbroken and he blames me – his beloved Esther – for his loss! How can I hope to be accepted back into the family circle after all that I've done?!"

Melinda said nothing, but her presence was comforting. With my warm home fading slowly into the land of the past, she was the only one still standing at my side.

"I understand, Estelle," she said. "I understand your pain. How about you try one more time? Send one more letter back home and see if time has wrought its magic. I'm sure your father misses you dearly and he doesn't intend to cut off contact forever."

I nodded perfunctorily, although I didn't place much hope in her convictions. *Tatte* was not prone to instantaneous decisions. If he had decided to send my letter back unopened, he wanted me to receive a message. He wanted me to know, in no uncertain terms, that my childish mistakes were irreversible. Unforgivable.

"And I must tell you, Estelle, how impressed I am with the progress you've made. After just two months at the Beverly School for Young Ladies, you've developed such poise and graciousness! And your accent, Estelle – it's nearly disappeared! All that remains is that charming lilt that sets you apart as an exotic foreigner.

"I took the liberty of booking an audition at The Opera House for tomorrow evening. This will be the first step in earning your way back home, Estelle."

At this point, I wasn't so sure if home would allow me back in, but I was too shattered to refuse. Tomorrow night I would audition at Melinda's theater and hopefully, I would snag a performing role. Before long, I would be able to return home without *Tatte*'s help.

And yet, the question remained.

Could I possibly go back home and risk Tatte's wrath? Could I place myself in a role that I had discarded so many months ago in favor of greener pastures?

I didn't follow through on Melinda's letter-writing suggestion. I couldn't muster the courage to send another piece of my heart out into the great world, only to have it returned without so much as a shred of response. No, I couldn't risk *Tatte*'s rejection again.

Zalmen, however, was different. I was certain that he

would respond to my overtures, even if it would come in the form of fiery admonition and a slew of blame-filled darts. At the very least, it would be a sign of life from my beloved family!

This second letter was penned with more thought and less emotion. I described what I had gone through and begged Zalmen to share with me the details of *Tatte*'s pain. I needed to know how much I had hurt the person whom I so desperately wished to protect. The promises I enclosed in that letter were effusive. I told Zalmen that I was still little Esther, the sister he so adored. I would be docile and I would toe the line. I would take over *Mamme*'s myriad tasks. I would agree to any match *Tatte* thought suitable and I would be a source of pride to the whole family.

If only they would want me back.

But this letter, too, was returned unopened. Zalmen's unspoken rejection cut me to the quick and I couldn't muster the courage to try again. If my greatest ally had turned his back on me, there was no hope. There was no going back.

After this second bout of disappointment, Melinda wisely maintained her silence. There was nothing to say. Nothing she could offer would ease the pain of familial rejection, so she kept quiet. Instead, she pulled me from one performance to another, dressing me up and placing me on stage to the admiration of cheering audiences and fawning producers.

I was Estelle Bonair, the new star on the New York theater scene. I performed before mixed audiences because Melinda told me to do so. After a mere few weeks, I had enough money saved up for a return trip to Europe, but I simply allowed it to accumulate. For all intents and purposes, I was an orphan, adrift in a world I detested.

Tatte! I screamed inwardly while waiting for the opening number of a grand performance. *Look what has become of your beloved Esther! I am standing here, before a mixed audience, singing for all I'm worth. Yet your face dances before me, Tatte! I see your rejection wherever I go, and I feel your fury at every step. Don't do this to me, Tatte! Call me back home before I get lost in this abyss of depravity!*

But *Tatte* didn't call me home. Neither did Zalmen, nor any of my sisters-in-law. In Plawo, I was an unwanted memory, while in New York, I was a star.

Melinda was proud. It seemed that my appearance on the opera scene had greatly boosted her musical career, and for that she was thankful. She complimented me after each performance, and soothed my ruffled feathers whenever I felt slighted.

And yet, I was alone. Achingly and desperately alone.

*   *   *

Several years later, when I stood under the *chuppah* at Barry Bonair's side, I felt the loneliness more strongly than ever. Melinda was walking me down the aisle, along with her sister-in-law, Barry's mother. They propelled me forward, step by step, tearing me away from the past with bone-chilling finality.

I walked towards my future, seeing nothing save for *Tatte*'s blazing eyes. I felt his tears searing my face, and I sensed his anguished heartbeat beating alongside my own.

I don't have a choice, Tatte! Do you want me to remain a performing spinster for the rest of my life?! At least I know that Barry's Jewish...and a fine, upright individual.

My children will make you proud, Tatte, I vowed. *I'll raise them with knowledge of our beautiful past; of you and Mamme. Please, walk with me down this long aisle,*

Tatte! I need you here!

But *Tatte* remained out of reach. I didn't feel his presence during the entire ceremony, much as I tried to conjure up his image and hear his gentle voice.

I hoped that Barry's ebullience covered up some of my turmoil, but Melinda's worried glance told me that my emotions could not be concealed. This was my wedding day! This was the day I had dreamed of back in Plawo, when Chaim'l the Shadchan started knocking on our door. It was the day every young girl imagined with wistful dreaminess.

Why, then, did I feel like a spectator at my own funeral?

Why, indeed, Esther?!

Part IV:
Plawo, Poland
May, 1912

Chapter Twenty-One

Rap. Rap. Rap rap.

Mrs. Hofert sighed. The neighbors were all well-meaning and concerned, but it was difficult to get settled with the constant comings and goings. Without Esther at her side she felt so exposed and vulnerable. Would the Plawo community give her the space she needed to come to terms with her loss?

Rap. Rapraprap!

"I'm coming, I'm coming," she mumbled, pushing aside her uneaten breakfast in favor of the unidentified visitor.

"Who is it?" Mrs. Hofert asked.

"Open up already! Do you think *shidduchim* wait around until you're good and ready to welcome them in?!"

Chaim'l the *Shadchan* tapped his foot impatiently, annoyed at the attitude he was being served. No one made Chaim'l wait outside. His visits were long-awaited and kept strictly confidential. Yet the Hoferts could afford to have the entire Plawo know that a *shidduch* was being offered for their beloved Esther. They weren't concerned that the other side would turn down the suggestion, leaving them with the embarrassment of unfulfilled potential.

Mrs. Hofert opened the door ever so slowly and peered

up at the red-bearded *shadchan* in consternation.

"Wh...what are you looking for?" she asked, a tremor belying her inner turmoil.

In days bygone, such visits were par for the course. Esther was at the top of every *shadchan*'s list and the offers came pouring in thick and fast. Now, however, Chaim'l seemed out of place. His fiery red beard and broad-framed, loquacious presence were decidedly incongruous in this house of mourning.

"What am *I* looking for?" Chaim'l repeated, chortling at the bizarre inquiry. "The question is – what are *you* looking for?! What is your young daughter looking for?! That's what I'd like to know!"

Mrs. Hofert's eyes dilated in pain and she grasped the doorpost with fingers gone cold and unfeeling.

"Esther...I...I don't know. Wh-what is Esther looking for?"

"You're her mother, aren't you?" Chaim'l asked, a note of bewilderment creeping into his confident voice. "I've offered tens of *shidduchim* for that daughter of yours, but nothing has passed muster. This time I have an idea that neither you, nor your illustrious husband, nor your wonderful daughter will be able to reject."

He doesn't know! Mrs. Hofert realized. *Chaim'l hasn't heard that Esther...that Esther will never need a shidduch. He doesn't realize that I returned home while she...she remained somewhere at the bottom of the ocean.*

"I don't think - "

"Don't wave it away so quickly," Chaim'l trumpeted, getting into his notorious *shadchan*-mode. "I've done all my research and everything checks out, Mrs. Hofert. If perfection would be a possibility, this would fit the bill!"

"Ah...I just came back from - "

"I know, I know," the matchmaker interrupted. "As soon as I heard that you had returned from your journey,

I made my way over. I mean, *shidduchim* don't wait. Not even for a trip on the most luxurious ship man has ever seen!"

"You don't understand," Mrs. Hofert tried again. "I came back but Esther...my dear, innocent Esther...did not."

Chaim'l was stumped, but any sign of confusion would ruin his carefully-cultivated image.

"No problem, Mrs. Hofert. No problem at all," he rejoined. "You and your husband can check out the suggestion so that when Esther comes home, things will be ready to move."

"Esther is not coming home," Mrs. Hofert flatly stated. "Never."

"What are you saying?" Chaim'l blustered. "She took a job as a stewardess? As a sailor? Why isn't she coming home?!"

"The Titanic hit an iceberg. Many people were killed... or lost. Esther was...was one of them."

Without another word, Chaim'l the *shadchan* turned on his heels and fled. His cheeks matched the color of his beard, but his feelings of sympathy far surpassed the load of shame chasing him down the street.

How was I to know that the Hoferts traveled on the ill-fated Titanic? It didn't dawn on me that their luxury trip was taking place on board that monstrosity, he thought as his feet pounded the cobblestoned street. *So R' Shimon Hofert lost his youngest daughter. Aiy aiy aiy...*

Chaim'l leaned against a tree and pulled his trusty notebook out of his pocket. He deliberately crossed out *Esther Hofert* from the first page. The finality of his pen-slash was heart-wrenching, making him feel as though he were affixing his signature to a death certificate.

"Good morning, Chaim'l!"

The perturbed *shadchan* guiltily stashed his notebook

back into his pocket and looked up at Zalmen Hofert with discomfort. Did this promising young man know about the blunder he had just made? Was he aware that he had inflicted additional pain upon his suffering mother?

But no, that was impossible. Zalmen was headed in the direction of his parents' home. He hadn't heard anything from his mother, and knowing Mrs. Hofert's legendary self-control, he would never know what had transpired.

"Zalmen!" he exclaimed, reclaiming his characteristic exuberance with ease. "It's...ah...a nice day!"

Zalmen nodded and rushed on ahead. He had to know what *Tatte* had heard from the Rav. Would the family be sitting *shivah* this week for little Esther'ke? His heart contracted at the thought of *Tatte*, *Mamme*, Menachem and himself sitting on low chairs in their spacious dining room. Esther would be the only one missing; the only one marring the complete family picture.

Then again, wouldn't that be preferable to remaining in limbo until some more concrete facts came to light? How could they forge ahead when Esther's absence was reduced to a flickering, unrevealing question mark?

Zalmen shook his head. *Tatte* had gone to the Rav for guidance and his decision would be adhered to. When he pushed open the door of his childhood home, he sensed immediately that *Tatte* had already returned with an answer. The doubt that had lingered heavily in the air that morning had all but disappeared.

"*Tatte*," Zalmen called out.

"Come into the kitchen, Zalmen," his father responded.

Tatte and *Mamme* were sitting at the table, which was laden with an untouched breakfast spread. Standing at the doorway, Zalmen gazed at them with concern and affection. How *Mamme* had aged! Her eyes bespoke such depths of pain that it was simply agonizing to meet her gaze. *Tatte*, on the other hand, sat straight-backed and strong, like a soldier mounted on a prize-worthy steed.

For that is what *Tatte* truly personified. He walked through life as a soldier in Hashem's army, doing what was expected of him without complaint and without regret. Under such awful circumstances, he took orders from the general and strengthened himself to meet the Commander's expectations.

"The Rav ruled that we cannot sit *shivah*," *Tatte* said. "We do not have any concrete proof that Esther is...that *shivah* is actually required, so we must wait. And pray."

Mamme sighed, and Zalmen understood. It was difficult to lose a child and then be denied the chance of mourning her absence. She had been on-site when Esther'ke had been lost to them...maybe forever.

"I should have gathered my strength and searched for her on deck," *Mamme* moaned, repeating herself for the umpteenth time. "Weakness is not an excuse for abandoning one's child."

"*Mamme*, you know that was impossible," Zalmen said. "You were saved in the last moment! Had that kind steward not carried you up the stairs and deposited you in the last collapsible, you would have...it wouldn't have ended so well."

"Who would have believed it," *Mamme* quietly reminisced. "Mr. Barlow, of all people, had the presence of mind to look after his charges instead of abandoning them to their fates. And I had accused him of wanting to steal my belongings on that first day..."

Her voice trailed off as she pictured Esther's stifled smile in response to her own paranoia. Esther had understood that Mr. Barlow wanted to help them. Yes, there were many things that Esther had understood.

"You couldn't have done anything, *Mamme*," Zalmen

reiterated, desperate to ease his mother's burden. "We're thankful to Hashem that at least you were rescued."

"But what is my life without Esther'ke?" *Mamme* moaned. "Zalmen, you should never know how heavy the burden of guilt can be. This guilt will accompany me every day of my life, Zalmen. Every day!"

Father and son exchanged a meaningful glance; a glance that bespoke pain and understanding. They had tried to talk *Mamme* out of her self-induced agony, but she wouldn't listen.

"Esther's death - "

"Don't say that, Dina," *Tatte* quickly interjected. "The Rav said that we must assume she is alive until more proof is procured."

"Esther's disappearance will blot my soul and stain my heart," *Mamme* said. "I could have saved her. If only I hadn't succumbed to my weakness...Now I can rest all I want, but on that fateful night I should not have rested. I should have saved my only daughter."

Another laden glance passed between the two men, and they wordlessly adjourned to the living room. *Mamme*'s wracking sobs could be heard through the walls, expressing their feelings with pathos. *Tatte* placed his hand on Zalmen's shoulder and closed his eyes for a long, tense moment.

"Zalmen, *mein kind*," he whispered. "The Rav said that we must be prepared for a lifetime of not knowing. *Halacha* mandates that we believe Esther to be alive unless proven otherwise...but we may never know. We may travel through the years with the constant 'maybe' shadowing every *simcha* and occasion.

"Promise me that you'll be strong, Zalmen," *Tatte* continued, his voice breaking. "I cannot be strong enough for all of us. *Mamme* will need our support, and I...I, too, will need your encouragement."

Zalmen swallowed, trying in vain to get past the porcupine that had lodged itself in his throat. Never before had *Tatte* shared his innermost feelings and fears.

"*Tatte*, you know that I am always here for you," he quietly replied. "Miri and I will do all we can to help *Mamme* reclaim her life. And the children...my innocent *kinderlach* will surely work their magic on their beloved *Bubbe*."

"We must send a telegram to Menachem," *Tatte* said. "He is waiting to hear the Rav's decision."

"Will Menachem come to Plawo?"

"I don't know," *Tatte* said. "It might be advisable. We haven't seen him since Sukkos, and I'm sure that a visit would do *Mamme* a world of good."

And you, as well, Zalmen thought but did not say. *You also lost a daughter, Tatte, yet you're trying to hold our family together by sheer force of will.*

"I'm going to send the telegram," *Tatte* said, donning his overcoat and heading towards the door. "You're staying with *Mamme* until I get back? I don't want to leave her here alone these first few days."

"I'm here, *Tatte*," Zalmen replied. "I don't have to give the *shiur* until late afternoon. In any case, I told Miri to come over with the children as soon as she can. They should be here shortly."

"Good, good. The *kinderlach* should bring their light into our darkened home."

Tatte turned to go, and in that last glimpse, Zalmen saw the mountains of pain that had piled up behind his eyes. The pain was begging for release, but *Tatte* restrained it forcefully for *Mamme*'s sake. He wouldn't burden her with his anguish when she was barely managing to hold her own.

Miri showed up just as *Tatte* was trudging heavily down the stairs. He bent down to smile at little Chaya'la and solemnly shook Naftali's and Dovid's outstretched hands. As soon as Miri stepped through the door with little Shmuel in her arms she looked at Zalmen with a questioning gaze.

"No *shivah*," Zalmen whispered. "The Rav said we must wait until more proof is found."

Miri silently prodded the children to join their grandmother in the kitchen, while Zalmen hung back. He was concerned that *Mamme* would not take kindly to their childish chatter when she was so immersed in grief.

But he needn't have worried. *Mamme* took Chaya'la onto her lap and buried her face in the little girl's hair.

"Chaya'la *zeeskeit*," she crooned. "You came to visit *Bubbe*?"

"*Zeide* and *Bubbe* and Esther!" the child proudly proclaimed.

Mamme stiffened noticeably, but she did not say anything. Instead, she turned her attention to the two boys standing rigidly at attention behind her chair.

"Naftali! My big *cheder* boy! Come, come to *Bubbe*. And you, Dovid – you're almost taller than me already!"

The boys shyly approached their grandmother, seeking their mother's permission.

"It's alright, children," *Mamme* said with a smile. "You're allowed to talk and run and play like only you boys know how."

She leaned over and whispered conspiratorially into their ears, "Never mind all those warnings you were given. *Bubbe* is ready for your antics!"

The boys grinned cheerfully and wriggled out of their grandmother's grasp. Within moments, their exuberant cries could be heard emanating from the living room, where they were ostensibly jumping on the beautiful armchairs.

"Don't worry," *Mamme* told Miri. "Let the boys enjoy themselves. It's not every day that I get the pleasure of their company!"

The baby gurgled happily and *Mamme* leaned over to chuck him under his chin.

"You'll join your brothers when you grow up, won't you?" she asked. "Only Chaya'la will stick around to help her mother."

At the mention of her name, Chaya'la ran into the room, clutching a small, leather-bound *Tehillim* in her hands.

"Look what I found, *Bubbe!*" she cried. "It was in Esther's room, on her desk! And I reached it, all by mine self!"

Mamme reached over to take the precious *Tehillim*, but Chaya'la refused to relinquish her find.

"Give it to *Bubbe*, Chaya'la. It's...it's Esther's."

"But Esther lets me *daven* with it," the little girl protested. "She said that if I'm careful I could even hold it myself!"

"Give it to *Bubbe*," *Mamme* repeated hoarsely. Turning to Zalmen, she explained, "*Tatte* gave Esther a beautiful, new *Tehillim* before we set out on our journey. This is...this is very precious to me."

Amidst tears and tantrums, Chaya'la gave up her find and buried her face in her mother's lap.

"Her room must stay the way she left it," *Mamme* whispered. "When she gets back, Esther will want to slide back into routine without any fuss or fanfare."

"*If* she gets back," Zalmen gently amended.

"Yes. Yes, *if* she gets back. My baby daughter, Esther."

Mamme kissed the small *Tehillim* and held it lovingly in her hands. It almost seemed as though she were rocking a newborn to sleep, with the gentle movements and tender glances that mothers reserve for their sleeping children.

"It's time to go, *kinderlach*," Zalmen called into the silence. He waited for a response from the living room, and was rewarded by indignant stomping.

"So soon?! We barely arrived," Naftali protested.

"We're leaving *now*," Miri stated, brooking no argument.

Dovid peeked out from behind an armchair, but upon seeing his mother's determined look, he abandoned his post.

"Bye, *Bubbe*," he called out, rushing to be the first one at the door.

Grinning victoriously, he pulled open the wooden door and nearly collided with Maria, who was standing hesitantly at the entrance.

"Naftali!" Dovid called out. "I'll race you to the Lefkowitz's house!"

Without so much as a glance at the befuddled washer-woman, he sprinted down the steps and set off at a rapid clip before his brother even offered a response. Maria looked after him disapprovingly, and then ventured into the house she had come to know better than her own home. She fearfully glanced inside, wondering what sort of reception awaited her. Would the mistress want to be bothered with something as mundane as laundry in the face of such unspeakable tragedy?

"I...er, excuse me," she muttered, as Miri brushed past her with a bawling Chaya'la in tow.

Her mistress was sitting at the kitchen table, clutching a small book and crying. Maria watched as Zalmen whispered something and then turned to leave. His mother did not bother responding.

"I don't think it's a good time for a visit," Zalmen said, when he spotted Maria standing in the hallway.

"V-visit? No, I...Uh, laundry."

"Who's there, Zalmen?" Mrs. Hofert asked.

"It's me, Maria!"

Mrs. Hofert stood up ponderously from her seat and motioned for Maria to enter. Sighing heavily, she led the washer-woman upstairs and allowed her to fill the laundry basket with whatever she could find at a moment's notice.

"That's enough for today, Maria. Go...go on your own."

Maria couldn't look her mistress in the face. Grabbing the basket in her strong arms, she marched downstairs and out the door. Even from this safe distance, she couldn't block out the tremulous wailing that emanated from within.

"Esther! Esther'ke, I'm sorry! Don't think your *Mamme* abandoned you. I couldn't, *tuchter'l*! I tried to get up and find you but I couldn't!"

Wracking sobs wafted out into the balmy spring sunshine, highly incongruous in a world awakening from its winter slumber. Maria shuddered and gripped the basket tightly. She had been unable to decide whether it would be appropriate to show up today for her weekly chore, but an ingrained sense of responsibility had propelled her here despite the discomfort.

"Esther'ke!"

The cry reverberated in the deserted street, and Maria quickly made her escape. Clutching the laundry basket as though it was her ticket to freedom, she rushed along the Plawo streets like one possessed. Once she reached the path leading to the river, she slowed down and took a deep breath of cleansing air.

Here she would be able to relax. The solitude at the riverbank was like a tonic that calmed her spirit whenever she was experiencing turbulence or challenge.

She had forgotten about Anna; that talkative young girl who had turned the solitude of the riverbank into a long-forgotten dream.

Chapter Twenty-Two

*S*he really doesn't know, Maria realized. *She isn't pretending!*

"Do you mind...could you repeat yourself, please?" Anna asked, her mouth moving too slowly to pronounce the questions cartwheeling through her mind.

"I said that your friend Esther never came home from the trip."

"Oh. I thought you said something else. So she decided to stay on a bit longer in glittering, glamorous New York, huh?"

A touch of humor sparkled in Anna's speech and Maria looked at her in confusion. What was going on here? A moment ago, Anna had been the picture of distress, but now she was happy as a lark.

"So, tell me, when is she coming home?" Anna asked.

Maria was exasperated. How many times could she repeat the tragic news?!

"Never!" she said abruptly. "She's never coming home."

"Never?!"

"She drowned! How do you expect her to come home?!"

Anna dropped the sheet she had been scrubbing and watched with marked disinterest as it sailed to its grave in the river's murky depths.

Much the same as Esther did, apparently, she thought. A shiver of horror gripped her, and she turned away from Maria for an interminable moment.

"I don't know why you're so surprised," Maria irritably continued. "When you heard that the Titanic sank, didn't you think that Esther may have been one of the victims?"

"The Titanic – sank?!"

Maria raised her hands in defeat. She would never understand this strange girl, nor would she fathom what Esther had seen in her. With mounting distress, she rubbed and scrubbed the perfectly-clean laundry Mrs. Hofert had absentmindedly given her to rewash. If the girl wanted to be obtuse, she would have to do it by her own sweet self. Maria had had enough of her fooling around.

"I...I didn't know," Anna stammered. "I heard nothing about it! How could such a huge steamer sink? It was supposed to be unsinkable!"

Maria stubbornly maintained her silence, but she didn't count on Anna's obstinacy.

"Please, tell me more details!" the girl pleaded. "You have to understand. In my home, we don't hear any of the world news. My father allows nothing to filter in."

Maria shrugged. Let the girl get her information from somewhere else. She had a chore to complete.

"How can you do this to me?!" Anna cried. "Esther is my friend! She means so much to me! You must tell me something...anything!"

With a sigh of annoyance, the washerwoman put down her linens and turned to face the distraught young girl. A twinge of sympathy appeared in her eyes as she glanced at Anna's terrified face.

"I'll tell you everything I know," she finally conceded, "although it's not all that much. The Titanic hit an iceberg sometime Sunday night and it sank a few hours later. They tried to save as many people as they could, but there weren't enough lifeboats."

"And?"

"And nothing. Some people survived, but fifteen hundred others didn't. So now you know. Mrs. Hofert came back home yesterday...without Esther."

Anna turned on her heel and ran. She ran along the grassy riverbanks, startling the chirping birds with her frenzied flight. She ran away from the horror, but the horror chased her with a cackling laugh and black fangs. Anna covered her face in desperation, trying to block out the whirling images of Esther – good and innocent Esther – flailing helplessly in the merciless ocean waters.

It was all for naught. Esther stared at her from her watery grave, sadly pointing an accusatory finger in her direction.

"It's your fault, Anna," the ghostlike apparition intoned. "You made me go to that first Zionist meeting, and then the second. It's your fault that I got trapped in their net...and forced my parents to send me on this trip. You, Anna! You are to blame!"

"NO! Esther, I tried saving you!" Anna cried, placing her hands over her ears. "I told your parents that they should do something before it's too late...but I didn't...I didn't mean for this to happen! Esther, don't look at me like that!"

With a cry of torturous pain, Anna sat down on a severed log and buried her face in her arms. The tears, however, refused to come. Now, when she needed them to cleanse her quivering heart, they remained firmly entrenched inside. Even the relief of crying was denied her.

Sitting there amidst the chattering birds and blossoming trees, Anna determined that she would have to pay the Hoferts a visit. She had to excuse herself to the bereaved parents. Esther had meant so much to her!

How could her well-intentioned revelation have caused so much heartache?

They won't want to look at you, a small voice insisted. *You sent their daughter to her death. Do you really expect them to welcome you in with open arms?*

"But I must! I have to do this," Anna said out loud. "I need to know what Esther did during her last few days... Was she happy? Did she enjoy herself? How did she fare during those last tumultuous hours before she lost her life to a hulking iceberg?!"

Her decision was made. Later that evening, when the Plawo streets would bed down for the night, she would once again approach the stately Hofert residence. This time, however, she wouldn't have to worry about Esther's sudden appearance. No, Esther would never again show her face in the home that had seen her progress from babyhood to young adulthood.

It was the right thing to do, but that didn't make it any easier. When Anna walked stealthily through the streets under the cover of darkness, she felt herself being pursued by a slew of demons.

Murderer! Murderer, they screamed wickedly. *You sent a young girl to her death – for what?! For some foolish argument that has no bearing on your life or hers?! How could you, Anna?!*

Now, at the most inopportune time, the tears came. They flowed from her eyes, blurring her vision and streaking her cheeks. With uncontrolled force, the tears spurted out of her heart and made themselves visible to the world at large.

Anna concealed herself behind a towering tree and tried to stem the endless flow. With her eyes closed and her hands clenched, she forced herself to picture Esther's laughing eyes and smiling mouth. It hurt.

Esther, I'm sorry, she mouthed silently. *I know that*

it's too late for that, but I...I must say it. We were young and foolish, Esther. I thought that all the world was a debating arena...but see where it led you...and me. Your life was cut short and my life has been forever afflicted with a strain of guilt. For that, I'm sorry, Esther.

Gulping on the last residues of sorrow, Anna swiped her arm over her eyes and resolutely marched forward. She would visit the Hoferts even if it resulted in finger-pointing and blame-throwing. They would be right in their reactions, though it would be nearly impossible to endure.

Upon reaching her destination, Anna did not allow herself even a moment of hesitation. She walked up the steps and knocked on the door, awakening memories of a different visit...a visit that had brought her friend's life to a screeching halt. Had it only been five weeks ago? It seemed as though a lifetime had elapsed since that self-righteous revelation.

Open up! Please, Mrs. Hofert, open up the door! If I don't do this today, I don't think I'll ever muster up the courage to try again!

In answer to her fervent pleas, the door was pulled open quickly by an unknown hand. Anna fearfully stepped back, unsure of the reception she would be accorded.

"Yes?"

It was Esther's father. He peered at her questioningly and Anna quickly pushed the tasteless words out of her mouth.

"It's me again," she said. "Anna. Esther's friend from... from the river."

He continued standing at the door, neither welcoming nor evading.

"I...Can I come in?"

The man sighed heavily and opened the door a tad wider.

"If you must," he said, leaving her in the hallway while he went to summon his wife.

Anna stood statue-like on the doormat, expecting the worst. Within seconds, Esther's mother would appear and she would rightfully throw the blame directly upon Anna's narrow shoulders.

What will I tell her? Anna fretted. *Will I try to white-wash the role I played? Ridiculous. After all, I was the one who alerted them to the damage I had wrought. So...why am I here?!*

Mrs. Hofert approached the young girl thoughtfully. She wondered what could have prompted her to return, on this day of all days. Nothing could be less inviting than the home of her deceased friend. Of that, Mrs. Hofert was certain.

"Good evening, Anna," she greeted her cordially. "Won't you come in?"

No! I don't deserve to sit in your living room like an honorable guest. I'll stay here, at the entrance to your home, where I feel that I am not impinging on the sorrow I caused, Anna cried mutely.

"Come, Anna," Mrs. Hofert softly cajoled. "This is no way to conduct a decent conversation."

Powerless in the face of the woman's graciousness, Anna followed her into the living room. Memories of her previous visit assailed her, and she cringed at their jeering overtones.

"Mrs. Hofert, will you...could you possibly...forgive me?"

Anna felt those tactless tears threatening an exposure, and she harshly admonished them to stay in place. This was not the way she had envisioned tonight's meeting. Then again, nothing about the situation resembled anything she had envisioned.

"Child, I don't understand," Mrs. Hofert said gently.

"Why are you asking my forgiveness?"

"I sent Esther to her death!" Anna blurted, allowing her emotions to run the show. "I forced her to attend those Zionist meetings, and then I even told you about it. It's because of me that Esther went on that ill-fated journey!"

"How pretentious you are, Anna."

Pretentious?! Of all words to choose, this would certainly rank among the least applicable, Anna thought.

"I...I..."

Mrs. Hofert held up her hand to stem her confused babble.

"Do you truly think that Esther's fate was decided by Anna, a young girl from Plawo? Is that what you were taught to believe?"

Anna shook her head miserably.

"The One Above led Esther precisely where she was supposed to be at the moment of the crash and in the hours immediately thereafter. You, dear child, cannot take credit for that."

It was a relief. The words hung in the spacious room like a friendly, cumulus cloud on a sunny day. They wrapped their cottony arms around the two guilt-ridden conversationalists, attempting to stem their emotions with the cork of reason.

Mrs. Hofert closed her eyes and a small smile appeared on her drawn face. It was apparent that she was drawing strength from the words of comfort she had offered to her young guest.

"May I...may I ask what Esther was doing during those last few days?" Anna ventured. "I mean, only if you feel comfortable sharing with me and...and if it isn't painful to bring up the memories."

"You're a good friend, Anna," the woman declared, gazing thoughtfully at the girl sitting tensely across from her. "You truly cared about my Esther."

"I still do, Mrs. Hofert. Nothing will change that!"

"You would be surprised at what time could accomplish, child," she said. "I, too, wait for the passage of days to work their magic. But let me answer your question. You wanted to know what Esther did aboard the Titanic."

Anna nodded eagerly.

"I'll tell you the truth," Mrs. Hofert admitted quietly. "I don't really know. From the moment that the Titanic set sail, I was confined to bed with an awful case of seasickness. I could barely lift my head off the pillow, let alone venture a walk on the Titanic's enclosed promenade.

"Oh, how Esther begged me to accompany her on a short stroll. 'Just on the promenade, *Mamme,*' she urged. But I couldn't."

"So Esther sat in the cabin all day?"

"No, not my Esther. She found her way around perfectly fine without me. In fact, I believe she even struck up a friendship with a nice Jewish woman from America."

"Really? Who?" Anna asked curiously.

"Now, what was her name again? Linda...Linda... Bonair! That's it. She spent her time with Linda Bonair in the first-class compartments. I don't even know how she entertained herself those first few days."

Anna noticed Mr. Hofert standing at the entrance to the living room, listening avidly to his wife's account. It suddenly dawned on her that nobody had wanted to probe into the last few days that mother and daughter had spent together. They hadn't wanted to pick at festering wounds.

"And on that last night, Mrs. Hofert, where was Esther? I heard that...that it was pretty late at the time of the collision."

"Yes, it was close to midnight," the woman replied, her eyes closed in painful recollection. "I was lying weakly in bed, dreaming of our first moments on dry and stable ground, when several jolts pulled me out of my reverie. I noticed that Esther was not in the cabin and I vaguely remembered her saying something about a band performing upstairs."

"You think she was watching the band's performance?" Anna probed carefully.

Mrs. Hofert nodded, looking at her hands as she contemplated this fact.

"Yes, that's probably where she was. I should have gone upstairs then, to make sure that my Esther was alright...but I couldn't. Anna, do you hear me? I couldn't do it! I was bound to my bed by such indescribable weakness!"

Anna placed her hands on the older woman's trembling hands and looked deeply into her eyes.

"Didn't you tell me that the One Above is the sole conductor of our world, Mrs. Hofert? Esther was precisely where she was meant to be, and your illness was part of a plan. A master plan."

The bereaved mother leaned her head against the cushioned armchair and inhaled deeply. With a look of newfound respect, she gazed at the young girl who had finally unlocked her memories of the fateful journey.

"Things happened so quickly after that," she continued. "I felt the ship tilting dangerously and I heard water streaming in somewhere beneath my cabin. I tried getting up, but fell back repeatedly. Lack of nutrition and severe dehydration held me captive in the sinking inferno.

"A bedroom steward saved me from certain death. He pulled me up the stairs to the last collapsible boat still waiting to be lowered into the dark waters. I didn't see Esther anywhere and there was no time to look...no time to ask...I just went."

Mrs. Hofert's voice cracked dangerously, but she regained her self-control.

"The question plagues me endlessly. Was Esther somewhere in the vicinity when I was placed on the lifeboat? Could she have been saved?!"

Anna looked at her with compassion, feeling her pain and experiencing the severe twinge of regret. If only...if only...

"The officers in New York asked me questions but I didn't understand what they were saying. They were talking to the survivors, writing down information quickly and efficiently. They pointed to me and demanded something but I couldn't answer. Then I saw the lists.

"I checked all the lists, Anna. I wanted to find some proof...something to tell me what happened to my darling Esther. I needed to know how my beautiful rose had been plucked from this world...But nobody knows. Her name doesn't appear on the list of survivors, and it's not on the list of identified victims. She disappeared, my Esther'ke. Hashem took her back without leaving us even a wisp of a memory."

From the doorway, a strangled sob was heard followed by a man's heavy tread. Mr. Hofert made his way into the study, accompanied by his wife's compassionate gaze.

"It's difficult, my child," she whispered. "Esther was our whole life. She was a dream...a dream that came to an abrupt end."

Part V:
Manhattan, New York
1942

Chapter Twenty-Three

*P*eople. *So many people milling around and making a ruckus. I can't even concentrate upon the moment we've all awaited since Lisa started attending college.*

"So, Estelle, it's actually us in the parents' stand this time!"

I smiled at Barry and delighted in the proud, fatherly expression he wore as a badge of honor. Lisa had done us proud. As a graduate cum laude of Sarah Lawrence College, she had much to show for her years of toil.

Aren't you proud of your granddaughter, Tatte? I asked myself, anticipating the familiar twinge of pain the thought evoked. *She's graduating today, as a fully-accredited science major. It's quite an accomplishment, Tatte.*

And Mamme, you're certainly looking down at us from on high. Do you see the mixed feelings I'm trying to hide from everyone – myself included? I'm so proud of Lisa. She worked hard and she achieved what few others have managed to accomplish. And yet...and yet, I envisioned my daughter differently. When she was born, I promised her that she would learn to appreciate her roots. She would be a source of pride to you and Tatte.

Are you proud of Lisa, Mamme?

"I still can't fathom why Lisa didn't register at Harvard," Barry muttered. "She would have graduated at the top of the class there, too."

I sighed. This argument had been laid to rest four years previous, when Lisa began her college studies. Why did it have to rear its head at the most momentous of occasions?

"You know that Lisa was dead-set against it," I said. "She wanted to attend an all-women's college."

Barry shook his head regretfully.

"Pity. Lisa could have been a Harvard graduate. She could have done her Daddy proud."

"Don't knock her accomplishments, Barry," I pleaded. "Lisa graduated with honors, and they say that Sarah Lawrence is on par with all other colleges out there."

A slight smile adorned Barry's face as he focused his gaze on the graduates crowding the front of the room.

"My daughter, the scientist," Barry proclaimed. "Who would have believed it?"

"And don't I count?" Dave asked, smiling impishly at us.

"My son, the soldier," Barry generously added. "You'll beat those Germans with everything you've got, won't you?"

I shuddered upon hearing the easy banter. Davey was slated to go off to Europe with his platoon sometime next week, and I was downright nervous. The news filtering in from across the Atlantic was horrifying, to say the least. Thousands of dead and wounded soldiers were constantly being shipped back to the U.S. – and I was actually sending my only son into the minefield.

Since President Roosevelt had amended the STSA in December, following the attack on Pearl Harbor, every able-bodied man from eighteen to sixty-four was required to register. Millions of American citizens had registered, but not all of them were drafted. Barry had been spared the induction, thank goodness, but little Davey had already received his marching orders.

It wasn't as though I had much of a choice, but the reality of his departure was weighing heavily upon my mind. Little Davey was donning the khaki U.S. uniform and sauntering into a battle he viewed as nothing more than a training exercise. He was innocent, my little boy, and he thought that he would come back much the same as when he went off.

I knew differently. I had heard enough from my friends to know that battle-weary soldiers came back without the joie de verve that characterized our American youth. They had all stared death in the face too many times to count, and they had watched their closest comrades fall prey to enemy fire.

"Dave, you're sure you can't get an exemption?" I asked yet again.

Dave laughed.

"Of course not, Mama! And even if I could, I would never do it. I want to show those bloodthirsty German cannibals a thing or two, and then I'll be ready to come back home."

Davey is going to Europe. He will be treading the blazing soil of European countries. Who knows? Maybe his platoon will be stationed in Poland...near Plawo.

While my family celebrated Lisa's achievements, I traveled back to Plawo. I peeked into *Tatte*'s study and saw him swaying over a *sefer* with that sweet singsong chant I could never forget. Rushing along the familiar streets, I took a moment to glance at Zalmen's lively brood, before heading towards the riverbank.

There was Maria, struggling to lug a basket of wet laundry. Anna was sitting nearby, looking toward the distant horizon while she rubbed a large sheet without much enthusiasm.

They were all still there, safely ensconced in Plawo. The awful news reports were just exaggerations aimed at raising American morale.

Whom are you trying to fool, Estelle? You know good and well that your family is being hounded for the mere fact that they are Jewish. The rumors you heard about those horrid concentration camps may be exaggerated... but they're not completely false.

"Dave!" I whispered desperately. "Promise me that you'll look them up once you get there!"

"Huh?"

Dave was riveted to the goings-on up front, but I couldn't wait for a more opportune moment. I needed to procure his promise, and I needed it immediately.

"Dave, remember I told you about my elderly father living in Plawo?"

He inclined his head slightly.

"And about Zalmen and Miri and their four little children," I continued. "Actually, they're not so little anymore. Naftali and Shimon must be big, strapping young men by now. And Chaya'la – she's certainly a young, married woman with children of her own. The baby, Shmuel...I wonder whom he looks like. He must have dropped his babyhood title way before you were born, Dave."

I was rambling, but I had to get Davey to identify with my family; his family. He was going to be in close proximity to them. Maybe...maybe he would be able to save them...Maybe he would make amends for my abysmal failure aboard the Titanic.

"You told me all this yesterday," Dave said. "I'll look them up if and when I have a free moment. The army is not exactly a resort experience, Mama."

I winced at the lack of interest he unwittingly conveyed.

"Davey! This is your grandfather I'm talking about!

You hear that? Your grandfather and your uncle! Your first cousins! You can't just try...You *have* to succeed!"

"Shh...," Barry shushed us impatiently. "They're distributing the awards now and Lisa is sure to be one of the recipients."

Barry's confident prediction was right on the mark. With grace and dignity, Lisa walked towards the podium to accept the framed document her esteemed professor held aloft.

My daughter is a queen.

The thought struck me in the most vulnerable section of my heart, and I felt myself basking in the glow she exuded. Lisa carried herself with effortless dignity that bespoke refinement and inner tranquility. She was happy with herself and with the path she had chosen.

She was most definitely not a spoiled princess. I had made sure of that.

Despite the abundance of household help we were able to afford, Lisa and Davey were expected to fulfill their assigned chores every day. If they didn't make their beds in the morning, the maids were instructed to leave them unmade. When their school projects required extensive work, I made sure that they slaved over their assignments instead of copping out and asking their tutors for assistance.

I had decided early on in my married life that my children would never know the angst of being superfluous. They would be needed, as per their individual capabilities and interests.

Barry thought my methods highly ridiculous considering our social standing and financial largesse, but he gave me free rein when it came to their upbringing.

"You want them to work hard?" he asked whenever he saw Lisa clearing the table after dinner. "Isn't that why we hired another maid?"

"It's important to me," I insisted, ignoring Lisa's exaggerated groans. "Some minor household chores never hurt anyone."

Not that I would know, I acknowledged in the privacy of my mind. *I never lifted a finger when I was growing up. I was a spoiled princess...and it didn't do me any good.*

Here she was, my grown-up little girl. She walked towards us at the conclusion of the formal ceremony, blushing self-consciously as she made her way through the crowds.

I was so proud of her, I thought I would burst. Barry was smiling broadly, enjoying every moment of his daughter's glory. It was a butterfly family moment, fluttering its wings gracefully and alighting upon our hearts with ease.

"Lisa, my girl!" Barry trumpeted. "You've gone and done it!"

"Oh, Daddy! I could barely believe it myself."

Dave stood off to the side, giving his sister her well-deserved moment in the sunshine.

"You really made me proud, darling," I whispered. "I don't know what else to say. I am just so inordinately proud of you!"

At twenty-two years old, you're not the little girl you once were. Hold onto your innocence and happiness, Lisa! Don't let anyone take that away from you!

"You're making me feel inferior," Davey said, grinning widely at all and sundry. "How could my sister graduate with honors when I'm still plodding along as a lowly sophomore?"

"You'll get there, son," Barry promised. "Lisa's two years older than you. Nothing you can do about that fact."

Thank you, Dave. I knew you would be able to lighten the atmosphere.

"Auntie Melinda isn't here," Lisa suddenly remarked.

Barry theatrically put his finger to his lips and waggled his eyebrows with the comic dramatics he displayed all too seldom.

"Your graduation is a state secret," he intoned. "Aunt Melinda must remain in the dark at all costs. The Pine Acres Home wouldn't let her out after that asthmatic episode she suffered last week. I can't say I blame them. I wouldn't want to take responsibility for her fragile health, either."

"So...you didn't tell her that I'm graduating?"

"No. She would have put up an awful fuss about attending. It's better this way, dear. Believe me."

We stood around some more, a model family living the American dream. Barry's gold cuff-links glittered flamboyantly, while my exquisite get-up received its fair share of envious glances. We had made it in corporate America.

Do you see what they all see, Tatte? Your little Esther is a template for others to emulate. I have it all – good husband, successful children, palatial dwelling and loyal household help. I have everything...except my past. Only you can give that back to me, Tatte.

Savoring our last moments in the limelight, we slowly meandered through the crowded aisles. It was time to go home. Barry had to rush back to his bank, and Dave was intent on repacking his army rucksack for the umpteenth time. As for Lisa – she probably wanted nothing more than the solitude of her room and the comfort of her home.

Homey comforts, however, were not hers for the taking. As soon as we stepped through the door, Gallita thumped down the stairs in her trusty clogs and greeted us breathlessly.

"Oh, you're home! I'm so glad. So relieved. You have no idea, Madame Bonair! It's just frightening! How could they take such a little boy and send him away? I don't understand it. It's all because of those despicable Germans!"

Davey rolled his eyes theatrically and ambled towards

the kitchen. Before he could help himself to the freshly-baked pastries he'd been eyeing earlier that morning, Gallita had waylaid him.

"How can you do this to your Mama?" she asked, standing before him with her hands on her hips. "Don't you understand how difficult it will be for all of us?"

"I have no choice, Gallita," Davey replied good-naturedly. "I've told you so many times already. This is a time of war and President Roosevelt wants us all to do our share."

"But why can't you do...other things for the war. Like...like the Salvation Army. You know, gathering donations and clothing and food and sending it off..."

Davey laughed out loud and even I had a hard time controlling my mirth. The loyal maid was miffed by our amusement, and my kindhearted son hurried to soothe her ruffled feathers.

"It's alright, Gallita. You have another few days to hound me about my conscription and then I'll be out of your hair for several months...or years."

"Another few days, huh?" Gallita huffed. "Don't be so sure, David Bonair."

With a flourish, she pulled out an envelope that had been hiding in her apron pocket. It was evident that the seal had been tampered with, but I chose not to make an issue of her annoying habit.

"You read this letter, boy, and tell me how much time you have left."

Davey looked in my direction and I saw an unmistakable flash of fear glistening in his eyes. He was afraid, despite his declarations to the contrary. My little boy was going to war.

Deftly, he withdrew a solitary paper from the torn envelope and scanned its brief lines. Without glancing at the offending document, I knew. I knew that this was the dreaded notice giving Davey his date of departure.

"Tomorrow, Mama," Davey said slowly. "They want me to come to army headquarters tomorrow."

"They'll probably brief you on army protocol and then send you back home," I said, forcing my heart to believe the unrealistic.

My carefree little boy only shook his head in gentle negation of my motherly instincts.

"No, Mama. I'll be assigned to a platoon and shipped out almost immediately. I'm going to Europe."

Barry! Where are you when I need you most?! Our Davey is going to the bloody battlefields and I can't stop him!

Without so much as a word of apology, I left Davey standing near his long-awaited snack and repaired to my room. I couldn't put up a pretense of tranquility when my only son was slated to leave within twenty-four hours. The years I had spent in the most elite circles of society had schooled me to hide my emotions, but they hadn't prepared me for this most wrenching of farewells. They hadn't given me experience in dealing with a child's departure into a world gone completely insane with bloodlust and barbaric cruelty.

I pulled aside the brocade drapes to revel in the glorious sunshine spilling like molten gold over our well-manicured lawn. Nature was so beautiful and breathtakingly simple when left to its own devices. Why did man think it important to take matters into his own hands? Why were the nations of the world snuffing out lives and pitting technology against humanity instead of building their futures?

Acting on impulse, I pulled the drapes back in place in an attempt to conceal the annoying scene of serenity. It didn't seem fair that the birds were privy to more contentment than I, the belle of every American ball.

Davey is going to Europe, Estelle, I told myself. *This is your opportunity! Tatte didn't want you back...but by now he certainly changed his mind. After all, he's an elderly man hitting the eighty mark! Don't you think he regrets the chasm?*

I uncapped the monogrammed pen Barry had recently bought for no occasion at all, and proceeded to jot down names and addresses on a small sheet of paper.

Tatte. Zalmen. Miri. Their children – Naftali, Dovid, Chaya'la and Shmuel. Other children, whose names I don't know. Menachem, living in Krakow. His wife, Devorah. Their children...their children.

Why can't I remember their names?! Menachem already had five children when I departed on the Titanic. Only boys, if my memory doesn't deceive me. They're my nephews, for goodness sake, and I can't even name them!

Anna.

Anna?! Do I really expect Davey to find a lone Polish woman out in the Plawo countryside?

I resisted the urge to cross her name off the list. Anna would remain there, for all that was worth. Shakily, I reached into the uppermost shelf of my armoire and pulled out two letters bearing multi-hued stamps and markings. The envelopes were becoming ragged at the corners, but they were mine.

"Dave!" I called out, suddenly impatient. "David Bonair!"

I hurried down the stairwell and I wasn't much surprised to see Dave lounging at the kitchen table with a pile of pastries stacked before him. That boy could eat in one sitting what most people would consume in several days.

"Dave, this is an important list," I said. "You have to take this along when you join the army."

"Sure, Mom. I'll take it."

"No, no. You can't just take it. You must memorize

the information and...and do something about it!"

Dave took the paper from my hands and started reading my frenzied scrawl aloud.

Shimon Hofert, Main Street, Plawo. Zalmen –

"Mom, what exactly is this gibberish supposed to mean? Is it some sort of code?"

"David!" I cried, horrified at the extent of his ignorance. "Those are your relatives! You can't – you can't call them a code!"

He leaned forward earnestly and pushed aside his overloaded plate.

"Tell me everything, Mom," he pleaded. "You can't expect me to know these...these people, if you never bother describing them."

Dave was right. I had refrained from sharing my most cherished memories with the children because I couldn't explain the reason for our separation. There was no way I could tell them that I had caused my mother's death and incurred my father's justified wrath.

"I don't really know how to begin," I admitted. "Plawo is this beautiful, pastoral town. It's...very pure. You know what I mean? It's serene and...and comforting."

Dave looked at me intently, but I detected a glimmer of impatience in his eyes. He wanted details...not emotions.

"We sometimes referred to Plawo as a carousel. You know, those things that go round and round..."

"I know what a carousel is, Mom!"

"Right. Of course. Plawo is a round little town, bordering River San. And...and it's my home, Davey. My home."

I couldn't look at my earnest young son, with his cropped haircut and designer shirt. I couldn't tear my eyes away from the winding streets of my childhood.

"Mom, you wanted to tell me about your family," Dave gently prodded.

"My father, Shimon Hofert, is an elderly man by now. He must be close to eighty years old, but I'm sure that he maintained his dignity which always set him a cut above the rest. Zalmen, my brother – your uncle, Dave – is a devout Jew with a wry sense of humor. And his wife, Miri - "

It was too much. I couldn't describe people I hadn't seen in three decades and the feeling of absolute disconnection was impossible to bear. I blocked them all out – *Tatte,* Menachem, Zalmen, Miri, and even Dave. For a long ten minutes, I allowed myself the luxury of tears. My immaculate kitchen had never seen its mistress breaking down – but today was different. Today I was trying to give Davey back his birthright, and I was failing miserably.

"Mom, it's alright," my son said, obviously frightened. "I'll look them up for you. I gather that I'm looking for religious Jews with the sideburns and everything else."

I nodded.

"I'll do everything I can to bring them back here, Mom. Please, just stop crying. If I get anywhere near this area of Pla–whatever, I'll try to save them."

I nodded once again, only slightly aware of how unreasonable my request really was. Dave would try. He would go back to Plawo and he would look up *Tatte* and bring him back to America. He would save them all from those terrible Germans.

"What are those?" Davey asked curiously, pointing at the two envelopes still clutched between my fingers.

"These? Oh, nothing much. They're letters I once wrote."

Davey laughed.

"You wrote them but never bothered posting them, Mom? That sounds like something I would do!"

"I sent them out," I corrected him, "but they were returned to me."

Davey looked at the letters and laughed yet again.

"Well, of course, Mom!" he chortled. "How do you expect the postmasters to know where Plawo is located?!"

I looked down at the addresses I had so carefully penned when hope had still fluttered merrily in my heart.

"Mom, when you send a letter overseas, you have to indicate its destination! Otherwise, the envelope is shuttled around the U.S. until it's returned to its sender."

Davey stood up, taking his plate along with him. I didn't bother calling him back, even though I was a stickler for keeping food in the kitchen...and not in the bedrooms, where my darling son was headed at that very moment. I heard him murmuring to himself lightly, probably rehashing the absolute naïveté of his clueless Mom.

I looked down at the cream-colored envelopes. Was Davey right? Had my letters never even reached their destination?

Tatte! Is it possible? I spent all these years wallowing in self-pity because my own father had rejected me outright. Maybe...maybe it wasn't so.

Then again, maybe Davey's hypothesis is totally off the mark. It stands to reason that a postman seeing the inscription 'Plawo' would understand that it's an address overseas.

Tell me, Tatte! Did you reject me?!

Do you miss your Esther'ke?

Chapter Twenty-Four

*H*is writing is that of an old man.

That was the first thought that crossed my mind after reading Dave's missive from Europe. He was a soldier, fighting for his life in the European battlefield. Over the years, I had gotten used to the chatty and fluffy-aired letters Dave sent from college. Nothing had prepared me for the severity and earnestness that peeked through every word he had carefully penned during one of his rare moments alone.

Then again, he had never stared death in the face nor scrutinized its ugly countenance. In his coddled American childhood, the most urgent battles he had fought had been staged in Speyer School's baseball courts.

They're killing them...murdering them in cold blood. It's not them, Mom. It's us, Davey wrote. *They're killing us – the Jews! And do you know why? For no other reason than the fact that they were born to Jewish parents. Little children, Mom. Innocent little faces peek out of cattle-car windows...and there's nothing we can do about it.*

Lisa! All those rumors you refused to believe...they're all true. They really do have huge ovens – crematoriums, they're called – to burn the Jews. Can you imagine? Which human being could throw wailing infants into a burning oven?! They're not human, Mom! They're monstrous, barbaric animals!

We're trying to push the Germans back into their own territory, but they're an obstinate lot. Until we get rid of them, we cannot penetrate those horrific camps where Jews are being killed even as I write.

Mom! Do something! Don't you realize that it might be your family looking out mournfully as the trains take them to their final destination?! I don't know what happened between you, Mom, but this is the end! The Germans want to rid the world of every last Jew. That includes us all, Daddy, even you!

I keep on repeating those words you always say, Mom. For some reason I cannot begin to fathom, they give me strength to go on. Hashem is good and all He does is good.

The letter ended abruptly, as though Davey had lost his stamina after pouring his emotions onto the crumpled paper. Methodically, I folded the paper, one crease after another, and slipped it back into the envelope. Barry would be interested in hearing news from the front...although I wasn't sure how he would react to the horrific details.

Where was Barry, anyway?

It's Monday and J.P. Morgan is swamped with its usual post-weekend business. Barry won't come home until early evening. Lisa is still at her interview. I can't stay here alone, in this big, empty house – just me and the horrific letter!

Desperately, I foraged around for a solution and found one named Melinda. I hadn't visited her since the previous week and she would be a wonderful distraction until the others returned. After she had moved into the Pine Acres Home, I had promised to visit her at least twice a week. It was shameful how quickly good intentions could disintegrate.

I donned one of the ostentatious shawls Melinda had

purchased for me, knowing that she would derive pleasure from seeing it wrapped around my shoulders. Whispering 'goodbye' to the bare rooms and the European ghosts occupying my house, I opened the door and stepped out. It was just a short walk to the Pine Acres Home, and I covered the distance in record time.

"Estelle!" Melinda exclaimed as soon as I entered the room. "Maybe you could help me! This nurse is fussing around and she is making me uncomfortable. I don't need her here."

Oh no. It's one of those days again. When Melinda gets into her cantankerous states, nothing can calm her down.

"A new nurse they assigned me!" she fumed. "A new nurse who just stepped off the boat! What kind of treatment is that, Estelle? You would think I was living here as a charity case instead of funding most of the building!"

The nurse was methodically changing the bed linens, ignoring the woman's tirade. From the rapid twitching of her eyes, I realized that she understood every word being said.

"I'm sorry," I whispered to her. "My aunt gets that way sometimes, and nobody is immune to her furious complaints. Believe me, I've been on the receiving end more times than I'd care to remember."

The new nurse looked at me strangely, her deep-blue eyes scrutinizing my face. I felt decidedly uncomfortable, but she quickly averted her gaze and nodded in appreciation.

"Thank you," she said simply.

"What are you whispering behind my back?" Melinda demanded. "Estelle, now that you finally remember to visit me, don't fritter away your time with that new nurse. New nurse, indeed. Doesn't the administration understand that a woman at my age and stage cannot take changes easily?! What else am I paying for, if not some decent service?!"

The nurse eyed me sympathetically and quickly made

her escape. As soon as the door closed, Melinda winked. I wasn't sure if I had seen that mischievous glint, but her burst of muted laughter removed all doubt.

"Sure got rid of that one, didn't I?" she asked gleefully. "I don't know how quickly she'll return to this room!"

"That wasn't nice," I reprimanded, although I couldn't restrain the smile that insisted on ruining my admonition. Aunt Melinda was just incorrigible.

"At my age, dearie, you could forget about bothersome niceties and courtesies. I am what I am, and everyone else can very well dance to my tune."

You've been saying that all your life, Melinda, though not in so many words.

"Tell me what's doing on your end, Estelle," she demanded.

"Nothing much. Lisa's still searching for her perfect, plum job and I told you that Davey's serving in the army..."

My voice trailed off at the mention of his name. Davey, my little boy, was witnessing horrors that I couldn't begin to contemplate. He was seeing the annihilation of our nation first-hand. My family was being led to –

"Estelle! What's gotten into you?!"

"Wh – It's my *Tatte*," I blurted helplessly. "My *Tatte* is...being killed!"

"What are you talking nonsense, my girl?" Melinda retorted. "You haven't heard from your father in thirty years. I should know!"

"B-but Davey is there now, in Europe. He sent me a letter describing the horrors being perpetrated against them...against us...against my family!"

"Oh, you mean the Germans," she said.

"My *Tatte* is an old man, Melinda! What do they want from an elderly man who never hurt anyone?! And Zalmen is too young to die. His beautiful children are so innocent...so pure. They can't, Melinda!"

She stared back at me, speechless. It had been a long time since I had broken down in her presence. I realized that my emotional outburst was making her uncomfortable, but I couldn't stop. It was like trying to hold up the Niagara Falls with one hand.

"So many years," I lamented. "So many wasted years."

Melinda didn't respond. I thought she would remind me about the letters that my father and brother had sent back unopened, but she maintained an uneasy silence.

"I think...I think they never got my letters," I explained, although she hadn't mentioned them. "*Tatte* doesn't even know that I tried to contact him."

Melinda said nothing. Her fingers tapped a staccato beat on the armrest of her chair, while her eyes roamed around the luxurious suite she had ordered custom-made to her specifications. Several minutes elapsed, and neither of us tampered with the prevailing silence.

"Now they're all being targeted by the Germans," I finally said, modulating my voice to appear controlled. "*Tatte*, my brothers, my sisters-in-law...everyone is in the line of fire."

"Have you also heard those ridiculous rumors about wholesale murder going on there in Europe?"

"Those aren't rumors, Melinda!" I cried. "Davey said so. He insists that Jews are being burned in ovens!"

"I don't know," she said. "It doesn't sound right. Do you think the Germans would really stoop to such barbaric means? What do they have against innocent civilians, anyway?"

"They're Jewish, Melinda. That's their crime."

"This war-talk is depressing me," she petulantly exclaimed. "Tell me about your life, Estelle. Did you do anything interesting recently?"

I groaned. Melinda had always lived precariously through me, but the situation had been aggravated when she moved into Pine Acres. Now that she was faced with monotonous days running viscously into each other without so much as a gossiping neighbor to ease the boredom, I was responsible for providing entertainment.

Every ball I attended was discussed in minute detail, as were the tea parties and shopping expeditions. Melinda wanted to know what I purchased, how much I paid for it, where I bought it and why I needed it. After hearing all the details, she invariably proved that I could have gotten a better deal at a different department store.

She saved your life, I berated myself. *Don't you dare forget that, Estelle. The least you can do for her is offer some fascinating tidbits of conversation.*

I tried. I really did. That day, however, my best attempts fizzled out into nothingness. Melinda was preoccupied with some weighty matters that she wasn't inclined to share with me.

"So Lisa is going for another interview today," I said. "I hope she gets the job she's pining for. It's so hard to stand on the sidelines while she traipses from one place to another, seeking the position of her dreams."

"She's spoiled, Estelle," Melinda muttered. "In my days, girls took the first job they were offered. How do you think I ended up as a musical director in The Opera House? I didn't land the job as a young, twenty-year-old whippersnapper!"

"How indeed?" I asked, sensing an opening to a lengthy discussion.

"I worked my way up! I worked, Estelle. Today's youth doesn't know what that word means!"

Dead-end. I've only been here for an hour and it would be impolite to leave at this point.

"You did your share later on," Melinda continued.

"I – what?"

"At one point my job was on the line, Estelle. It was

before Bill and I left to Europe on that ill-fated journey."

"But you kept your job for many years thereafter," I protested.

"It was all your credit, my dear," Melinda said. "When you finally agreed to audition for the opera, the producers went wild. They couldn't thank me enough for the star I had whisked out of thin air, and my career stabilized. I was given priority, because of your remarkable talent. By the time you got married, I was once again firmly ensconced as musical director at the Opera House."

Oh.

"And then you threw it all away, Estelle. I never understood what prompted you to drop a promising career mid-stream!"

"Well, after I got married there was simply no point," I explained for the umpteenth time. "Barry was doing extremely well at the bank and our finances did not need my measly opera contributions."

"The payments were not measly by any standard," she huffed. "And it's just an excuse, Estelle."

"Truthfully, it was really *Tatte* who convinced me to drop the performing arts," I said impetuously.

Melinda glared at me.

"Leave your father out of this," she hissed. "There was no communication between the two of you. He doesn't even know you exist!"

She was furious, leaving me no choice but to explain my enigmatic words.

"Melinda, I'm sorry. I wasn't trying to fool you. It's just that I saw *Tatte*'s disapproving eyes at every performance and...and I couldn't bear his disappointment. I *had* to give it up."

What a day. It started with Dave's disturbing letter and it's ending with a full-blown argument way out of my league. I wonder what the evening will bring...

"You're making me tired," Melinda complained. "I think I'll rest now. Summon one of the nurses to help me into bed."

I rushed to comply, breathing a silent sigh of relief at the abrupt dismissal.

"And don't allow that new one to enter my room!" she yelled after me. "I've had enough of her doting services!"

The new nurse was standing just outside the door, poised to knock. A streak of mischief urged me to allow her inside, but I suppressed it with force. Melinda was in an explosive mood, and it wasn't fair to put the inexperienced staff member directly in the line of fire.

"Uh, I don't think you should go that way," I said hesitantly.

The nurse turned towards me, her mouth twitching in what looked like a suppressed smile.

"And why ever not?" she asked, her voice soft and gentle like rolling waves at sea.

"Melinda is not...up to it today," I stammered. "She really prefers to be serviced by someone familiar."

Why am I so self-conscious in her presence? She's just a nurse! It doesn't befit someone of my stature to be intimidated by a new immigrant like her!

"You would be surprised," she said, her laughter tinkling and shimmering in the empty corridor. "She'll learn to get along with me, for better or for worse."

I glanced at the woman standing before me, trying to place her in an age bracket. She appeared young and sprightly, but her eyes betrayed the many years that hid beneath her youthful veneer.

"Consider yourself warned," I said, shrugging in defeat.

The nurse's tinkling laughter sounded once again. It accompanied me as I walked home, granting me a strange feeling of security and contentment.

Chapter Twenty-Five

*I*t was a rare moment of quiet. Barry was sitting in his favorite armchair, his arms folded behind his head and his eyes closed in languid contentment.

"They complained about Lisa today," he said, drawing the words out with effort. "Bernard Hackney told me that she's ruining the atmosphere."

"Hackney...Isn't he the big name there at the Lab?"

"Uh huh. He's the sole proprietor."

"Barry, why would someone complain about Lisa? She's working there for two weeks already and she must be their greatest asset!"

I knew that I sounded like an overprotective mother hen sheltering her offspring, but I couldn't help it. Lisa was a hard-working individual. With her natural acumen and sharp intelligence, I had no doubt that she was making her mark in the world of science. What was all this nonsense about complaints and atmosphere?

"Of course he's not complaining about her job performance," Barry confirmed. "You should have heard how he lauded her abilities and powers of concentration!"

He fell silent, savoring the moment of fatherly pride he had come to expect from his eldest child.

"But," I prompted.

"But Lisa is being...what was the word he used? She's being...stand-offish. That's it. Hackney says that she keeps to herself and doesn't join in the office chatter."

Having never worked a day in my life, I couldn't peg this behavior in any way. Was it absolutely unheard of for an employee to keep to herself? Was this a breach of office etiquette?

"Why, she didn't even want to join them in their pre-holiday bash!" Barry continued. "Hackney says that this bash is the highlight of the employees' year. Lisa, apparently, thinks otherwise."

Good for you, darling! I didn't realize what you would be dealing with in the great, big world, but you're managing perfectly fine on your own. I'm proud of you.

I didn't dare voice my thoughts aloud because Barry was sure to shoot them down with complaints about my old-fashioned child rearing and outdated ideas of propriety.

"You know what I told him, Estelle?"

I raised my eyes to see what, precisely, was making him so jovial. His beloved daughter had just been criticized by an esteemed researcher, and he didn't seem in the least perturbed.

"I told him that Lisa is Jewish. He has to give her some space and let her create a niche for herself, because she's Jewish. And her mother is Jewish...very Jewish."

"And her father?" I dared to ask.

"Oh, her father's as Jewish as one can get," Barry laughed. "But I meant Jewish in a...different kind of way. You know what I mean?"

No, I wasn't sure what he was referring to.

"I mean that you taught them how to be Jewish like... like European Jewish. Lisa is just acting on the upbringing you gave her, Estelle."

Barry didn't seem upset at the startling revelation. In fact, I would even venture to guess that he was proud of the way his daughter maintained her dignity despite the prevailing sense of informality.

"I fought you tooth and nail, Estelle," he said, grinning ruefully. "But something about your convictions filtered through to them."

"Er...Barry..."

Barry held up his hand theatrically.

"Oh, no you don't!" he said quickly. "Don't start again. We are not going to change anything in this house, Estelle. I need my weekends and my food and my comforts... Don't think I'm giving in just because I approve of our children's refinement."

How did he know precisely what I was getting at? At least the children identify with their heritage. Just think – Davey's Yiddishe neshama is being awakened by the horrors in Europe and Lisa is maintaining her dignity despite the awful American freedoms. Tatte would be horrified if he set eyes on them...but...Hashem knows just how much it took to reach this point.

I wonder what Mamme would say. She was always adept at looking past outer appearances and discerning the kernel of truth concealed within. She would have loved Lisa. They're so alike...

"So, she's reasonably happy," Barry was saying.

"Why shouldn't she be?" I replied, trying to cover up my lapse in attention. "She got herself a plum job with more benefits than nearly anyone else we know."

"Good evening, Madame Bonair," Barry laughed. "I'm talking about Melinda. I closed the previous topic while you were daydreaming about something very compelling."

I had the grace to look apologetic, though this happened often enough when I was conversing with Barry.

"I was talking about Melinda," he explained. "She seems happier lately. That new nurse is doing her a world of good."

"Who would have believed it? I can still hear Melinda's vociferous complaints ringing in my ears. She was so annoyed that the administration had foisted an inexperienced staff member on their most respectable client!"

"I don't know how they got from there to here," Barry said, "but they're getting along famously now. You should have heard the conversation I was privy to the last time I visited."

This is going to be a long one. When Barry gets into his storytelling mode, he tends to get lost in the echoes of his own voice.

Helping myself to a cup and saucer from the coffee table, I settled down for a lengthy discourse. It was a good thing Gallita had prepared some refreshments before repairing for the night.

"I was there two days ago," Barry said. "It was a quiet day at the bank and I grabbed the opportunity to wriggle myself back into Melinda's good graces.

"When I got there, she was engrossed in conversation with that new nurse. Annie, I think she called her. Melinda waved to me as I walked into the room and then – wonder of wonders – she turned right back to her companion and continued talking! I was flabbergasted...and slightly annoyed. Here I had given up my extended lunch break for my poor aunt's sake, and all she could spare was a hand-wave and a small smile."

"Barry, you know she thinks the world of you," I interjected. "She's just excited about her new acquaintance."

"It's not a mere acquaintance, Estelle. Melinda was bombarding the nurse with details of her life that even I had never heard before!"

He looked at me strangely, gauging my reaction.

"This pertains more to you than to me, Estelle. Our dear aunt was discussing her Titanic experience and the events that led up to your adoption."

"I was never adopted, Barry."

"Whatever. Official or unofficial, you became a Bonair because of Melinda's...schemes. I'm not sure if I should be repeating this," Barry admitted, crossing his legs first one way and then the other. "Melinda must be losing her famous iron grip if she allowed these tidbits to slip out in my presence."

The revelations of the past few weeks made me suspect that Melinda was not the guardian in angel's robes that I had always thought her to be. And yet...I wasn't ready to give up on the only mother figure I had merited in my adult years. Melinda had been my anchor for so many excruciating years.

Barry forged ahead.

"I'll repeat her words as accurately as I can, Estelle," he said.

*   *   *

"It was on the Titanic that I heard her sing for the first time," Melinda said. "That voice...it was otherworldly. I couldn't understand the words she was singing, but the voice captured me from the very first moment. She was a sweet young girl, innocent and untarnished by the world at large. Her mother was awfully seasick right from the start and I took her under my wing."

"This is your niece you're talking about, correct?" the nurse interjected.

"Niece, daughter...call her whatever you want. In actuality, we weren't blood relations at all. But it never mattered. Estelle is mine."

"Oh. I see," she said slowly.

"Anyway, I tried getting her to sing in public but she was so stubborn. You have no idea how stubborn some people can be! Remember I told you about my wobbling career? I thought Estelle would be the answer...but her obstinacy told me that I would have to seek a solution elsewhere.

"On the night of the crash, everything changed. I forced Estelle to get into the lifeboat, even though she had this ridiculous notion of saving her mother. I did it for her...only for her. At the time, I wasn't thinking of myself. I just knew that if Estelle would try to find her mother, they would both perish.

"Estelle was saved. When we arrived in America, our names were put on a list and I figured that if her mother survived, she would look us up. She didn't."

"That's queer," the nurse said.

"Why is that queer? Her mother died and dead people can't search for their daughters."

The nurse nodded in understanding.

"I got Estelle to attend school and to audition at the opera," Melinda continued. "She saved my career and I will always be grateful for that. Never mind that she abandoned the opera as soon as she married him," she concluded, pointing in my direction. "You wouldn't believe how strongly she held onto her family's traditions. She obviously couldn't keep them all, but she insisted that her children would be different. They would be a source of pride to her...parents."

"I don't understand," the nurse said. "Didn't your niece have any other family members? Why did she opt to stay with you?"

"Of course she had – or has – family, somewhere in Europe," Melinda retorted. "But she never...uh, she never made contact with them."

"She never tried to reach them?!" the nurse asked in disbelief.

"She did, maybe," Melinda stammered. "It was something with the letters and the addresses...I wasn't sure if it was written correctly and I didn't really bother looking because...because I figured that maybe it would be better if...if she stays with me."

The nurse was horrified, but Melinda quickly jumped in to whitewash her words.

"It's not like I tried to prevent her from contacting them," she asserted.

"You just didn't help her," the nurse said matter-of-factly.

"Correct."

"And they didn't check the lists to see whether she was listed as a survivor?"

"Do I know what they did?" Melinda impatiently replied. "I don't know these people! I don't know what they tried! I'm pretty sure her name was on the list...After all, I registered her at the docks..."

Melinda's voice trailed off and it was obvious that she had just remembered a significant detail.

"You registered her," the nurse prompted.

"Yes, yes I did. The officer changed her name from Esther to Estelle for some reason, but that wouldn't stop them from finding her, would it?"

"No, it wouldn't," said the loyal nurse.

"I...don't remember clearly," Melinda said with a wavering voice. "Did I say Esther? Maybe Estelle? No, it was definitely the officer's revision. And the last name..."

At this point, Melinda fell silent and no amount of prodding could convince her to resume. She had just one line to add; a line that concealed more than it revealed.

"That was a mistake. It was an honest-to-goodness mistake and by the time I realized, it was too late to turn back. Her name was written on the list...under the letter B. Bonair."

*　　*　　*

"The nurse looked at Melinda and suggested that she take a nap. Melinda happily agreed, ignoring my presence," Barry said. "I was hurt, Estelle. I was hurt for your sake. I just left Melinda to her beauty sleep and stalked out of the room."

I sat there, cradling my cup in both hands, trying to feel some of the indignation Barry was professing. All I felt was a devastating load of emptiness. My heart was emptied out, beating mindlessly on thin air. My veins and sinews all seemed to contract, as though they wanted to shut out the unwanted information and protect me from its repercussions.

In actuality, nothing earth-shattering had been revealed. Since Dave had pointed out my naïve mistake, I had suspected Melinda of...something. I just wasn't sure what precisely she could have done to hinder my efforts.

She's not a bad person, I told myself. *Melinda lost herself in the heat of the moment. At the docks, I believe that she listed me as a Bonair by mistake. Simply because that's what came naturally to her.*

And when she ignored my futile attempts at letter-writing, she surely struggled with her conscience. She needed me to save her career but she couldn't deny me the right to a family.

I saved her career...and I lost my family. Melinda did her best to make it up to me. I see that now. She arranged that I should marry Barry, her successful and beloved nephew, so that I would never again feel need or want.

But I need, Melinda. I need my family. I need the purity and beauty of my childhood. I need so much that you can never give me.

"Let's think of it this way," Barry gently interrupted my ruminations. "Had you returned to Europe, Estelle, who knows what would have happened to you during this awful war! Melinda saved your life on the Titanic, without any ulterior motives. At that point, at least."

I didn't want to hear his logical explanations. I wanted to wallow in self-pity and regret. I wanted to dream of what could have been, if only Melinda hadn't placed her needs squarely above my own.

"Hashem is good," Barry continued slowly. "All He does is good."

Don't say that now! I wanted to scream. *Don't tell me about how good this is…when it could have easily been avoided.*

"You can't pick and choose, Estelle," he persisted. "Didn't you tell me that when the stock market crashed on that Black Tuesday, so many years ago? I told you that I would thank Him when things worked out, but you said it's hypocritical. You told me that we must thank Him at all times, even when we don't necessarily see how something is for our benefit."

I shrugged my shoulders, once again a young girl balking at her brother's instructions and advice. It was easy for Barry to be so cheery and faithful. He hadn't lost his entire family to the machinations of a selfish woman.

Don't call her that, Estelle, I reprimanded myself. *Melinda gave you everything she could here in America. She made mistakes. Didn't you make some errors of your own, back in Plawo? Don't focus on hers while conveniently ignoring your own!*

"Hashem is good," Barry repeated.

It was so pleasant to hear those words coming from my husband's mouth. I had repeated them endlessly throughout the years, and the children had picked them up by osmosis. Barry, however, had resisted their influence. This was the first time he gave me the pleasure of verbalizing what I knew he really believed.

"So tell me," I whispered. "What's so good about all this? Melinda fooled me! She led me to believe that *Tatte* had rejected me...that he couldn't find it in his heart to forgive his only daughter. She prevented them from finding me, Barry!"

"She saved your life," Barry said futilely.

"For that one moment of self-sacrifice, do I really owe her a lifetime of gratitude?!"

"She's saving your life right now, as we speak," he continued.

"What are you talking about?"

"Listen carefully, Estelle. You know what's going on in Europe right now. Towns are being razed to the ground. Fields are being trampled and set on fire. And the Jews – who can even think of what they're going through? Davey's descriptions don't even describe the full extent of horror and persecution they're being dealt."

I nodded. We had discussed all this in detail over the past few weeks. What had prompted Barry to bring up the topic again?

"You could have been there, Estelle," he said with a steely edge to his voice. "Had you gone back to your father, who knows where you would be now? Who knows whether...whether you would still be alive?!"

I shuddered. Barry was right. Had I returned to Plawo, I would be just another Jewish number waiting to be processed by the German death machine.

"It doesn't justify Melinda's mistakes in the least bit," Barry continued. "But your life has been saved, Estelle. Hashem is good and all He does is good."

Could I truly accept that? Hashem, You know how difficult these years have been for me. I was fighting a losing battle against America's free-thinking society. So many mitzvos fell to the wayside because I just couldn't do everything! My children are...Americans. They're wonderful, refined children but they would be an embarrassment to Tatte and Mamme. I tried, Tatte in Himmel! You led Me-

linda to keep me here by force and You know that I would have done anything in my power to return home...to return to You. But all You do is good, Hashem.

Melinda was just a messenger. I know that I should forgive her.

"But I can't!" I blurted.

"Can't what?"

"I can't forgive her! She altered my life to suit her own!"

"It will take time, Estelle," Barry said. "I think that Melinda is beginning to understand just how deeply she wronged you. Her conversations with that new nurse are bringing up long-forgotten memories."

"It will take time," I agreed. "For now, I'll have to continue acting the part of the dedicated niece who obediently visits her aunt every few days."

Barry didn't respond. He understood my feelings but there was nothing he could do to alleviate them. This was something I would have to untangle on my own.

"I think I'll bring her a gift," I murmured thoughtfully.

"You don't have to go that far," Barry objected. "Just be nice and polite. Things will straighten out on their own. You'll see."

I laughed, enjoying the sensation of my lips turning upwards to smile at the world.

"Not a gift for Melinda!" I exclaimed. "Not yet, anyway. I was thinking of buying the nurse a gift. She's working wonders on your aunt and it's only proper that I acknowledge her efforts. I also want to thank her for...for giving me back my family."

Barry raised his eyebrows but wisely remained silent. I didn't feel like explaining my convoluted emotions. This nurse had gotten Melinda to admit how she had foiled my efforts at reunion and how she had stymied *Tatte* as well. They didn't reject me.

I was still their beloved Esther'ke, as I had always been.

"I think the nurse is approximately my age," I continued. "What would a fifty-year-old woman appreciate?"

Barry tuned out. He never enjoyed giving his opinions on matters completely unrelated to him.

"I wonder if she has a family. It makes a difference, Barry. If she has a husband and children, she would appreciate something warm and homey. Then again, if she's alone in the world, she would probably prefer something personal. An accessory, or a piece of jewelry.

"She doesn't strike me as a jewelry-person," I quickly amended. "But maybe I could find a…a clock for her mantelpiece."

"That's assuming she has one," Barry interjected.

"I don't know," I finally conceded. "Melinda is much better at these things than I am."

I was surprised at how quickly Melinda's name slipped out of my mouth. Viewing her simply as a messenger who fulfilled Hashem's plan made it easier to avoid the cycle of anger, rancor and regret.

"I think I'll just get her a gift card," I concluded.

Barry nodded perfunctorily, engrossed in the newspaper. Our conversation had derailed his nightly routine, and he skimmed the pages quickly before calling it a night.

"Do you want me to deliver the gift?" he asked considerately.

"I'll do it," I said quickly. "It would be best if I face Melinda as soon as possible instead of stewing in anger for the foreseeable future."

Chapter Twenty-Six

I had never chosen a gift so randomly and haphazardly. After walking into Macy's Department Store and greeting the sales ladies courteously, I had wandered from one aisle to the next, but nothing struck my fancy. The nurse was an unknown entity. I had no idea what her life outside of the Pine Acres Home's walls was like.

I finally settled on an elegant set of teacups and saucers. Everyone could get some use out of them, I figured. Never mind the fact that it would only interest one who entertains guests in her home. If the nurse never did any entertaining, she could always display it on her mantelpiece as an acquisition of beauty.

To cover my bases, I made sure that the gift could be exchanged if need be. The gracious cashier assured me that anything Madame Bonair purchased would be taken back, no questions asked.

Money certainly wielded its power in these upper-class haunts.

Now, as I tentatively approached Pine Acres, the gift felt exceptionally clumsy in my hands. What had I been thinking? The nurse would take one look at my pretentious offering and inwardly thumb her nose at the rich

American's ridiculous taste. Maybe it would be wiser to conceal the box behind some shrubbery before venturing inside.

"Estelle!" Melinda called out. "Estelle, I'm over here."

So much for any plans of concealment. I turned towards Melinda, who was sitting under a beautiful weeping willow. She looked like a queen, reigning in great splendor over a profusion of servants.

"Oh, hello," I murmured.

Act natural, Estelle! This is the drama of a lifetime. You know that Melinda wronged you, but petulance and revenge won't get you anywhere. Smile to the lonely old woman.

So I smiled. I smiled and grinned until I thought my face would remain plastered in that ludicrous contortion. Melinda did not seem to notice my discomfort. She had probably forgotten that Barry had overheard her revealing conversation.

"How is everything? You heard any news from that son of yours?"

"Dave writes very infrequently. The army doesn't quite offer a vacation package," I said stiffly.

"And Lisa – how is she doing?"

"Good. She's enjoying her job and her employers are satisfied."

Melinda nodded and glanced around for something to discuss. Despite my good intentions, I couldn't bring myself to fritter away the next few hours with empty chitchat. It felt as if I would be betraying *Tatte* by enjoying the company of the woman who had separated us for good.

"You didn't ask how my life here is going," Melinda complained.

"I'm asking now," I said patiently.

Melinda looked away, obviously miffed by my disinterest. It took only a moment, however, for the thunderclouds to clear and for her eyes to regain their spark of life.

"How are you today, my dear Melinda?"

It was the new nurse. She had this uncanny sense of knowing when her presence was needed most. With admiration bordering on envy, I watched her gentle interactions that immediately soothed my crotchety old guardian.

"I'm alright," Melinda smiled. "I even merited a visitor on this lovely morning."

The nurse turned in my direction and a flash of recognition indicated that she remembered me.

"This must be your niece," she said softly. "The niece whom you saved while the Titanic was going under."

Melinda shifted in her seat, but the nurse took no notice.

"I'm not her niece," I pointed out stiffly. "It's just...a...a figure of speech."

"Oh, I know that. That's just the way Melinda refers to you."

The nurse eyed me intently, and I fought to keep my gaze steady. Without much forethought, I extended the gift I had brought along.

"It's for you...uh...I'm sorry. I don't know your name."

She ignored my implied question and wordlessly accepted the gift.

"Is it your birthday?" Melinda asked, desperate to be included in a drama that even I couldn't really understand.

"No, it's not," the nurse replied. "Estelle should know that."

I glanced at her sharply. Those deep-blue eyes stared into my own, willing me to grasp the unspoken. What was it about her that made me so...uncomfortable? There was a certain familiarity that I couldn't place; a snippet of memory that her presence evoked.

"Shouldn't you know when my birthday is, Estelle?"

"I...I assure you that I don't," I said nervously. "Did... is there any reason why you think I should?"

"I believe we've discussed this in the past."

This was too much. I hadn't exchanged more than ten sentences with the woman, yet she was insinuating that our relationship was a thing of substance.

"Didn't we, Esther? I think it was on a Wednesday morning while I was scrubbing my family's laundry and you were supposedly supervising the washerwoman..."

Anna! Those deep-blue eyes could only belong to one person...one individual. And that laugh...the tinkling chimes that always lifted my spirits. I knew that it had a familiar ring...

Anna looked down at the unwieldy box I had given her and she laughed.

"Come on, Esther. Can you really see me playing around with one of these delicate teacups?"

I was struck dumb. Anna was standing composedly before me, conversing as though we were both sixteen-year-old innocents lounging at the riverbank.

"You figured it out a while back," I said hoarsely. "You recognized me."

"It took me a few days," Anna admitted. "When I first saw your aunt's name on the door, I remembered your mother telling me about this woman, Linda Bonair - "

"My mother?! My mother told you?!"

"No need to get so uptight, Esther. It was just a short conversation."

"Since when do you converse with the dead, Anna?"

The buzzing in my head intensified a thousand-fold, but Anna appeared utterly unfazed. At my side, I sensed Melinda's drooping eyelids even before I looked in her direction to ensure that she had fallen asleep.

"Slowly, Esther," she said. "Let's backtrack. I spoke to your mother."

"But...but how?!"

"Err...I walked over to your parents' home and knocked on the door. Then - "

"Stop it, Anna!" I screamed, losing every last bit of composure I had managed to maintain. "Talk to me!"

This time, Anna was the one crowned with a look of bewilderment.

"*Mamme* died! She drowned in the Atlantic when the Titanic went under!"

"Nonsense," she quickly retorted. "I spoke to your mother after she returned...without you."

"But...but she wasn't on the lists," I whispered. "Her name wasn't recorded on any list."

"Neither was yours, Esther. Do you have any idea how bitterly your parents mourned your death?"

My name was there, I fumed inwardly. *It was there under an alias. It was inscribed under the name Melinda had decided to impose upon me.*

"They were wonderful, your parents. I cannot tell you how strongly they accepted the Creator's will. It was hard for them, not knowing precisely what happened to you, but they accepted it."

I couldn't bear to listen, but I wanted Anna to continue talking...forever. I needed to hear every detail of the life that should have rightfully been mine. Anna, however, abruptly fell silent and none of my silent cues prompted her to resume her narrative.

"Where are they now, my parents?" I asked. "*Tatte* and *Mamme*...how are they holding up in the Nazi inferno?"

Anna turned her head away and her fingers restlessly toyed with the box she had reluctantly accepted.

"Anna, talk to me!"

"Before I go on," she said, "I need to ask you something."

I nodded impatiently.

"Do you blame me?"

I stared at Anna in astonishment. Carefree, joyous Anna was struggling with...guilt? Guilt was my personal domain in the past three decades. She had no connection to that awful planet.

"Don't just look at me," Anna pleaded. "Answer me! Tell me that you've been blaming me every day of your American life! Throw the shameful guilt in my face so that it could be some sort of atonement."

This was too much. Why was my dear friend berating herself for something which rested on my shoulders alone?

"I know that I was the one who sent you to that first meeting," she whispered. "I know and I will never forget."

"B-but Anna!" I finally blurted. "This is not about you! It's about me – only me, Esther Hofert. I was young and foolish and I allowed myself to be swept up by a passionate storm."

"But I sent you there," Anna repeated. "I sent you."

"I have never blamed you, Anna, and nothing you will say will change that. Quite the contrary, in fact. I've often wondered what happened to you and whether my disappearance had affected you in any way. I hoped that you managed to maintain your joy of life despite everything."

"I tried, Esther. Your *Mamme* helped me."

It's not fair, an infantile voice bawled deep in my mind. *Mamme should have been helping me, her only daughter! Why did Anna merit what I was denied?!*

"She was so strong. Even now, when the Germans led your family to the ghetto - "

"Ghetto? What's that?"

Anna's eyes widened in shock.

"You don't know, Esther? You really don't know what's going on back home?!"

"I know...something. My son, Davey, is an American soldier and he sends me information from time to time."

"The Germans relocated all the Jews to ghettos so that they should be...uh...easier to...access."

"Tell me the truth, Anna," I pleaded. "I'm big enough to handle it. I'm not that *Spoiled Princess* you remember!"

A twinkle appeared in my friend's eyes, and I warmed myself in its glow. Something told me that I would need all the strength I could muster in the ensuing moments.

"Uh...the Germans are very efficient. They figure that by concentrating the Jews in one place, it will be easier to have them all...liquidated."

"*Tatte* and *Mamme*," I prompted hoarsely.

"I was there when they were all taken away," Anna admitted. "I couldn't stay home while these atrocities were taking place. I went into Plawo proper and stationed myself near your parents' house. No one looked in my direction. Why would they be interested in an old spinster, who was also a schoolteacher to boot?"

Anna never got married. And she's a schoolteacher... just as her father had predicted

"Your mother walked out like a queen, resisting the Germans' efforts to urge her forward."

"And *Tatte*?"

"He...didn't go to the ghetto."

The sigh of relief died on my lips when I saw Anna's pitying glance.

"Your father was spared the agony, Esther," she said quickly. "He merited a Jewish burial, with hundreds of people in attendance. He didn't have to see the horrors perpetrated against his beloved brethren."

"How could that be? *Tatte*?!"

"He was an elderly man, Esther. You know that."

I didn't know that. *Tatte*, in my eyes, had remained the youthful and energetic activist who flashed his coal-black eyes when he wanted to make a point. His posture had remained erect in my imagination, and he had always been there, in Plawo, waiting for my eventual return.

And now, he was no more. He merited a Jewish burial, Anna said. He was one of the lucky ones.

But what about me, little Esther?! Where did that leave *Tatte*'s little girl?!

Suddenly, I had to know everything.

"Zalmen and Miri. What happened to them? And Dovid? Did Naftali escape? What about little Chaya'la and the baby? Actually, he's not a baby anymore. But what happened with them? Do you know where Menachem and his family were taken? I need to know, Anna!"

Anna simply spread out her hands and shook her head.

"I'm sorry, Esther. I don't know. After Plawo's Jewish quarter was emptied out, I left the country. I couldn't remain in that ghost town, especially since I had nothing keeping me anchored to home.

"I want to tell you what your mother said as she was leaving the house," Anna continued quickly. "She saw me standing in the shadows, and she winked to me to come closer. The Germans, surprisingly, allowed this sprightly old woman to have her last say before she was herded into the truck idling a few paces away."

"You saw *Mamme*," I whispered, envy obscuring every other detail of the horrifying occurrence.

"She looked me in the eye and she said, 'Hashem is good'. She said it once, and then again."

What the devastating spate of news hadn't accomplished, *Mamme*'s faithful declaration did. In my mind, I saw *Mamme* walking towards her fate, proudly proclaiming her belief in Hashem and I cried. I cried for the lost opportunities and I cried for the opportunities that would never be. I cried for the guilt that weighed heavily upon so many people, marring our lives with its distinctive stains. I cried for my elderly *Tatte* who had died without knowing of my existence, and I cried for dear *Mamme* who had suddenly come to life and just as suddenly been snatched away again.

"Your *Mamme* told me something else, Esther," Anna said gently. "She said something about you. 'I don't see Zalmen and his family,' she whispered. 'Menachem is far away. But Esther I'm taking along. Esther is with me all the time.' And then she left, a serene smile adorning her gentle face."

Thank you, Mamme. At least I know that you still kept me in your heart. You weren't upset at me. You didn't blame me.

Anna tactfully stood up and started wheeling the sleeping Melinda Bonair back into the Pine Acres Home. After she departed, I remained sitting on the white wicker chair waiting for the return of my childhood friend.

Her reappearance had given me back my past. She was the only one on the entire North American continent who knew me in the guise of Esther Hofert, innocent young girl from Plawo, Poland. Only she could seamlessly combine my youth and my high-flying, American present.

Anna returned, as I knew she would. Without a word, she sat down near me and put her arm around my shoulders.

"I must return to my duties, Esther," Anna said. "But I want to hear everything. Don't leave out a single detail, from the moment you left Plawo on that midnight train until the day you met me at Melinda Bonair's side."

I stared straight ahead, trying in vain to conceal my turbulent emotions.

"You'll visit, won't you?" Anna prodded.

She lifted the heavy box I had given her what seemed like a lifetime ago, and laughed. Leaning back in my chair, I closed my eyes and allowed the tinkling laughter to transport me back home.

"At least now I have an excuse to use these beautiful teacups," Anna remarked. "You'll enjoy your gift, Esther!"

She left me sitting in my place, hiding in the shadows of the weeping willow.

How apropos, I pondered. *I am that weeping willow. My tears will never dry up, though they may not be evident to the world at large. But, at last, I am a blossoming tree. I am a tree with a past and a tree with a future. Anna has given me back my roots.*

I will spare no efforts in tracking down my family... or what remains of them. But for now, I relish the feeling of belonging. Of being understood. Of having a Tatte and Mamme who always loved me and who are certainly looking down at me with compassion and concern.